RACING Dirty SERIES
TURBULENCE
THE FINAL RIDE

(Racing Dirty Series book 3)

By J. Lynn Lombard

Published by J. Lynn Lombard

Copyright owner J. Lynn Lombard 2018

All rights reserved. This book is a work of fiction. Names, characters, places and events are the product of the author's imagination or used in a fictitious manner. Any resemblance to actual person, place or events is purely coincidental.

No part of this book may be reproduced or used in any manner without the written permission of the publisher, except by a reviewer who may quote brief passages for review purposes only.

Cover Design by Literary Designs

Also written by J. Lynn Lombard

Racing Dirty Series

Thrust (book 1)

Torque (book 2)

Turbulence (book 3)

Savage Saints MC Series

Kayne's Fury (book 1)

Blayde's Betrayal (book 2)

Stryker's Salvation (book 3)

Rooster's Redemption (book 4) coming soon

Ace's Ascension (book 5) coming soon

Royal Bastards MC Series

Blayze's Inferno (book 1)

Capone's Chaos (book 2)

Capone's Christmas (book 3)

Torch's Torment (book 4)

Derange's Destruction (book 5)

Aftermath's Exposure (book 6)

Jaded Red (book 7) coming July 2024

Prologue

Nolan

The evil I buried in the past is heading right for me. Like a freight train with no brakes, crashing into everything I've worked so hard for. The day I left New York City, I changed my name, buried my past, and broke away from everything I'd been programmed to do. I vowed to myself I would never return, exploding from the binds they had on me.

Wiping the sweat from my brow, I jump down from the elliptical in my personal gym. I've been struggling to come up with ideas to keep my past in the past, but the walls are closing in on me, suffocating me. They're growing closer and closer to finding me. I have no one I can turn to for guidance anymore. It's just me and my demon locked away, demanding to break free.

I peer into the full-sized mirror against the gym wall, staring at the scars that mark my body. I tried to cover most with tattoos, but there's too many to hide, too many to cover. I run my palms across my chest. One pink scar stands out two inches above my heart. It's four inches long, stretching from my armpit to my neck, and required several stitches. That scar almost cost me my life, and it's the worst one marking my body. There are shallow cuts or cigarette burns that needed no stitches, cascading down my chest and back. I've learned to cope with the pain of my past by turning everything into jokes, but after what happened to Xavier and Izzy, something in me snapped. Gone went the humor I've always used.

    Striding out of the gym, I walk up the softly carpeted stairs in my loft and into my bedroom. It's just me here. Ashley's back in L.A. and I'm moving my business out there, so we can be together. With this current information coming into play, I need to take care of my past before I can move on in my future.

Chapter 1

Nolan-2 months ago

I'm startled awake by the buzz of a cell phone. My mind is foggy as I slap my hand on the nightstand next to my head. My phone crashes to the ground and the buzzing finally stops. I turn onto my left side and wrap my arms around Ashley's sleeping form, pulling her tighter against me. We're in the room Natalia gave to us when we all went back to her place. After everything Ashley's been through the last few days, she's still my light in the darkness that's closing in on me.

I still haven't revealed everything in my past to her. Eventually, I will, but right now I need to savor this moment. I want to relish the way she looks at me like I'm her everything. The love in her eyes will change to disgust or pity and I'm not ready for that yet.

My phone chimes with a voicemail, but I ignore it as I bury my nose in Ashley's hair, inhaling her strawberry essence. I'm painfully hard as she brushes her ass against me in her sleep. I run my hands down her stomach and play with the band of her shorts. She whimpers and nestles closer. I kiss the side of her throat, my free hand drifting down further. My favorite place to be. She rolls over and spreads her legs. I kiss and lick the outer edge of her ear, knowing it's driving her nuts.

Ashley's honey brown eyes open, meeting mine. She smiles at me and rests her hands on the stubble growing on my jaw. "Good morning," she whispers. Her voice is husky, sending chills down my spine.

"Morning, beautiful."

I lean in and explore her mouth with my tongue, caressing every inch she gives me. Our tongues battle for dominance as I grind my hips into her. Her fingers run through my hair tugging me harder against her.

"Fuck," I growl.

I'm already naked, preferring to sleep this way when I have Ashley next to me. I grasp her legs, spreading them wide open for me. I run my eyes up her perfect body until I lock onto her light brown ones. Desire flows through my body as her long dark lashes cover her eyes, hooded with desire.

I grip my shaft and she watches me, licking her lips. "Is this what you want?" I ask.

"God, yes. Quit teasing me," she growls out.

Every thought or worry disappears as I bury myself deep inside of her. I lean back down and cover her with my body. We're chest to chest, skin against skin.

"God, you feel so good," I hiss through clenched teeth. Fire rips through my spine as I find my own. Breathing heavy, I stop moving and hold myself up with my elbows. Not ready to leave the warmth of her body just yet.

"You're going to spoil me," Ashley giggles.

"Can't help it. When your ass rubs against my dick, he kind of takes over." I roll off her and watch as she gets up from the bed. With a groan, I sit up and swing my legs over the side. I find my phone and check to see who called. Xavier's name flashes across my screen and I hit the voicemail button.

"Hey, Nolan. I'm just calling to check on you guys. I haven't heard from you and wanted to make sure everything is all right." There's a hesitation before he continues. "Look, I'm sorry we took off the way we did. Something came up, and we had to leave. I can't explain it right now. But I will soon. Just take care, watch your back, and I'll talk to you soon." I replay his voicemail as Ashley comes out of the bathroom. There's something off in Xavier's voice and I can't put my finger on it.

"Who's that?" Ashley asks, sitting on the bed next to me.

"X, he called to see how we're all doing, but something sounds off. I don't know. Maybe I'm being paranoid."

"Do you want me to call Izzy?"

"Nah, I'll talk to him when I head back home in a few days."

"I don't want you to go," she says, resting her head on my shoulder.

"I know. I don't want to either, but I have to tie up loose ends before we make the move out here."

"Are you sure you want to do this? It's a big step." Ashley asks.

I wrap my arm around her bare shoulder, pulling her against me. I kiss her on top of her head. "More than sure. Wherever you are, so am I. After everything that's happened, you can't leave. Your family needs you here and the only thing I have back in Michigan is Xavier and Izzy. Maybe they'll move out here too. Who knows?"

"I'll miss you while you're gone." There's a sadness in her voice that breaks my heart.

"I'll miss you too. It'll only be for a couple of months, maybe less." I reassure her.

There's a knock on our door and we both get dressed quickly. She has on a pair of dark blue jeans and a blue tank top over a white one. I put on a pair of jeans and a black shirt. I open the door and come face to face with Ashton. There's a darkness in his eyes I've only seen a few times, and this can't be good.

"We have a lead on Marcus," Ashton says.

"Good, we'll take care of it from here. I don't want you guys involved in what's going down. Keep it quiet and no one besides the three of us and Ian knows what I'm about to do." I tell Ashton.

"Got it."

I walk back into Ashley's bedroom and pick up her phone. I hand it to her, "It's show time."

Chapter 2

Nolan-Present

Looking out the huge bay windows of my office, I pull myself from the memories of that night Ashley and I sought revenge on Marcus Dual, when there's a knock on the oak door. Ashton sticks his head in my office. I had to come back to Michigan to wrap up some loose ends before we make our move to the west coast. I'm not letting Ashley out of my sight ever again.

"Hey Nolan, I have some news." Ashton says walking into my office and taking a seat in the chair.

"What is it?" I ask.

He sits down on the plush leather chair in front of my red oak desk, shifting uncomfortably before speaking. "I don't know how to tell you this," he takes a deep breath.

"Just spit it out, Ashton." I growl, irritated.

"Switch." Ashton finally blurts out.

All the color drains from my face as I hear the name from my past. My heart skips a beat and there's a pounding in my ears. Ashton knows all my secrets and what this guy has done when I was a teenager. All the scars that mark my body. I tune everything out he says. I can see his lips move, but no sound penetrates my ears, as my mind wanders back to the most horrible time in my life. Where I thought I left it burned and buried.

"He's coming for you," Ashton says quietly.

I heard that loud and clear. I take the file he's trying to give me with shaky hands. I open it and there, inside the file, is a picture of Izzy and Xavier. Izzy's green eyes are filled with fear and Xavier's are filled with rage, staring into the camera. Below this picture is an address I know all too well.

Dropping the file onto the oak desk, I grab my phone and dial Xavier's number. It rings a few times and goes to voicemail. I try again, strumming my hands on the desk. After the fourth ring, I give up all hope he will answer. A male voice on the other end greets my ears and panic sets in.

"Well, well, well. It's about time you called. I was starting to worry you didn't get my package. That wouldn't bode well for this hot piece of ass I'm staring at."

"What the fuck do you want, Switch?" I growl into the phone.

"I want you out here. You know where to go," Switch replies, casually.

"You better not lay a fucking hand on them." I state through clenched teeth. My hand grips the phone so hard, I'm shocked it hasn't snapped.

"I guess you'll have to come out and see for yourself." There's a pause. "Oh, and Nolan? Come alone if you want this hot piece of ass and her guard dog back in one piece." Switch hangs up before I can respond.

White hot anger flows through my veins and I slam my phone down on the desk cracking the screen.

"I'll get the guys around." Ashton says, standing up and walking towards the door.

"No, I need to do this alone." I declare.

Ashton stops at the door and whips around in my direction. He's pissed. "No, you're fucking not. We're in this. All of us. Izzy and Xavier are our family too."

"If you guys come with me, he will kill them. I can't take that chance." I answer, standing up. I grab my suit jacket off the back of my chair and throw it on. "Call ahead and get my plane ready. I'm leaving now."

"Nolan, this isn't a good idea. You need back up. What if he gets back inside your head again?" We're standing toe to toe. Ashton's nostrils are flaring with each breath he takes.

"He won't. I'm not some young, naïve teenager anymore. He can't fuck with my head. I won't let him." I push past him and out into the plush carpeted hallway. "Get my plane ready." I demand, over my shoulder.

Pushing the button to the elevator, I wipe the sweat from my brow with shaky hands. Switch wants this, but if I take my team with me, Izzy and Xavier will die. I've seen and experienced it too often. When Switch gives an order, you follow, or pain becomes your new friend.

The elevator doors whoosh open and I step inside. Hitting the button to the ground floor, I glance up. Ashton is standing in front of the doors, his arms crossed over his chest. Anger is radiating from every pore in his body. He narrows his eyes in my direction, shaking his head.

"It'll be fine, Ashton. Trust me." I tell him as the elevator doors close between us.

I breathe a sigh of relief when the elevator starts it's descent to the lobby. I walk quickly through the lobby, my dress shoes echoing off the marble floors. I make my way to my car parked out front and climb inside. Cranking the key, I rev the engine and shoot off into the traffic, weaving in and out, racing towards my past and the demon I've kept locked away for the past two months. He's pounding against my chest, straining to break free of the chains I wrapped around him.

Chapter 3

Nolan

The plane ride was smooth as we touch down at John F Kennedy airport, a few hours later. Powering my phone back on, it dings with several missed calls and text messages. I shove it into the pocket of my jeans, not ready to check them yet. I changed from my suit and tie to a pair of faded blue jeans, a black shirt and black racing boots on the plane and make my way to the passenger terminal. The white marble floors glisten as my boots tap against it. Chatter from fellow passengers raise the hair on the back of my neck and my eyes scan everything and everyone passing me by. My body is on high alert. Everything is bright and cheerful, opposite of the way I'm feeling.

Not wanting to drive, I bypass the car rental area and step out into the bustling drop off and pick up zone. The air is warm against my skin for mid-March. Yellow taxis and shiny cars assault my vision in the bright sun and I put my aviator's on, blocking the shimmering light. Hitching my go-to bag over my shoulder I hail a cab. One switches the light off on top and races towards me, slamming on the brakes at the last second. I climb in the back seat, the hard-plastic digging into my legs and back and give the cabbie directions near the motel I'm staying at.

"First time in the Big Apple?" The cabbie asks me in a heavy Arabic accent.

"Something like that," I respond.

I take my phone out of my jeans pocket and scroll through the messages. Most are from Ashton and Ashley. Not finding anything from Switch, I shut my phone off and jam it back into my pocket. Running my fingers through my hair, I blow out an irritated breath. My anxiety is picking up as we grow closer to Manhattan, the place where it all began.

******

Nolan 10 years ago (Age 15)

The music coming from the living room in our tiny apartment vibrates in my ears. My mother is having another "party." It's her way of telling me to stay the fuck out of the way so she can get high and screw whoever brings her the drugs she craves. I can't take any more noises coming from outside my bedroom door, so I open my window and crawl out onto the rusty old fire escape. The warm breeze drifting over my skin is a small reprieve from the stuffy apartment and I inhale a deep breath of the city air. I sit on the cold metal for a moment thinking about how we ended up here.

My mother went into rehab and stayed sober for about four months before she met Marcus Angelo. A well-known drug runner for the Corridore Rosso, an Italian gang. She was working as a waitress in a seedy bar when he charmed the pants right off her and two months later, here we are in a rundown apartment building in the heart of the Manhattan. My mother slipped back into her old habits.

My grandfather disowned my mother when he discovered that she started using again. He tried getting me out, but the state kept siding with her. She's never been arrested or in any legal trouble, so they made me stay with her.

I stand up from my spot on the fire escape and slide my way down the rickety old ladder. I walk down the dark street and make my way to Times Square. Peddlers and street performers are all over the place and the billboards are so bright, it's hard to know how late it is. I take a seat on one bench and watch the people go by.

There are so many types of people and cultures here in the City, it's a sensory overload. I watch as families stop and see what the street performers are doing. One group catches my attention and I make my way over to them. They're doing a bunch of flips and dance moves to music drifting out of their boom box. People are applauding and cheering them on, one kid goes around with a backpack and collects money from them. A quick way to earn a buck in this expensive city.

I leave the bright lights and bustling area behind me and walk down a dark side street. Yelling, horns *honking, and police sirens fade in the distance as I make my way over to Little Italy. It's quite a distance from Times Square, but knowing my mother, she will never know I was gone and it will be a while before she's done doing whatever she does.*

There's a group of teenagers dressed in black t-shirts, jeans and red bandanas around their heads or biceps sitting on concrete steps of an apartment building. They're eyeing me as I walk past them. One of them gets up and follows me.

"Hey kid, wait up," he says, trying to draw my attention.

I keep walking with my head down, acting like I didn't hear him when he falls in step next to me. I slow my pace and look him over out of the corner of my eye, trying to assess what he wants. I have no money on me and the only thing worth anything is my pocket watch my grandfather gave me. That's tucked deep in a secret spot in my blue jeans.

"Hey, I've seen you around before. You know it's not safe to be out this late at night alone." the guy says, standing in front of me.

I stop walking and raise my head to look him in the eye. He's about three inches taller than me, maybe a year or two older and has an air of authority about him. His dark skin and black hair standing out under the street light. His black eyes look me over and it appears he's decided.

"What does it matter to you?" I ask. I look around to see it's just the two of us and breathe a sigh of relief when it is.

"Hey kid, I know where you're coming from. Broken home, no dad, mom a druggie. Am I right?"

I clench my fist at my side, anger brewing under the surface of my skin. I look at him dead in the eye before I speak.

"It doesn't matter where I come from or what's going on I'm not interested in anything you have to offer." My voice full of rage and hate. I hate this city. I hate my mother. I hate my father.

"Actually, it does. You see we can help," he gestures to the others. They're now standing on the steps watching us.

"How?" He's got me intrigued now.

"We are a family and that means something to us. Once you're in and prove your loyalty to us, we have your back no matter what. Why don't you come back and I'll introduce you to the rest. What's your name by the way?"

I look behind me at the other kids watching us. It would be nice to have someone to hang with. It's been lonely being in a big city, surrounded by people but no one giving you any attention or acknowledging you exist.

"Nolan Sherwood," I answer. I hold my hand out and he takes it and gives it a good handshake.

"Well, Nolan Sherwood, good to meet you. Mine is Switch. That's what everyone calls me. C'mon I'll introduce you to the rest."

We walk back over to the other teenagers and they all watch me with caution as we approach.

"Everyone, this is Nolan Sherwood. Nolan, this is everyone," Switch says.

Some give me a nod, others keep watching me like I'm some freak show, cautious but curious. I give them my best smile.

"Hey everyone." I say. I put my hands in my pockets unsure on what to do next.

"C'mon Nolan, relax. We just hang out here when things get hard at home and we can't stand to be around our family." Switch says, throwing an arm around my shoulder.

I stiffen at his touch and he removes his arm immediately. I don't like to be touched. I've always been that way since I was little, and I think it's from lack of affection from my parents. They never showed me love or *attention and when someone touches me, my reaction usually isn't good.*

A girl I didn't notice before comes out from behind the other boys and makes her way over to me, a look of something in her hazel eyes I can't quite place. She stands close enough I can smell her raspberry body wash, but not touching me. She has on a black tank top, black skin-tight jeans and a red bandana around her left leg. She has light skin, long blonde hair and big hoop earrings. Her face is covered with make-up, hiding a bruise I can faintly see under her right eye. She pops her strawberry flavored bubble gum before she speaks.

"Name's Tatiana, but everyone calls me Wrath." she says with a thick east coast accent. Her hazel eyes looking into my brown ones.

"Why do they call you Wrath?" I ask her.

She rolls her eyes before answering me. "Because if you piss me off you meet the ends of my fists. Wrath of fury. This bruise is nothing compared to what the other guy looks like." Wrath answers pointing to her eye.

She doesn't look like she could do some damage, but her knuckles are scarred and bruised. She cracks them while watching me and I swallow a lump in my throat. She's hot and my teenage hormones kick in at her being so close, but not touching me. Wraths' soft body sneaks closer so we're only a hair's breadth apart. She's got me under a spell I can't shake and frankly I don't want to right now.

"This is going to be so much fun," Wrath says giving me a wink.

****

"Sir, we're here," the cabbie says, yanking me out of my memories.

"Thanks." I reach into my pocket and slide the money through the bulletproof glass separating me from the driver.

"Enjoy your stay," The driver says as I get out of his cab.

He flips on the light above his taxi and speeds away, into the bustling street of Mid-town. My eyes search the surrounding area, making sure no one is following me before I walk. Skyscrapers greet me as I make my way down the familiar streets of New York City. People are milling around me with earbuds in, ignoring everything around them and drowning out the horns and sirens floating around them. The tourists are easy to spot, stopping every few feet to snap a picture or pointing out massive skyscrapers in an expression of awe. If they only recognize the dangers that lurk around the corner, they'd follow the people who grew up here and keep their heads down.

The tourists were easy prey for us when I was a teenager. We'd get them to watch one way, while we'd pocket what cash they'd have in their wallets. It was exhilarating and nerve wracking the first few times, but after doing it for a while, it became second nature. The guilt eating away at my subconscious stayed tucked in the back of my mind until I finished the job.

Now, watching these kids approach the tourists, I have the desire to run over and shout to get away. I know they're probably just like I was, lost and alone, but I still wish someone would have told me back in the day, how wrong it was and guide me in the right direction. Exhaling a deep breath, I continue to walk down the busy sidewalk, leaving a part of my past behind me. I'm here to save Xavier and Izzy, not tumble down the rabbit hole I once was in.

Approaching an intersection, I stop and wait to cross the street. People all around me are doing the same, waiting for the signal to cross. They're all like sheep, being herded and following directions. A boy around eight years old, with brown shaggy hair and light brown eyes, captures my attention. He's standing next to a girl who looks to be around fifteen. She's tugging on his shirt, trying to make him follow her down the alley. His familiar eyes connect with mine, a look of shock written all over his face. The girl tugging on him follows his sight and she does a double take when she sees me standing away from the rest of the crowd. Her golden blonde hair and familiar hazel eyes widen in surprise. She whispers something to the little boy and nudges him away from me. They take off at a fast pace down the alley, out of my sight. Once the shock wears off, my feet are moving in their direction, eating up the pavement. I turn down the alley they disappeared to and they're nowhere in sight.

I pull my phone out of my pocket and try to calm my racing heart. What the fuck was that about? Dialing Ashton, I strum my fingers against my jeans, keeping an eye out for the kids again. Pacing back and forth, I run a hand through my hair while I wait for Ashton to pick up.

"Nolan, fucker. You can't do that. Where are you?" Ashton says when he picks up the phone.

"Listen, I need you to run a check on a woman named Tatiana. Street name Wrath. That's all I know."

"Are you going to tell me what the fuck is going on? Ashley is on her way here. She's pissed."

"No, not yet. I need you to run a full check and get back to me A.S.A.P." I answer, hanging up the phone before he can reply.

I walk back out of the alley and cross the street. Fuck this waiting bullshit. Horns blare in my direction, but I'm done being a sheep. One menacing glare from me has the drivers laying off the horns and throwing their hands up in the air. That's right motherfuckers, I'm back and I'm out for blood.

Chapter 4

Ashley

The commercial plane touched down at MBS airport and Redline and I make our way through the terminal towards the waiting area. Rush and the rest of my crew are getting a direct flight to New York City in a few days. Ashton is pacing back and forth next to a set of black plastic chairs. The closer I get the deeper the stress lines appear on his handsome face.

"Ashton, what's going on?" I ask as he pockets his phone.

"It's not good. C'mon I realize you're jet lagged but hang in there. The jet is fueled and ready to leave. You can nap on the flight over."

Redline grabs our bags off the conveyor belt and drags them behind him. We make our way to a private terminal and Ashton opens the door for us. A gentle breeze greets my skin and the sun warms my face when I step outside. I inhale the country air and a peaceful serenity wraps around me. I love this about Michigan. You don't find this sense of peace anywhere else. I soak it in for a few seconds before all hell breaks loose.

A white, shiny jet waits on the tarmac. The door is open and I walk up the steps and into the beige, plush interior of the jet. Nolan's woodsy scent wraps around me like he's standing right next to me. I close my eyes and inhale his essence deeply. Opening my eyes, I move to a double seat on the right side of the plane, next to the windows. Peering out into the bright sunlight, I wish Nolan wouldn't have left without us. I wish he would have confided in me to help. That hurts the most, but he was there for me when I needed him. So, I'll be here for him, even if he pushes me away. I will not lose him to his past.

The doors close and the seatbelt sign lights up. The captain's voice comes across the speakers and I tune him out. Redline takes the spot next to me and settles his hand on my clenched fist. Ashton takes the seat directly across from me and scowls at Redline.

Redline and I have come a long way from where we once were. After the whole Shaun incident, he finally realized something misguided his heart. We were never meant to be together and once he figured that out, things have been great between us. He finally sees me as the leader and sister I was always meant to be, not a lover like he thought. Someday he'll meet his other half and when he does, she'll knock him on his ass.

Familiar voices to the left of me snap me out of my daze and I peer over Redline's massive body. Mia and Christian come into view and she lets out a squeal when she sees me. When did they get on board? God, I'm losing my mind. I need to stay alert if I want to help Nolan.

"Ashley? Oh, my God. You're here!" Mia squeals again. She forces her way over to our seats.

"Hey Mia, how have you been?" I ask.

"Better now you're here. Who's this?" she asks, cocking an eyebrow at Redline. She dyed her short black hair red and blue this time. Last time I saw her it was all assorted colors.

"This is Redline, he's part of my crew. Redline, this is Mia, Izzy's other best friend." I introduce the two.

"Good to meet you, Redline. Now move it or lose it." Mia says, propping her hands on her hips and cocks one to the side. "Ash and I need to talk."

"Well, it's nice to meet you too." Redline's rich voice responds. He releases my clenched fist and stands up.

"Oh, good looking and a deep voice. The ladies must fall at your feet. Now move it." Mia says. I try to suppress a laugh bubbling up my throat but fail miserably.

"It's all right Redline, go sit next to Christian. Mia and I need to talk." I reassure him. He grunts a response and moves. Mia quickly plops into his seat. She's a ball of energy and does it gracefully. She gently lifts my hand and I relax my grip.

"How have you been?" she asks.

"OK. Just going through a lot right now and Nolan pulling this stunt threw me for a loop. Scared we won't make it to him on time. Worried he won't be the same after this. Terrified for Izzy and X." I answer, shrugging my shoulders.

I lean my head back in the seat as the jet takes off, the ascent dips my stomach to my toes. Mia does the same and we both stare off into the distance, lost in our own worlds. She is the only person who can make you open up about things you rarely talk about. She lets out a little sigh and swings her head in my direction.

"Are we ever going to get a break and just enjoy life?" she asks.

"I don't know. I hope so, but I doubt it'll be soon. When was the last time you talked to Izzy?"

"A couple of weeks ago. She called and told me she was heading back to L.A. to visit you, now I feel horrible for not seeing this."

"Hey, it's not your fault." I cover my hand over hers and squeeze gently. "I thought they were back here with you. Living it up and having a good time. I had no idea Nolan's past put them in jeopardy. I wish I knew how they were taken."

"I know," Ashton mumbles.

"How?" I ask, snapping my eyes in his direction.

Christian and Redline are leaning towards us from the seats across the aisle and Ashton gestures to them to come over too. Mia stands up and Christian slips into her seat, pulling her down onto his lap. Redline takes the seat next to Ashton. I'm not sure where the rest of their crew is.

"A couple of weeks ago, Xavier received a phone call. I'm not positive what they spoke about, but whatever it was had them boarding the first flight to New York City. From what I could dig up, they hailed a cab from the airport and traveled into Manhattan. From there, they went into a decrepit apartment building, the same one Nolan grew up in, and the rest we all know. I'm thinking it was Switch that called him. He might have threatened Nolan's life or someone else." Ashton takes a deep breath, folding his big hands in front of him. "Being the type of guy Xavier is, I would stake my left nut Switch threatened Nolan, and Xavier thought he could deal with it. Only thing is that Switch has been in the life for a long time and knows how to manipulate people. He can bend them to his will, and they don't stand a chance. Which is why I didn't want Nolan going by himself. They have a terrible past and Nolan's come a long way from where he once was."

Ashton stares at me. I know what he means, and I shake my head. They don't need to learn what kind of torture he's been through and how hard he fought to get out. He assumed he was protecting me by not telling me everything, but I know. I have my own ways of finding things out. Which is another reason I hopped on the first flight here. We need to work on this together. Bring Nolan back home to us. He will be battling his demon, and I'm the only one who can talk him off the ledge. I'm the only one who can break through and reach him. He's my other half and I'll do whatever it takes to make these assholes pay for forcing him to go through this. That's right motherfuckers, I'm coming for you at full throttle.

Chapter 5

Nolan

I walk three city blocks in both directions near the motel I'm staying at before entering. I wanted to make sure no one was following me and honestly, I was also hoping to see those kids again. I don't know why, but I'm still shocked at seeing that little boy. There's something about him that caught my attention. The girl is a spitting image of Wrath, but there's no way she's her kid. She was fifteen when we met and had no kids. Maybe it's a little sister or something. Ashton still hasn't called me back with the information I asked for.

I glance up at the building and take in the surrounding sights. I've learned to tune the noises of the city out, so instead of constantly hearing horns blaring, people talking or sirens going off, it's all white noise. From my time spent here, I know this place used to be an apartment building back in the day. Someone bought it and turned it into a motel. It's tucked between several other buildings in the heart of Manhattan. If I look just right, I can see the Empire State Building, towering behind it about four blocks over. The warm sun shines down upon me and I walk inside the dark building. A security guard stationed at the door gives me a once over and then continues reading his paper.

Approaching the counter, I set my bag down on the dingy carpet in front of my feet. The smell of Lysol trying to cover up body odor overruns my senses. The woman at the desk eyes me up and down, shamelessly. Her dark eyes appraise my body before resting on my face.

"Can I help you?" she asks in a seductive voice.

"Need a room for a week. Top floor if you have one." I grunt out in response.

After blatantly staring at me and licking her red lips for a few minutes, she turns to the computer. I've seen this look from many women in the past and I roll my neck on my shoulders, making popping sounds, trying to keep my temper in check. Exasperated at this woman's intense ogling, I knock my knuckles on the fake wood, making her jump.

"Are you done checking me out or do you need more time?" I ask.

Her cheeks turn a shade of pink at my blunt question and whirls around so fast, her dark hair whips from side to side, to the key cards in the fake oak cupboard behind her. She grabs a sleeve and turns back around. Eyeing me again, she slides the cards towards me with a pink, polished nail.

"That'll be seven hundred. Name for the reservation?" she asks.

"Ryan," I grunt out. Less is better.

"If you need anything, Ryan, I'm just a phone call away," she says, lowering her lashes.

"That won't be necessary," I grunt again and snatch the sleeve off the counter being careful not to touch her.

I pull my business credit card out of my wallet and slide it across the countertop and she gently takes it, sliding it through the reader. She doesn't slide it back across the counter this time, but holds it in her hand, forcing me to take it out of hers. She licks her red lips again, trying to make eye contact with me.

"Room fifteen-fifteen, enjoy your stay, Ryan." Her flirting is making me on edge and I just want to get to my room.

I snatch my credit card out of her hand and pick up my duffle bag on the floor. Not saying another word to the receptionist, I walk to the grey elevators and push the button. The doors open with a loud bang and I walk inside and push a button for the fifteenth floor, praying the old dingy piece of shit doesn't give out.

I'm the only one in here as the doors close and the elevator begins its rickety ascent to the top. One quirk when I stay somewhere is that I have to have quick access to the roof. The top floor is what I always choose. If it's not available, I stay in a motel where it is. I need to be able to escape in a heartbeat if the walls close in and the top floor is the quickest way to get there.

    The elevator dings and the doors groan in protest as they open, greeting me to my new home for a little while. Walking down the hallway, my boots are quiet on the thin brown carpet. There are several doors on each side and visitors occupy some. I can hear T.V.'s on behind them. I find my room in the middle and slide the card through the reader. At least the smell isn't as bad up here. I flip on the light and shut the door behind me, turning the top lock and sliding the chain. It's a small twenty by fifteen room with a bed right next to the door and a closet next to it. There's a full bathroom on the other side of the door. It's actually an afterthought in the room. There's a tiny kitchen and a black mini fridge diagonal from the bed. There's a thirty-inch T.V. mounted to the brick wall separating my room from the next and a tiny fold up table pushed against the wall. Tossing my black duffle bag on the twin bed, I walk over to the window and open the curtain. There's a little sliver of sunlight streaming in between the three brick buildings on the other side. I hope my claustrophobia won't kick in. I know I get what I pay for in this city. I wanted to stay close as possible, without Switch knowing I'm here. All I can see as I look out the window, are buildings surrounding me. The little sliver of light is warm against my skin. I close my eyes and steady my breathing, leaning my head against the window. I give myself a minute and wish Ashley was here with me. It's been two months since I've seen her or touched her and there's a sudden ache to have her here with me. Before I realize what I'm doing, I have my phone up to my ear and it's ringing on the other end. Ashley's voicemail picks up and her beautiful voice floats in my ears telling me to leave a message.

"Hey, Ash. Just want to call and tell you I miss you and I love you." Exhaling a deep breath, I hang up the phone. Allowing myself a moment of weakness, I shake my head and steel my nerves.

Time to get down to business.

These motherfuckers will pay for messing with my family. I unzip my bag and pull out my laptop. Next, I take out my favorite Smith and Wesson .40 caliber handgun. The sleek black grip is weightless in my hand and I cock the slider back and chamber a round into it. I set it on the bed next to the laptop and take out my Ruger .45 caliber pistol. The chrome slider shines under the lighting. I cock it back and chamber a round before setting it down on the bed, next to the other one. One thing about New York City and New York State is that you're not allowed to conceal carry unless you have a special permit. Since I own A.R. Security, I have all special permits needed in every state.

I fire up the laptop and settle in for some recon. I know I can't go in half cocked and take the chance Switch will kill Izzy and Xavier when he knows I'm coming. I have to work my way back into their world and there's only one way to do that. It's another dark tunnel I don't want to go down, but I have no choice.

After searching the internet for two hours, I finally find what I'm looking for. I mentally note the address listed and crack my neck from side to side. Time to get the show on the road. Closing my laptop, I stand up and holster my weapons. I tuck a knife in my boot for backup. Ashley taught me that. Always have a spot for a knife. It saved her life and if I need it, it might save mine too.

Once I'm locked and loaded, I head back down the hallway and call for the elevator. I put on my black hoodie and baseball hat, keeping the brim low on my forehead. It makes a dinging noise and groans open. The doors close after I step inside and begins its descent down to the lobby. I stare at myself in the dirty mirrors around me. The man glaring back at me is someone I haven't seen in a long time. Massive muscles tense and ready to strike. I clench my fists at my sides, the haunted but deadly look in my brown eyes and a wicked sneer on my lips should be enough to show these guys I mean business. I'm not some stringy teenager anymore. I'm strong, independent and ready to feel bones crunching under my fists. The demon is ready to play and they won't know what hit them.

Chapter 6

Ashton

Our plane ride is quiet once I revealed how Switch captured Xavier and Izzy. The plane dips and hits turbulence occasionally, shifting in the air, but other than that, it's a smooth flight. Ashley's curled up in the seat across from me, sound asleep. Mia's next to her, resting her head on Ashley's side, also sound asleep. Christian and Redline are talking in hushed voices across the aisle from me.

In another time, another life, I would be over there joining them. I was the outgoing one, Christian was the shy one growing up. Girls saw him as Ashton's younger, dorky brother with long, skinny arms and legs, no muscle build, an awkward teenager. Living in a small southern town it was hard to escape the stereotype and being four years older than Christian, I already developed my body and build. The elderly people in our town always compared us, asking him why he can't be like his older brother? Why aren't you following his footsteps and joining the service? No matter how pleasant and nice he was to everyone, they constantly turned their noses up at him and used him to get to me. He hated me for it and needed some kind of outlet to get rid of his anger and aggression and he found that in Maui Tia boxing. Christian grew up while I was in Iraq and since I've come back from my two tours, we've grown apart. I've done things overseas I'm not proud of, taken many lives more times than I can count, and it's hard to be the man you once were when you've seen and done things that can't be unseen or undone.

I stare at my hands, lost in thought when Christian sits down next to me. He nudges me with his massive shoulder. "Hey bro, you all right?" he asks.

"Yeah, why wouldn't I be?" I claim, shaking my head clearing it of those younger years.

"You're acting distant. I want to help and don't leave me in the dark this time." Before I can rebut his statement he cuts me off. "I realize we're not as close as we used to be, but Ashton, you're my brother. I'm here for you. There are things you don't know about me and things I don't know about you." He settles his palm on my shoulder, giving it a squeeze. I stare into his familiar brown eyes, his gaze not leaving my face. It's my fault we're not as close as we should be and that's on me, not him. I nod my head.

"Thanks, man. Look, there are things you don't realize I went through in Iraq and I hope one day I can talk to you about it, but today isn't that day. We need to focus on getting Nolan, Xavier, and Izzy back safely. My team will meet us in the City once they have the other cases we were working on closed. I don't know how long that will be, but in case they aren't here on time, I need you to be prepared for what you're about to see. It's not going to be pretty."

"I can handle it. Since meeting these guys, I've realized everything isn't black and white. There's a grey line I've had to toe. Honestly, it felt good, not always being straight and narrow. So, whatever you need, I'm ready."

My face must have displayed my shock because Christian lets out a quiet laugh. My brother, the straight shooter, always doing the right thing, will cross a line he can't come back from. This won't be grey, it will be black, so black that once you get a taste for it, it'll be hard to give up. I don't want to change the way he sees things. That'll be more guilt I have to deal with.

"Don't even think about it," Christian responds with a shrug.

"Think about what?" I ask.

"I can handle it. I've seen some dark shit on the police force. That girl right there," Christian says pointing to Mia, "is my light. I didn't want her to come, but she's a stubborn one. I know what we're walking into and trust me, brother, I'm ready. Xavier and Izzy have become a part of my family and these assholes just fucked with the wrong guys."

"You do know, if mom heard your mouth, she'd break out the Dawn dish soap," I say with a shudder. Christian mimics my reaction.

"That shit is so gross. I can still taste it from when we were teenagers and thinking it was cool to swear." We both laugh and I scrunch my nose. That shit's nasty. "All I want is for us to be in this together. I'm here Ashton, no matter what."

"Thanks, man. What's going on with Redline?" I ask the question that's been bothering me since I saw him get off the plane with Ashley. We both look over at Redline. He's sitting next to the window with his eyes closed, not paying us any attention.

"Rush and the rest of Ashley's crew had to stay behind a day and he didn't want her coming alone. He told Redline to come with her and keep her safe. I don't know for sure. What do you know?"

"Between the two of us? He had a massive crush on her for years. I don't trust him nor like him very much. Something about him rubs me the wrong way. I hope I'm mistaken but keep your guard up around him. Ashley trusts him and she's a good judge of character, so I hope it's just my paranoia kicking in and he's here for the right reasons. I hope he isn't here to drive a wedge between her and Nolan, but here to help. I guess we'll find out soon enough."

I rest my head on the back of the seat and stare out the plane window. The clouds break apart under us and the Brooklyn Bridge comes into view. The sun is glistening off the Hudson River, causing the bridge to shine. The landscape is breathtaking. The two new twin towers loom in front of us, shining in the sunlight.

Sometimes it's hard to believe so much evil lurks beneath something so beautiful. I know first-hand how something so beautiful can be so deadly.

****

Ashton, Iraq-2 years ago

The stink of burning flesh fills my nose and awakens me. I jolt upright but quickly realize I'm still tied to a metal chair. Memories of the last couple of days assault my mind and I squeeze my eyes shut, struggling to block them out. Images of a beautiful woman with long black hair, piercing blue eyes and secrets of her own. Owning her body, the way she owns my heart when I take her away from her suffering with my hope and dreams of us escaping her personal hell. I don't know what happened to her because these men came into her room in the dead of night and knocked my ass out with a blow to the back of my head.

Black boots stomp on the dirt floor into my line of sight. I keep my head down, trying to play it off like I'm still sleeping, but my body aches all over from the massive beatings I've received. The black boots stop right in front of me and I coil my muscles. A reflex ingrained into my mind by my drill instructor.

"Well, well, well, look who's finally rejoined the party." A dark voice says off to my right.

I don't move a muscle. Keeping absolutely still, I wait for the man to finish talking. He isn't done yet. That's all this man does is run his mouth and his voice is grating on my nerves. I can't wait until it's my turn to give him the same torture he's inflicted upon me. Not answering him pisses him off and I'm waiting and ready.

"Do it again," he commands. *The sting of a whip cracks across my exposed skin. Pieces of flesh rip from my body and boots keeps going repeatedly.*

I don't say a word as the whip keeps shredding my flesh. Burning agony fires through my body until I can't take any more pain and pass out with one thought on my mind. Revenge. It's a bitch, motherfuckers.

****

The plane starts its descent onto the runway. The dip it takes snaps me out of my memories. I reach across the seats and gently shake Ashley awake. She jerks her head up and her reflexes kick in, ready to pounce. Once she has her bearings, she blinks her brown eyes and relaxes back into the seat. This woman has seen and done so much in her short life, it hurts to see her like that. The vulnerability on her face is heartbreaking.

"Have you heard from him?" she pleads with a sleepy voice. I shake my head and her face settles into a frown. "How are we supposed to find him in a city full of thousands of people?"

"We'll find him, trust me. I can find anyone, anywhere. Even if they don't want to be found. It's what I do." I answer with a shrug.

I give her the famous line we always say and she responds by rolling her eyes. It's true though, it's what I do. I've been trained to kill someone with my bare hands and find anyone, anywhere. All I need is internet access and a few minutes.

The plane lands and rolls down the runway before coming to a complete stop. The seatbelt light flashes off and we all get up. Mia is a little slow since I forgot to wake her. Christian is by her side, steadying her sleepy form. I grab my black duffle bag and swing it over my shoulder. Redline takes Ashley's and his own bags and we all exit the plane into the airport. The sun is shining brightly off the white marble floor through the massive floor to ceiling windows as the five of us make our way to the car rental counter. They hang back off to the side of the crowd as I get our car. A few minutes later, I make my way back to them and we exit out the doors.

The city sounds assault my hearing when we walk out into the parking lot, making me flinch. Taxis are lined up, waiting for someone to flag them down. Horns are blaring, and sirens are going off in the distance. This will take some getting used to. I sneak a glance at the others behind me and they have the same reaction as I do.

Locating the black SUV, I hit the key fob and the rear hatch pops open. Redline and Christian throw their gear in the back and I set my duffle on top. I have important things we'll need while we're here and I want none of it broken. I unlock the doors and we all climb inside. Redline, Christian, and Mia get in the back and Ashley takes the passenger seat. She lets out a yawn and stretches her hands above her head, arching her back. I glance in the mirror, while she does this, and watch Redline. He's facing the window, staring off into his own world, not paying her any attention.

"Where are we heading?" Ashley asks quietly.

"We're going into the lion's den, but first we need to locate Nolan." My phone dings in my pocket and I pull it out. "Got him. He's staying in a motel in the heart of Manhattan."

"How do you know?" Ashley asks.

"I have an app on my phone that tells me when the company cards are being used and he used it two hours ago at a motel in Manhattan. He knows I have the app so that tells me he wants us to find him. If he didn't, he would've used a different card." An email icon lights up my phone and I click on it. The information he wanted about Wrath fills the screen. This bitch is dangerous. The police arrested her several times for fighting in the last seven years. The last time, she did a stint in county for a year. The guy she beat the shit out of ended up in a coma. When he came too, he dropped all charges, and they let her out. She has a younger sister and a little boy around eight years old. I click on the attachments and suck in a deep breath.

"Holy shit," I whisper, staring at the image on my phone.

"What is it?" Ashley asks, cocking an eyebrow.

"Nothing, it's nothing. Just some information on another case." I answer quickly, closing the image staring back at me so she doesn't see it. Fuck, fuck, fuck. Now what?

I start the SUV and pull out into heavy traffic heading into the heart of New York City. Things will be brutal and I have no doubt, once this is over, every one of us will be different.

Chapter 7

Nolan

I walk down the city streets, searching for the address I found online, trying to blend in as much as possible. It's hard to accomplish with my height and build, but I'm doing the best I can. The tourist area has thinned out and there are more rundown apartment buildings I pass by. I keep my hat down, covering my eyes, hoping to blend in. I have a red bandana tucked into my front pocket and I pray I don't have to use it. It's the same one Switch gave me when I was initiated into the gang.

I didn't know at the time it was a gang, but after receiving that bandana, my entire world changed in a heartbeat. Women would take one glimpse at it and throw themselves at my feet. Fighting became second nature, fucking every time I needed to take the edge off and my mother never even knew. She was so wrapped up in drugs and fucking, she didn't give a shit. Wrath was my go-to girl, but occasionally, she'd have a guy she was fucking, and I had to take the edge off with someone else. Being a teenager is tough, but what I had to do the more time I was them, was tougher. I cut off all communication with my grandfather, never saw my mother, unless she wanted money for drugs, and my father didn't give a shit.

The only ones who seemed like they cared at the time were Switch and the rest of the gang. I became their enforcer. I trained to fight and was an unrelenting force. One glance at me coming down the street, with my bulging muscles and a pissed off expression, people were too frightened to cross me. I was the best at what they trained me to do, which was fuck up anyone who owed us money, either it was for drugs or security. Sometimes I'd beat the shit out of someone just because they looked at me wrong. I quit school and spent a lot of time at a local gym, bulking up and learning the correct way to disarm someone or knock them out. I even learned how to kill someone with one blow.

Once I became the best, Switch introduced me to an underground fighting ring called The Circle. He also got me into stealing fast cars, teaching me how to outrun the cops. They only stopped me a handful of times and when I had to bail, Switch would get so pissed, he'd beat the shit out of me. Made me learn the hard way. Never bail on a job.

A dog barking in the distance snaps me out of my memories and I look around. I'm standing in front of a discreet brick building. Shit. I was so lost in my head I walked right up to the address. I wanted to do recon first, but with this guy about my size standing at the door, watching me with a cocked brow and shaved head, I have no choice but to approach him or he'll become suspicious.

"Looking for Amber," I deliver in a gruff voice.

That used to be the code for I want a fight. The bald guy crosses his arms over his heavy chest and glares at me. My palms are sweaty and my heart is knocking so hard, I swear he can hear it. I keep my composure, staring right back at him, into his black eyes. After a moment, the standoff is over and he opens the door.

"Hope you know what you're doing," he declares.

"If I didn't I wouldn't be here," I respond as I walk by him.

He slams the door behind me, plunging me into darkness. I can hear chants off into the distance as I make my way down the garbage littered hallway. Once I reach the end, the voices are becoming louder, coming from below my feet. I open a door to my right and walk down the metal stairs. Roars and cheers vibrate off the walls and barrel at me, forcing my heart to beat harder in my chest. The smell of sweat, blood, and body odor transports me back in time to my very first underground fight.

****

"Mayhem, Mayhem, Mayhem," the crowd chants my nickname as Switch creates a path to the center of the room. Their voices vibrate off the walls around me. They form a huge circle around us, giving me no room to escape. Adrenaline saturates my veins as I listen to the crowd roar for me. I'm scared shitless on the inside but

present no emotion on the outside. My opponent takes one glance at me and the hesitation that flashes in his blue eyes gives me an advantage. He doesn't want to go up against me. He quickly masks it and glares at me.

I stretch my arms above my head, flexing my shoulder muscles and rippling my abs. Sweat already covers my body, the dew is glistening the new tattoos that snake their path up my wrists to my shoulders on both arms. Switch grabs my fists and wraps them up. The only protection I'll have. Not breaking eye contact with my opponent, Switch shouts in my ear, over the crowd.

"You listening to me?" I nod my head. "Good, now go in there and show no mercy. Stay low, keep your guard up and stay on the balls of your feet. Aim for his gut and ribs first, knock the wind out of him, then deliver the ultimate blow. The one you've perfected." Switch grabs my shoulders, forcing me to stare into his cold, black, soulless eyes. "You win this and there'll be more money and more pussy than your little dick can keep up with. If you don't..." he trails off, glaring into my eyes.

Oh, I got the message. If I fail, he will hand me my ass until I submit.

"I'm not losing." My tone is low and savage. All the nerves wracking my body a few minutes ago disappear as I stare into Switch's cold, dead eyes.

"Good. Now go beat the shit out of this asshole." He shoves me away from him. "Oh, one more thing. He fucked Wrath two nights ago and wasn't gentle with her." He shouts over my shoulder.

I clench my fists tighter, crushing the tape around my hands and rage pumps through my veins. My muscles tighten in response and I zone in on the fucker in front of me. I want blood. When Wrath came to the apartment last night, she had fresh bruises all over her body and wouldn't talk to anyone. She sat on the couch tucked up into a little ball. She didn't make eye contact with anyone and when I tried to talk to her, she pushed me away and left. I knew something happened to her. This motherfucker will pay.

He's wearing a pair of black boxing shorts and no shirt, swinging his arms back and forth, glaring at me. His shaved head and tattoos are supposed to intimate me, but they don't. I lock my eyes on him and let the demon out to play. My body pulsates with rage and all I can see is this motherfucker in front of me. His blood on my hands.

He attacks first, running at me in fury. I watch his feet and his fists simultaneously. He steps with his left foot and swings with his right. I learn his pattern quickly. This will be too easy. I let a smirk cross my lips as I duck away from another jab and that pisses him off even more. He comes at me again and I deliver a shocking blow right to his gut and kick him away from me, sending him flying back into the crowd. He's struggling to catch his breath as the crowd shoves him back into The Circle with me.

Vibrations from the screaming crowd fuel me and I rapidly approach him delivering another slam of my fist to his stomach. He doubles over and the crowd goes nuts. I rear back and smash my fists into his face repeatedly. Bones crunch under my knuckles, blood spraying everywhere. I don't stop. I won't stop. I can't quit. He slumps to the concrete with a thud. Breathing hard, I tower over him. Sweat dripping into my eyes, I lean over and hoist him up by his armpits. His head rolls on his neck, but he's still conscious, just not for long though.

"Come near her again, and I'll fucking kill you next time." my voice is deadly in his ears. His one eye cracks open and shock registers on his face that I know. I deliver the heaviest blow I've ever flung in my life. All the anger, rage and aggression packed into one solid hit. His body twists around and he crashes to the floor again with a sickening thud.

The crowd goes wild and someone approaches me from behind. I'm still locked in the adrenaline thrumming through my body and whirl around, ready to punch the fuck out of who's touching me. Switch throws his hands up in the air in surrender and the beast I battle with every day takes it as a form of submission. I lower my fists and fight to control myself.

"C'mon kid. Let's get out of here before they ambush us." Switch shouts.

He throws a towel at me and we quickly exit the room and run up the metal stairs, shutting out the chants and the howling of the crowd. We reach the exit and once I wipe the sweat off, he hands me my black hoodie and hat. I put them on quickly, disguising myself in the dark of night.

****

Someone bumps into me from behind and I spin around to see who it was. A teenager with big hoop earrings, blonde hair, and familiar hazel eyes stare up at me, speechless. It's the same girl from the alley.

"Oh fuck," she mumbles, before darting back into the crowd.

Before I can stop her and discover who she is, she's gone. I rush the crowd searching for her, but she's nowhere in sight. Sighing in defeat, I turn back towards the circle of people, keeping my head down, my baseball hat sitting low. I push my way through the crowd and stand two rows back, watching the scene in front of me. Grunts and groans penetrate the air as two women battle it out in the middle. One of them has long black hair tied in a tight bun. She has on a black sports bra and green boxing shorts. She's sporting a cut above her right eye, bleeding into her vision. Her left eye is swollen shut, and she's swaying on her feet, on the verge of losing consciousness. The other woman has her back to me, wearing dark blue boxing shorts and a matching sports bra. Her long blond hair is tied in a loose ponytail. I spot a tattoo I've been very intimate with, peeking out from under the waistband of her shorts. She slowly shifts in my direction. My heart stops beating and the noises all fade away as her hazel eyes lock onto mine.

Frozen in place from shock, she doesn't see her opponent coming up behind her until her fist connects with the back of Wrath's head. She spins back around, ducking low and delivers the most powerful uppercut to the woman's face, I've ever witnessed. The other woman falls back and lands on the ground with a sickening thud, not moving.

Wrath spins back around in my direction, but the crowd swallows her up before she can break free. Finally snapping out of my daze, I turn around and push my way through the crowd and up the metal stairs, taking them two at a time. My heart is pounding in my ears and my body is shaking from head to toe. I need to get out of here fast.

I push open the door at the top of the stairs with unbelievable force and it slams against the wall behind it. I run down the dark hallway and shove open the door leading outside. I stumble onto the sidewalk as the sun blinds me for a moment.

"Rough time?" A deep voice asks me from behind.

I whirl around and see the same guy that let me in standing against the building. He has a cigarette in his mouth and crosses his arms over his chest, glaring at me.

"No, I'm good. Too many memories." I gruffly reply.

"Hey, kid. If you can't handle it, then don't come back."

"Oh, I can handle it and I'm not a kid."

I turn around and make my way back to the subway station. I pay for a Metro card and enter the underground trains. Taking a seat on one of the wooden benches, I rest my hands on my knees and keep my head down. Exhaling a deep breath, I compose myself. I need to get this shit under control. I didn't fight all these years to get out and only to be sucked back in again.

Ashton was right. I'm not ready to handle this on my own and what just happened back there proved it. Vibrations echo off the walls and a breeze blows onto the platform, tousling my shirt. A train is coming in. I look up and see it's the E train heading to Times Square. Once the train has stopped, my feet are moving me onto it. I grab a seat in the back of the car and hold my head down. Passengers get on and off the next few stops. I've looked up every few minutes, keeping my hat low over my eyes, observing and watching the other passengers.

When the ding sounds, signaling it's my stop, I stand to my full height and wait at the doors for them to open. People on the other side of the doors, waiting to get on, catch one look at me and step back as I step out. I can't even blend in down here, so I need to figure out a way to use that to my advantage instead of hiding from it.

Chapter 8

Nolan

The sounds of taxi horns blaring, and voices greet me as I stride up the concrete steps from the dark subway station. The sun is bright and the fresh air is a blessing in disguise. I look around at Times Square and the beauty still takes my breath away. Billboards light up the city blocks for miles on end. I approach a long plastic seating area and people move out of my way quickly. Sitting down, I rest my head in my hands and listen to the noises around me. This part of Times Square is shut down to cars and bicyclists. It gives tourists an effortless way to enjoy the sights around them. This is a beautiful city if you look past the evil lurking in the corners and dark alleyways.

"Alright, ladies and gentlemen. Listen up!" A familiar voice shouts from behind me. "We have a show for you today and this one's very special."

I stand to see what's going on, keeping my baseball hat low on my head. There's a crowd gathered around a group of guys and they're extending my way. The guys are wearing grey sweatpants and have yellow bandanas tied around their heads or arms. Their dark skin is glistening with sweat and none of them are wearing shirts. I swallow hard when their leader glances in my direction and locks his light brown eyes on me. Oh shit, this isn't good. I break eye contact with him and walk toward the back of the crowd.

"Hey," he hollers in my direction. "Where are you going? Don't you want to stay for the show?" Knowing I shouldn't engage with him, I keep pushing my way through the crowd, until a strong hand grabs my shoulder, whipping me fast around.

Throwing his grip off me, I give him a lethal glare. "Don't fucking touch me," I growl, fighting to keep my anger tamped down.

"We need to talk," he states and crosses his solid arms over his chest. A King Cobra snake tattoo coils up his right arm and spreads out across his dark chest, the mouth open towards his heart, ready to strike the black heart tattoo.

"No, we don't," I answer, low and deadly.

He looks me in the eye and slips a piece of paper in my hand. "Yes, we do," he insists. He turns back to the crowd and continues his speech like nothing happened. I tune him out and open the piece of paper in my shaking hand. It's an address. Underneath the address says *you need me.*

I need Ashton on this. I can't do this by myself anymore. Things are getting stranger and stranger by the minute. That guy is the leader of the Black Heart Crew. They're bad motherfuckers and I've had a few run-ins with them back years ago. They live up to their name, Black Heart. They don't give a fuck who you are or what gang you're affiliated with. They'll kill you for looking at them wrong, then send pieces of your body to your loved ones.

I walk away from the crowd and down a dark alley. I tuck the paper in my front pocket and keep my head down. Pulling out my phone, I dial Ashton's number.

"It's about fucking time." Ashton growls on the other end.

"Hey, I need your help. You're right, I can't do this alone."

"What happened?"

"It's a long story. One I don't want to get into on the phone. Can you meet me at my motel room?"

"I'm already here," Ashton quickly answers, taking me by surprise. "C'mon you should know I can track anyone, anywhere."

"I'll be right there." I sigh, hanging up my phone.

I smile to myself as I make my way back down the subway station. I can always count on him to be there. The train to take me to thirty-sixth street is just pulling into the station and I walk into the car. I find a seat in the back and kick my feet up on the bench in front of me. A woman huffs in annoyance at my move, but I don't give a fuck right now. Ashton is here and that means the rest of my team will be here soon and we'll figure this out together. I wonder if Ashley is here too. Pulling my phone back out, I click on her name and send a quick message. I can't talk down here, but I can send a text.

Me: I miss you.

Ashley: I miss you too, now quit being a stubborn asshole and tell me what's going on.

I smile to myself. She's a firecracker that's for sure. God, do I miss her like crazy. My phone chimes again with another message.

Ashley: Sorry, I'm just worried about you. I'm here and I'm not going anywhere. So, you better get used to letting me in.

Her message is cryptic. Does that mean she's here in the City or here in general? Fuck this woman keeps me on my toes. Instead of pondering her message, I slide my phone back in my pocket and watch the signs for my exit.

Thirty-sixth street looms ahead as the train slows down, its brakes squealing as it comes to a fast stop. I stand up and wait at the doors again. This time, instead of keeping my head down, trying to blend in, I keep it up high and make eye contact with everyone who looks in my direction. Something must appear on my face because when I look at someone, they quickly look away. I know I'm an intimidating guy, but that's just ridiculous.

The doors whoosh open in a hurry and I step out onto the platform. People make a wide berth for my massive frame as I pass them by. What the actual fuck is going on? I'm used to people moving away from me, but not like this.

Walking up the concrete steps into the city again, I can feel a tiny hand rest on my lower back. I immediately whip around and no one's there. Laughter floats in my ears and I close my eyes, trying to steady my erratic heartbeat. People pass by me as I stand on the steps, trying to gain control.

What the actual fuck? I'm finding myself saying this repeatedly since I've been here. Laughter floats around me again and I scan the crowd as I walk up the rest of the stairs.

"Sherwood, c'mon," a girl cries, catching my attention over the crowd.

I turn around and spot the same little boy with shaggy brown hair and the girl from the underground fighting ring. She's yanking on his sweatshirt and he's staring at me again. His whiskey-colored eyes are pleading with me to help him. She's dragging him down the street by the arm, disappearing into the crowd. My feet are moving at a rapid pace, trying to catch up with them, pushing my way past the mobs of people separating me from them.

"Move the fuck out of the way," I growl when a man steps in my path. I shove him hard and he loses his footing and hits the side of a brick building.

"Hey, asshole. Watch what you're doing." the man shouts.

I spin around, already on edge and fighting the demon inside, ready to punish his ass, when a warm, gentle hand grabs mine. I freeze from the contact and the voice I've been longing to hear floats in my head.

"Nolan, I'm here."

Chapter 9

Ashley

 I spot Nolan as his towering form walks up the steps from the subway station. He's battling something inside of him, I can see it in the way he walks. I had a feeling this is where he'd come out and I was right. His muscular legs eat up the steps as he appears from the dark stairwell. The sight of his broad shoulders and solid body makes my heart skip a beat. I missed him so much in the last couple of months, it's unreal and a little scary.

 A little boy gently touches his back, trying to get his attention and a girl with long blonde hair, big hazel eyes, and tons of makeup on shoves him away. They quickly make their way up the stairs as Nolan turns around, just missing her dragging him away. Nolan closes his eyes for a minute in the dark stairwell and walks up the steps. He's struggling, I can understand that.

 When the girl's voice floats our way, Nolan doesn't see me, but he locks eyes onto the little boy. I try to holler at him, but he's gone in a flash, heading in the direction the two kids went. He clenches his hands at his sides as he shoves everyone out of his way. One man steps in his path and I quicken my pace until I'm right behind him. Something in Nolan snaps at what the man says to him and I know I must intervene before he knocks this guy on his ass. I grab his hand gently in mine, the kids are long gone by now.

"Nolan, I'm here," I whisper.

His whiskey eyes, full of pain and rage, whip around to mine and he closes them briefly. When he opens them again, he's back in control.

"Ashley," he whispers my name.

"I'm here Nolan. Let's go back to the motel and regroup," I answer. I wrap my arms around his waist and pull him against me. His tense body relaxes against mine and he rests his arms around my shoulders, hanging on for life.

"You're really here?" he questions.

"Yes, I'm really here. I've missed you. Now come on before someone sees us."

"But I can't. That little boy..." he trails off, hurt and confusion cloud his voice.

"Shh, it will be OK. We'll figure it out." My heart is breaking from the sadness in his tone. I lean up and kiss him on the cheek. I cup his face with both palms and make him look at me. His eyes still take my breath away. "I love you, now let's go."

Not letting me go, he nods his head once. We turn back and head to the motel he's staying at. Nolan wraps a strong arm around my shoulders, keeping me close to him. We make our way through the crowd and into the motel lobby. He pushes the button and the rickety old elevator doors groan as they open. We walk inside and before the doors close, his lips are on mine, stealing the breath right out of my lungs. His hands roughly tug my head back and I open my lips to allow him access. His hot tongue invades my mouth and I release a whimper from the back of my throat. He rips his lips away from mine, both of us breathing heavy, trying to calm our racing hearts.

"I needed that," Nolan whispers, his eyes are full of love and lust.

"So, did I. I've missed you."

I wrap my arms around his neck, bringing our bodies closer together. His woodsy scent dominates my senses, his hardness digging into my lower stomach. His hands tighten around my hips as his mouth crashes down onto mine again. He picks me up and I wrap my legs around his waist. A low growl escapes his lips as his mouth moves to my neck, licking and biting.

The elevator groans to a halt and the doors creak open. Nolan sets me down on my feet and we make our way out. A tingling sensation builds between my legs and I huff out a breath in frustration. He pulls me against him and whispers in my ear, "I feel the same way."

He slides his key into the door and flips on the light. I walk in behind him and shut the door. Before I have the lock turned, Nolan is on me, picking me up again. His hot breath fanning across my neck.

"I need you," Nolan groans.

I grab his hair as he pushes my back against the door, trapping me against him. He thrusts his hips into my heated center. His mouth and tongue lick and bite my neck down to my heaving breasts. My heart is pounding against my chest and my body is overheating with want and desire.

A knock at the door breaks the lust craze we're both in and Nolan releases a deep grumble. He sets me back down on my feet and I open the door. Ashton, Christian, Mia, and Redline are all standing on the other side. Nolan's hot breath is fanning across the back of my neck, sending shivers down my spine. Mia raises an eyebrow.

"Are we interrupting something?" she asks in a teasing in her tone.

Nolan lets out a grumble, his hands gripping my hips. "No, not at all Mia. Glad you guys are here. Bad timing, but that's nothing new with you," he responds, moving us out of the way.

They all enter and suddenly it's tight in here with these massive men standing in the small room. Needing to get out, I gesture to Mia.

"Mia and I are going to get some air," I tell Nolan.

"Are you all right?" he asks.

"Yeah, I'm fine. I just need some air and you guys need to talk." I answer, resting my hand on the side of his face. Tingles work their way up my arm from the contact and Nolan nods his head, not taking his whiskey eyes off mine.

"All right just don't go far," he answers.

"We won't. I want to grab a coffee. Jet lag is catching up again. Do you want anything?"

"Nah, I'm good. Just be careful." He wraps his arms around me and pulls me against him, giving me a soul-stealing kiss. Breaking away, I rest my hands on his chest.

"I'll be back in a few."

Mia gives Christian a kiss and we walk out the door. She's quiet as we step into the rickety old elevator, which is unusual for Mia. The doors groan open when we reach the bottom floor and walk out of the lobby and into the noisy street. Mia and I make our way down the street to the nearest café. People are sitting outside, enjoying the warm weather after a harsh winter. We walk inside, and the scent of fresh coffee beans assault my nose, making my mouth water.

"Do you want anything?" I ask Mia as we wait in line.

"I want to know what the hell is going on." Mia answers.

"Not in here. I'll explain what I can in a minute." I respond, staring at the floor.

I'm still not clear why she's here. After everything we've been through when Izzy had that stalker, the last thing I want is for Mia to be around the danger looming ahead. I don't want her to see what I'm capable of. She's far too innocent and looks at life with a positive attitude. If she sees what goes down that will change her whole outlook on life and that's the last thing I want.

We approach the counter and I give the barista my order. Tapping my nails on the counter as I wait for my coffee, Mia's eyes are burning into the side of my face. She's ready to unleash holy hell on me. The barista brings my order out and I accept it with a smile. Adding sugar to my large coffee, I still avoid eye contact with Mia.

We walk out into the warm, spring day and find an empty wrought iron table away from everyone. I take a seat and Mia sits down next to me. She's bouncing her leg up and down and her eyes are still watching and waiting. I take a sip of my coffee and enjoy the bitter, sweet taste coating my mouth and throat, giving me a shot of caffeine. I set my cup down on the table and finally look at her. She's worried and scared, but she's pissed too. I swear you can see the steam coming out of her ears. Her crazy is showing.

"Ashley," she says gently. "Please tell me what's going on. Christian is being tight lipped about all of this, just that X and Izzy are missing, and Nolan needed him out here. I made him bring me with him. He was going to leave me at home." Tears are welling in her brown eyes. Well, shit. I don't want her to cry.

"Mia, it's not good. I love your outlook on life and I don't want anything to change that. You should have stayed home, stayed out of this."

"Izzy is my best friend and I want to help. We've all been through a lot the last year. Please don't push me away."

"It's not safe for you out here, Mia. I wish you would see this. I don't know all of Nolan's past yet, but if things turn out the way I think they will, it's going to come rearing its ugly head. I don't want you involved in this shit. It will get really nasty and real dark, fast. I want to protect you the best way I can. You're not ready for this." I plead with her.

"What if I stay at the motel? I want to be here when you guys get Izzy and X back. I want to be here for them. Please, let me help." she pleads.

Releasing a huff, I sit back and cross my arms. I look at Mia dead in the eyes. She needs to see what I'm capable of, what we're all capable of.

"Have you ever seen Nolan with his shirt off?" I ask. She shakes her head in confusion. "There's a reason for that. Mia, these people we're dealing with are not nice. They're worse than Marie. What Marie did to us, is child's play compared to what these guys will do to us if we're caught." I search around all the people moving past us, going about their business. "I will show you something, but you have to promise me you won't tell anyone. Not even Christian. If you think you can handle it, then you can stay. If not, I want you on the next plane out of here back to Michigan. Agree?"

"Yes." She doesn't hesitate to answer.

With shaky hands, I pull my phone out of my jeans pocket and pull up my email that Rush sent me. I had him do some research on the Corridore Rosso Gang Nolan was tied with. It took him some time, so he wasn't tracked. I show Mia the first image on my phone. She lets out a startled gasp and puts her hands over her mouth, her brown eyes are wide.

"Oh my God," she says, tears are running down her face.

The image I'm showing her isn't as bad as the others, but it's bad enough. This one is of a man who crossed their gang and didn't pay up. His face is bloody and bruised, unrecognizable. There are knife wounds marring his chest and stomach, bleeding. He's missing a few teeth and his eyes are swollen shut.

"Mia, do you understand now?" I ask.

She nods her head, tears are still streaming down her face. "Did they do this to Izzy or Xavier?" She asks the question I was hoping she wouldn't.

"I don't know. We haven't heard anything yet."

Mia composes herself and wipes her eyes. "What have you heard?"

"We've only seen a photo."

"So how do you know these people really do have them?"

I click on the next email and hesitate to show her. Staring at the same image Nolan received, tears well in my eyes. They don't deserve this. They don't deserve what's happening to them. Finally finding the courage, I slide my phone across the table towards Mia with an unsteady finger, my heart pounding hard against my chest.

She glances down and picks up the phone. Her shoulders shake and tears stream down her face.

"Oh no," she sobs. Mia runs a shaky finger down the screen. I scoot closer to her and wrap my arm around her trembling shoulders, pulling her against me.

"Do you understand now? Do you see why I don't want you to get involved? I want to protect you, Mia, not bring you into my world. It's bad enough Izzy is thrown into this shit, I'm scared something will happen to you too." I confess, rubbing her arms soothingly.

"Yes, I do, but Ashley, you have to trust that I can handle it." She responds through sniffles.

"Mia, there's more about me I don't want you to see. I'm worried if you see what I'm capable of, you'll never look at me the same again. I consider you one of my best friends." A weight lifts off my shoulders, confessing what scares me the most. It isn't about taking another life with no hesitations, it's about losing my closest friends.

"You should let me be the judge of what I know and don't know, Ashley. Give me time to absorb all of this. I'm going to head to a hotel and call Christian along the way." Mia says, standing up and stretching.

I grab my cup of coffee and follow her to the curb. She releases a loud whistle and raises her hand, hailing a cab. One comes speeding towards us and slams on his brakes right in front of her. She opens the back door and turns towards me.

"Ashley, get them back safely. I'll call you in a little while and tell you what I decide to do." She climbs in the back seat and gives the cabbie a hotel name. She pulls out her phone and dials Christian.

"Stay safe Mia and let me know when you get there."

"I will. Thank you for being honest with me and please be careful." She shuts the door and the yellow taxi pulls away, tires squealing.

I watch the taxi, until they're farther down the street, mixing in with the sea of yellow. A shiver runs down my back and I sink deeper into my hoodie, trying to shake off the cold that suddenly penetrates my bones. It's still really warm out for spring, but something is settling in my gut that things are going to be taking a turn for the worse really quick.

Chapter 10

Nolan

Ashley and Mia just left the motel room and Ashton is glaring at me, his nostrils are flaring. Feeling like a kid who stole some candy, I take a seat on the twin bed and hang my head. I know I've fucked up big time.

"Nolan, you've got to stop trying to deal with this shit on your own. That's what we're here for." Ashton scolds me.

"I know. It was stupid, but I thought I could handle it. I still can but can't do it alone. We need to regroup. Tell me what you know." I answer, looking up.

Christian is leaning against the wall with his arms crossed over his chest, looking just like his brother. Ashton is sitting in the tiny chair against the wall, his huge form taking up most of the small space. Redline is leaning against the door, his blue eyes are watching me. I didn't have time to wonder what he's doing here instead of Rush earlier, but now the question is running through my mind.

Ashton leans forward in the chair, his fingers are steepled in front of him. "I ran a check on Tatiana like you asked me to. She's been in and out of jail for several years for either fighting or illegal shit the cops couldn't pin on her.

She does have a little sister named Alessia. She's involved in the gang just as much as Tatiana."

"Anything about Tatiana having a little boy?" I ask, holding my breath.

"Nothing I could dig up yet. Marks is still searching, but he needs to do it carefully. They've got shit under control after you left. Any time someone searches for any of them, their security system flags it and alerts Switch. These guys have come a long way since you were in. We need to get someone to work undercover and penetrate their walls." Ashton responds. There's something he isn't saying. I can see it on his face.

"I'll do it," Redline says. "I can get in and out and they'd never know."

"I don't know Redline. These guys are dangerous. I think Ashley has to have a say on that. Your part of her family, which makes you a part of ours." I explain.

"Ashley won't care. Nolan, I need to do this. I need to do something. I feel terrible about the way things went down between us out in L.A. and this will be my chance to make it up to you." His blue eyes are pleading with me to let him do this.

"Let's talk to Ash first, then we can decide," I counter.

"Fair enough, but I want to do this. I can handle it."

Christians phone rings, breaking the silence that followed our conversation. He pulls it out of his jeans pocket. "It's Mia."

He swipes it and answers. "Mia, what's wrong?" He pushes away from the wall and paces back and forth in the small room.

"Are you sure?" he speaks into the phone. I can't hear what she's saying, but relief crosses Christians face. "OK. I'll swing by the hotel in a little while and check on you. Lock the doors and don't answer it for anyone but me, Ashton, or Nolan." He disconnects the call and looks at me. "Your girl is good."

"What did she do?" I ask, confused.

"She convinced Mia to stay out of this. She's on her way to The Plaza. Mia wouldn't tell me what Ash said or did, but I'm relieved. I couldn't talk her out of staying at home. Whatever Ashley told her worked. I'm going to swing by there and check on her when we leave here."

"We'll all check on her. Now, back to business. Redline, if you're serious there are a few things you need to know. The best way in is to fight."

"You mean like a street fight? Like walk up to one of their members and knock him out cold?" His eyebrows wrinkle in confusion.

"No." I shake my head, "That'll get you killed. Have you ever been underground?" I ask.

"No."

"There are no rules down there. Only bring what you got and go in hard and fast. I trained for months before going in, but we're going to have to get you up to speed fast. The longer they have Xavier and Izzy, the worse it is."

There's a soft knock on the door, interrupting our conversation. Redline moves out of the way and I open the door. Ashley is standing on the other side, relief written across her delicate face.

"Hey, I convinced Mia to head to a hotel. Did she call?"

"Yeah, she just talked to Christian. She's heading to The Plaza. What did you say to her?" I ask.

"Nothing much." She casts her eyes down onto the worn carpet. "I don't want her involved. I didn't tell her anything about you or your past. I just did what I had to do."

I grab her hand shoved in her jeans pocket and pull her into the room, shutting the door behind us. A passive look crosses her face and she glances up at Christian.

"I'm sorry Christian, but she can't see this side of us. I know she'd probably be able to handle it, but I don't want to take that chance. There's a lot of shit that will go down and I want to protect her from it. It's bad enough Izzy is seeing this side." Her bottom lip trembles at the thought. I wrap my arms around her and pull her soft curves against my hard body. Running my hands up and down her back in a soothing motion, Ashley relaxes against me.

"It's OK, Ash. I didn't want her to come in the first place. She's stubborn and strong-willed. I'm just relieved you could do what I couldn't." Christian says. "What did you say to her?"

Ashley looks at the ground and then meets my eyes before answering. "I showed her some pictures of what the Corridore Rosso's are capable of. They weren't as bad as what they've done in the past, but it worked."

"How did you get pictures?" I ask, baffled. My heart is pounding against my chest and my palms are sweaty. Has she seen what I've done? Does she realize how dangerous I really am?

"I have my own resources, Nolan. I know more than what you give me credit for and I'm still here." Her honey brown eyes bore into mine, revealing she knows about my past. How much? That I'm not sure on, but like she said, she's still here and letting me touch her, hold her. If it disgusted her, she wouldn't even be able to look at me. What's reflecting in her eyes is acceptance. She accepts my past and what I've done. There's a weight lifted off my shoulders and I swallow hard. A smile lights up Ashley's face and she rests her head on my chest, breathing my scent in.

"Uh, Ash...," Redline mumbles, breaking into our little bubble. She picks her head up and looks at Redline. "I have an idea and need to run it by you."

"What is it?" she asks.

"There's only one way into the Corridore Rosso Gang and that's through me. I can go undercover and penetrate their walls."

"What. No, no way." She shakes her head back and forth. "You're not putting yourself at risk. I won't allow it."

"Please, Ash. I need to do this. Not just for Nolan, but for me too. I acted like a complete ass to Nolan in L.A. and I feel this is the best way to make up for it, please." His blue eyes plead with her.

"I can't let you, Redline. You don't know what they're capable of and even if you did, how would you get in?"

"We've got that under control," I answer.

"You want him to do this?" she asks, peering up at me.

"No, but I don't see any other way. Ashton needs to be here with us and Christian is too much like a cop and they'll see right through that. I obviously can't go in and I can't let you. Redline is our way in. He'll be safe as long as he sticks to the plan and keeps his head down."

"Please Ash, I need to do this." Redline pleads again. Her body stiffens with apprehension before answering.

"Fine. But if they suspect you for anything, you get the fuck out of there. I don't care where you are or what you're doing. You get the fuck out, Redline."

"I will. Thank you," his blue eyes light up with excitement.

"First, you need to learn how to fight and it will have to be a quick lesson," I say holding up one finger. "Second, once you get in, keep your head down. They're going to make you do some shady shit and it will try to change you, possibly break you." I hold up two fingers. "Don't let it. Don't get sucked into that world, Redline. Once she sinks her evil claws in you, she won't let go. It's an adrenaline rush and one that's addicting. Third, you're going to want an outlet after you fight and there's one girl who can do that," I hold up three fingers. "That'll be your in. Cozy up to Wrath but watch your back."

"What can she do?" Redline asks, his sapphire eyes are wide, soaking in everything I'm telling him.

I hesitate to answer when Ashley splays her fingers along the worst scar marring my body over my shirt. The warmth of her hand encourages me to be strong. I lift my shirt up over my head and hear gasps coming from the room. I keep my eyes on Ashley as I speak.

"This one here," I say pointing to the long, jagged scar from my armpit to my collarbone. "Is what she's capable of when she's pissed. She used a dull knife and found immense pleasure in making it." I swallow hard and keep my eyes locked on Ashley as my mind drifts back to one of the worst days of my life.

Chapter 11

Nolan-17 years old

It's been two months since I've officially been initiated into the Corridore Rosso gang. I've had to do some shady shit to be wearing this red bandana, but the power that comes with it is like nothing I've ever experienced. I'm hooked, and I can't let go. The demon I've fought with every day is slowly taking over and he wants blood.

Switch and I are walking down the street, towards a bar called "The Rosso." It's where my mother has been bar tending and working under Switch's father Marcus Angelo. She doesn't care that I've been involved with these guys if I keep providing her money for her drugs. It's a warm spring day, but the light breeze blowing off the Hudson Bay sends a shiver down my spine.

Switch opens the heavy wooden door to the bar and it takes my eyes a second to adjust to the dim lighting inside. My mother is standing behind the bar, wearing a pair of short shorts and a black tank top that hangs off her slim frame. She's looking worse each time I see her. Her stringy brown hair is pulled up in a ponytail and her cheeks are sunken in. She's serving Marcus a beer, who's sitting at the end of the bar and he looks up when we come inside.

He nods his head at Switch and they go into the back room of the bar, out of sight. I take a seat at one of the scared round tables, near the door. My mother comes over and sets a Coke down in front of me.

"Looks like you can use this," she says and walks away.

I take a long pull, the cold liquid burning its way down my throat, looking around the bar. Shit, she's mixed some Jack in this Coke. There are just a few people in here watching me out of the corner of their eyes. They won't look at me directly, which is fine with me. Suppressing a cough from the strong mixture, I keep one eye on the door and stay aware of my surroundings. Leaving the drink my mother brought me alone, I play with the straw, waiting for Switch and Marcus to appear from the backroom. They do most of their business back there.

We just got done collecting money from our dealers and walked out with over fifty grand in cash. I had to use my fists only once when the asshole thought he could short change us. He'll be eating from a straw for a little while. I flex my hands and stare at the scars created by beating the shit out of people. Is this what my life has come to?

Switch appears from the backroom. He has a pissed off expression on his face and I immediately stand up. My head is spinning and my stomach is woozy from the drink. I never drink and my mother knows this. I need to keep my wits about me around these guys.

"Let's go now," Switch barks at me. Fuck, he's pissed about something.

We walk out of the bar and into the sunlight. The brightness is overwhelming, and I shield my eyes until they can adjust, stumbling a little on the cracked sidewalk.

"What the fuck's wrong with you?" Switch growls.

"Nothing. What's going on?" I answer.

"Bullshit. Don't fucking lie to me, Nolan. You can't walk a straight line."

"My mother served me a drink. Fucking shit, I don't drink. I'll be fine in a minute." I stumble again as we walk down the sidewalk.

"How many times do I have to tell you, don't take things from that woman? She's fucked up your ability to do your fucking job and we have another one." He stops right in front of me and I almost slam into him. "Don't fuck this one up. Marcus needs this money and if you fuck it up, you'll be sorry." The deadly look in his black eyes sobers me up immediately.

"Got it. I won't fuck it up." I answer, keeping my eyes locked on his. He must be satisfied with what he sees because he turns and walks away. I scramble to keep up. "What's the job?"

"You're going to go and collect twenty grand from this junkie named Tony. He's owed Marcus for a long time and we finally found out where he's been hiding. You do this job and I'll take you back in The Circle. You fuck it up, and you'll face me."

A shudder runs through my body at his parting words. My back is still healing from the last time I had to face him. I had a simple job to boost cars, but the cops were there and I had to abandon them. I didn't walk for a few days after Switch gave me a beat down of my life. One I never want to experience again. The bruises and wounds are still evident on my back.

"C'mon, we have a small window to deal with this asshole," Switch says, jogging across the street. Taxi horns are blaring at his disregard for the walking signal. I quickly follow and a grey sports car almost hits me. The man driving it blares his horn and slams on his brakes. I pound my fist on the hood of his car, causing a dent.

"Who the fuck do you think you are?" The man says, climbing out of his car.

"Someone you don't want to fuck with," I growl, glaring at him.

My body is shaking with rage. After a cold, hard, savage stare down with this guy, he finally gets back into his car. I'm still standing in front of him as he revs the engine. The demon inside wants to come out and play and *a smirk crosses my lips. This motherfucker thinks he's a badass behind the wheel of his shiny car, but I will teach him a lesson. I keep my hands spread out on the hood and lean forward, not breaking eye contact. I watch his juggler move up and down in a frantic pace, sweat beads on his brow and his breathing turns erratic.*

Switch grabs me by the arm and my head whips to the side. He holds his hand up in surrender when he sees how far gone I am. I've lost all control to the evil living inside of me right now.

"C'mon man, save it for Tony," Switch says. I cock my head to the side, watching and waiting. A smirk still on my lips. "Let's go. He's not worth it. Let's go get our money. Keep him out to play, but let's do this job."

"I'll do this job, but I want in The Circle, tonight." My voice is low and deadly. Switch backs away from me slowly, his hands are still up in surrender. I follow, watching and waiting. I'm the predator, stalking towards my prey with black hair and black eyes. Everything he's done to me in the past few months is in the front of my mind and I want nothing more than to shed his blood with my fists. My body vibrates with tension as Switch guides me to the sidewalk.

"You got it. Circle, tonight. You need to get in there and I have the perfect fighter." Switch agrees.

"Set it up, now," I demand through gritted teeth.

My eyes follow his movements, my body still vibrating with rage. I could easily end him right here, right now and I'd finally be free of him, but I can't. If I do, Marcus will kill my mother. He's already warned me if I do anything, she's dead. She might not give a fuck about me, but she is my mom and I have to get her out and far away first before I make my move. He slowly pulls his cell phone out of his jeans pocket and sends a text. He looks up at me and nods his head when his phone chirps in his hand.

"There, done. Now can we go?" He asks and shows me his message. The demon is satisfied for now and I'm able to pull him back and take control again. I hate it when that happens. I hate losing all control. I need to figure out a way to channel it and use it to my advantage. The more I fight it, the more I lose control. Closing my eyes, I take a deep breath and release it.

"Let's go," I agree.

We walk down the sidewalk in hurried strides and jog down into the subway station. A train is barreling through causing the wind to ruffle my hair. It screeches to a stop and we get on, taking a seat in the hard, plastic chairs. The locals give us a wide berth and keep their eyes down as the train shoots off into the darkness. Leaning forward, resting my elbows on my knees, I flex and unflex my fists, waiting impatiently for our stop. I can't fuck this job up. I need to get into The Circle tonight to keep the blood lust thrumming through my veins in check.

"We're here," Switch says, snapping me out of my mind.

We get off the train and make our way up the stairs, into the bright sunlight. The anger and rage are back, thrumming through my veins, watching Switch. I need to do something, anything to get away from him. The longer I'm in his clutches, the worse the evil wants to take over. Walking up to a rundown house on the outskirts of the city, Switch glances back at me.

"Ready?" he asks.

"Ready," I respond.

He jumps up onto the rickety old porch and kicks the door in. It swings wide and bounces off the wall, making the man inside jump up off the couch. He's about six-foot-tall with dirty blonde hair that hasn't seen a shower in a few weeks. His clothes are dirty and falling off his skinny frame. His dull green eyes are wide with shock when we come barreling in. Switch narrows his eyes on the guy and approaches him quickly.

"Where's my money?" he asks.

"What money?" The junkie's playing dumb. His eyes dart to the kitchen.

"The fifty g's you owe me, Tony. I suggest you pay up now or my man here will have some fun."

I crack my neck to the side and never take my eyes off the junkie. I give him a cold, hard stare and I swear he just pissed himself. His body is shaking, and the body odor stench is overwhelming when I stalk towards him. I try not to gag the closer I get, but it's hard. I grab the junkie by the throat and lift him off his feet. His jagged fingernails try to dig into my hand as I squeeze his windpipe closed with my fist. He swallows hard under my hand and his eyes dart towards the kitchen again.

"In the kitchen," I tell Switch, not taking my eyes off Tony the junkie. I can hear Switch leave the room and I tighten my hold on this guy's throat. His eyes bulge and his feet thrash, trying to connect with my shins. His face takes on a blue tint when Switch comes back into the room.

"Let him go," Switch says.

I drop him to the couch and he grabs his throat, wheezing and coughing. I'm not satisfied he received our message and my hands are shaking with rage, itching to spill blood. His blood, as his bones crunch under my knuckles.

"Let this be a lesson to you," Switch says staring at Tony still trying to catch his breath, on the couch. "You don't pay up when you're supposed to, I'm going to find you and let him," he says pointing to me, "loose next time. You'll be eating from a straw for the rest of your life."

Tony's green eyes grow wide again and he nods his head up and down. I turn my back on him and walk towards the door. Hearing a grunt, I whip around and Switch is on the ground with a knife to his throat. There's a line of blood trailing from the corner of his mouth. Tony is straddling him, pinning him down. In a quick moment, I have a choice to make. I can let this junkie kill Switch or I can kill the junkie.

Shit. With as much as I need to get out, I can't, not yet. I charge the junkie and throw him off Switch and he hits the wall with a thud. Without a second thought, I pick him up and pin him against the wall, the adrenaline flowing through my body leaves me no choice but to end his life. The demon I battle with daily is ready to wreak havoc on this guy. With surprising strength, he pushes off the wall and I lose my grip. He takes a swing and connects with the side of my face, making me stumble back. Blood fills my mouth and I spit on the ground.

"Wrong move asshole." I glare at Tony and am on him in a flash. My fist hitting his face with a satisfying crunch. He howls in pain, but I don't stop. I keep on raining blow after blow until he stops moving. Blood flying everywhere, hitting me in the face and arms. Hands grab my shoulders and Switch's voice is in my ear.

"Finish him."

Two words and my demon's happy. I grab the junkie's head and twist his neck until I feel the bones snap under my hands and his body goes limp. Dull green eyes stare back at me, unblinking.

Fuck, that felt good. Tony the junkie's blood has stained my knuckles and I've taken another life with the order from Switch. Another reason to get the fuck out. It's not the first time I've killed under his command and I have a feeling deep in my gut, it won't be the last. Standing up, I catch a glimpse of Switch out of the corner of my eye. He's pissed, holding his throat, pacing back and forth. I don't say a word. His black eyes lock onto mine, fury and rage pass across his face.

"Check for anything valuable, then destroy and burn it down. Meet me at the apartment when you're done." He gets right into my face. "If this happens again, you're fucking dead. You got me?"

I nod my head. He has control over my mind and can fuck with it whenever he wants. I might be stronger and bigger than he is, but he's in my head and I can't help but do what he says. He's programmed me to be this way and I can't fight it. I'm not strong enough. I need to channel the evil lurking below the surface. He's afraid of the demon, but he knows I have no control.

Several hours, one burned house, and dead body gone later, I finally arrive at the apartment where it all started. I'm completely exhausted as I walk up the brick steps and into the foyer. My defenses are down and my body's sluggish. Strong arms grab me from behind and something dark covers my head. A needle pierces my skin and I'm out cold before I have a chance to fight them off.

******

Awakening to a slap across my face, I try to open my eyes, but fail at the attempt. Tingles work their way up my arms as my body wakens. My hands are tied above my head. I try flexing my muscles but it's no use. White hot pain radiates through my chest and back. I can't see what they've done while I was unconscious, but the stink of burnt flesh finds its way to my nose.

"It's about time you join us. We had a little fun while we waited." Switch's voice penetrates through the fog in my mind. "Hope you don't mind, but I needed an ashtray and your back made a good one."

Opening my eyes, I finally get a look at where I am. Shit, this isn't good. The evil lurking under my skin wants to come out, but with the drugs flowing in my system, it can't. I'm in a cellar, tied upright to a metal beam, my bare feet are dangling inches from the floor. If I flex my toes, I can touch the ground. I only have on a pair of jeans. No shirt, shoes, or socks. The dampness surrounding me sends a shiver down my naked torso. A bright bulb is shining in my eyes and shadows dance in the corners, water drips from somewhere off in the distance. Electricity hums softly next to my head, running through the wires in the ceiling. Switch walks up to me, blocking the light and stares me dead in the eyes.

"You fucked up today, now you must pay for your mistakes. Good thing you're awake for this part." An evil sneer is upon his lips.

I try to open my mouth and respond, but no sound escapes my lips.

"Let me do it," Wrath says from somewhere in the shadows.

My body turns stiff from her comment. She's the last person who I thought would betray me. I assumed we had something special. All the times we've been together invade my mind. Each kiss and caress of her body, each time I've made her forget her own name, every time I brought her pleasure, flips through my head. I've been played by the one person I thought I could trust.

Wrath appears from the shadow directly in front of me. Pain and remorse flashes in her eyes and she shut's it down, turning her hazel eyes cold and deadly. Switch moves out of the way and she takes his place. She removes a knife from her pocket and flips it open. The dull metal gleaming off the single bulb. I swallow hard and can't seem to find my voice. The cigarette burns across my back long forgotten as my eyes widen.

"Nolan, I hate to do this to you, but you fucked up today. Now you must pay for your mistakes," Wrath whispers in my ear. "Don't fight it and it'll be over quickly." She kisses the side of my cheek and runs her hands through my hair before slicing a shallow cut across my chest. Pain like no other, radiates through my body, but I bite back a groan, keeping my eyes locked on hers. Her hazel eyes are hesitant to keep going, but her hands work quickly making several small slices across my chest. Blood is dripping down my torso after another sink of the blade. She slices again, deeper than the others and I bite back another groan fighting the pain and unconsciousness wanting to take over.

"More," Switch demands from my right.

Wrath sinks the knife into my chest, breaking through several layers of skin. Hesitant in her strokes as she makes several shallower cuts across my skin. I'm helpless and defeated to stop her and fight back. After another sweep of her blade, sinking deeper than the rest, I can't hold back the pain. Even the demon I battle with daily can't help me now. A low agonizing moan leaves my parted lips, my breath coming out in shallow spurts. Fire is blazing through my body and blood is dripping down my chest to the rhythm of my heart. My head drops to study the damage done and I suppress a groan.

She draws her blade to my flesh one final time before my mind slips into the darkness, blocking out the pain. Her blade plunges deep into my skin, starting at my armpit and splits my flesh away across my chest up to my collarbone. The stroke of the knife is slow and jagged as she rips away my skin. I struggle to lift my head and find her eyes, but the pain is too much to handle. I let out a blood curdling scream as my mind shuts down and I succumb to the darkness dancing in the corners of my vision.

Chapter 12

Nolan

Tears are in Ashley's eyes and her warm fingers are running gently across the scars left behind from that torturous night.

"How can you trust anyone after that?" she quietly asks. I kiss the top of her head before answering.

"It wasn't easy, but Izzy helped me trust again. She kept after me, when I moved to Michigan, and finally wormed her way into my heart. She's a light in the darkness. Xavier, Mia, and Izzy all helped me see that there's peace in a world of darkness and I learned to trust again." I answer.

"What happened after you blacked out?" Redline asks.

"I came too, next to a dumpster in an alley, rain pelting my skin causing more pain and washing away the blood. The pain thrumming through my body almost made me pass out again, but the will to survive took over and I crawled my way to the street. Some guy spotted me and ran over to help. I couldn't talk or move anymore. Drained of all my energy, I passed out again. I came to several times in the ambulance and once on the operating table. The doctors had to stitch up the worst cuts and repair the damage done to my muscles. If she would have gone an inch deeper, I wouldn't be here now. I spent several days in the hospital being questioned by detectives. My mother didn't show up once to see me and when they were getting ready to discharge me, my grandfather showed up. He got me my own place to stay away from everyone and hide while I healed." I haven't told anyone how I escaped the gang and I don't know if I ever will. If Switch discovers, he'll kill me for sure. "After I healed, I returned to the apartment Switch lived in and acted like nothing happened. I had no choice. If I didn't go back, then they'd find and kill me. Wrath tried to cozy up to me, but I threw her advances back in her face and only did my job while plotting a way to get out."

"How did you get out?" Christian asks. He's leaning up against the small window, his face is pale from my story.

"That's a long story I don't want to get into. It wasn't pretty, but a few months after the basement incident, I found my escape and took it. I changed my name, got my mother out and left. They had no idea where I went to and that worked to my advantage. As far as they knew, I was dead, and my body was never found." I look down into Ashley's light brown eyes filled with tears. "I understand this scares you and you don't want to let Redline go in, but I think it can work. We need to get inside and I can't do it. Switch still has control over my mind after years of being subjected to his hate. But if I have you by my side, I can fight him and together we can help Redline while he's in there."

"Ok, but we need to have a plan on how to get him out if things take a turn," Ashley responds.

I turn my head and look at our small group. Christian is now pacing back and forth from the window to the small table Ashton is sitting at. Ashton is on his laptop he pulled out, his fingers flying over the keys. Redline is leaning against the wall, lost in his own thoughts and Ashley is still leaning against me. Her hands are soft and warm against my bare skin.

"Redline, we need to find a gym to teach you the basics of being in a fight club. I need to see what you can do and who to match you with." He nods his blonde head, he looks scared, but that's good. He needs to remember it isn't all fun and games in The Circle. "Ash, how long until Rush and the rest of your crew get here?"

"I don't know. Let me call Rush and find out." She stops running her fingers across my skin and I immediately miss her touch. Before she can get her phone out, I pull her against me and my lips descend upon hers. She runs her hands through my hair, opening her mouth to allow me access. Slipping my tongue inside, she releases a whimper I swallow up as our tongues battle back and forth. My groin tightens and my heart stutters in my chest.

Pulling away our breaths are rapid against each other's lips.

"Hmm, what was I doing?" Ashley asks, trying to get her breathing under control.

"You were calling Rush." I answer with a smirk.

"Oh yeah. You've got to stop doing that." She responds, giving me a wink.

I watch her ass as she opens the door and walks out into the hallway. Closing it behind her, I thank God every day for bringing her into my life and loving me, scars and all. Ashton clears his throat and I drag my eyes away from the door towards his massive frame, sitting at the small table.

"I found us a gym and an apartment to rent right near the Corridore Rosso Gang. They won't know we're there as long as you keep a low profile. Christian and I will work the fighting scene, you stay out of sight and if you go anywhere, disguise yourself."

Ashley comes back in with a smile lighting up her face. "Rush will be here tomorrow. The rest of my crew needs to stay back in L.A. but he's coming." She looks at Ashton and his face falls for a moment before schooling his features. "Natalia asked me to tell you she'll see you soon, Ashton."

He nods his head and gets up from the table, closing his laptop. "Come on let's get to our new place." His voice is surly and disappointed. I would be too if the woman I wanted keeps skirting the attraction there. I'm still not happy with Natalia, but it's Ashton's life and he likes her, so he can do what he wants.

I grab my bag off the bed and we walk down the dirty hallway toward the elevator. I push the button and wrap my arm around Ashley as we wait. She snuggles into my side and my heart picks up speed. I hope we have separate apartments while we're here. I really need to get inside of her again. The tightening in my jeans is a sign it's been way too long. Her strawberry shampoo penetrates my nose and I inhale deeply as she lets out a soft sigh.

"What are you thinking?" I whisper in her ear.

"That we need our own place," she whispers back.

The elevator dings open and we all walk into the cramped space. The doors close and it groans as it begins our descent.

"I hope this thing holds our weight. It would suck if we all plummet to our deaths in here." Christian jokes.

"Ha-ha. I hate this elevator. It gives me the creeps." Redline says with a shudder.

It finally stops on the ground floor and the doors creak open slowly. Ashton and Christian step out first, their eyes are scanning the whole floor before letting Ashley and me out. When they're satisfied it's clear, they move out of the way. I kiss Ashley on the head.

"I'll meet you outside. I need to check out."

"OK, I'll see you out there." She responds by grabbing my face and kissing my lips gently. Blood thrums through my veins from her gentle touch. She releases me and walks with Christian and Redline out the door and out of my sight.

I hurry over to the receptionist and toss my keycard on the desk with a slap, making the receptionist jump. Ashton is right behind me.

"Checking out already, Mr. Nolan?" It's the same chick from earlier. She licks her lips as she looks up and down, then her eyes fall on Ashton's towering form behind me.

"Yeah, don't need the room anymore," I grunt.

"Bummer, I could have shown you a good time." She snatches the keycard off the counter with a pout and types on the computer. "There, all checked out. Here's your receipt and if you change your mind, my number's below."

She slides the receipt across the counter and sure enough, her number is written below. I say nothing and hand the receipt to Ashton. He barks out a gruff laugh at the receptionist and crumples the receipt.

"Sorry sweetheart, but my man here isn't interested."

"What about you? You look like you could give a girl a night of pleasure." She says batting her eyelashes.

"Barking up the wrong tree, sweetheart." Ashton throws his huge arm around my shoulders, trying not to laugh. "Ready babe?" He asks in a high pitch voice.

"Yeah," I answer, trying to hold my laughter in at the dumbfounded expression on her face. We turn from the counter and I punch Ashton in the stomach. "Dude, what the fuck?" I ask when we're out of earshot. He lets out a grunt.

"Sorry, she was laying it on thick and made my skin crawl. I couldn't help but fuck with her." He's not sorry, he's trying not to laugh.

"Just, bro, don't touch me. That creeps me out more than anything." I respond with a shudder as we walk out the door and into the bright sunlight. It's warm against my skin and all my worries melt away when I see Ashley. She's leaning against the brick building and has her head tipped back towards the sun, her Aviators are perched on her nose, blocking the light. She looks relaxed and ready. I approach her quietly and settle my hands on her hips, leaning against her soft body. Nibbling her neck, she releases a soft sigh and runs her hands through my hair, pulling me closer. I kiss my way up her neck to her lips and she shudders under my grip, connecting her lips to mine. Lust roars through my veins and I instantly hardens in my jeans as her soft velvet tongue invades my mouth. Her sweet taste overtakes my senses and I let out a deep groan from the back of my throat, forgetting we're in the middle of the street.

"Guys, we need to get moving," Ashton says behind me.

I drag my lips away from Ashley's and rest my forehead against hers. Her rapid breathing floats towards my mouth and I want nothing more than to rip her clothes off and have my wicked way with her.

"We'll pick this up later," Ashley says, breathlessly. I pull her against me to know how hard I am for her and she lets out a little gasp. "Definitely later."

I let go of her hips and we walk hand in hand down the busy street. I keep my head down and try not to make eye contact with anyone passing by us. I feel exposed out in the open and stop under a construction beam when we round a corner. Ashton, Redline, Christian, and Ashley stop with me, giving me a questioning look.

"I feel too exposed." I reach into my duffle bag and pull out my Detroit Tigers baseball hat and a black hoodie.

I put the hoodie on and pull the cap down low on my forehead to cover most of my face. "I'm ready."

"Good idea," Ashley says, as she snuggles into my side. I wrap my arm around her shoulders and we walk to the subway station.

Once we're down the steps, into the underground world of trains, bums, and entertainers, Ashley removes her Aviators and sets them on top of her blonde hair, discreetly scanning the people walking past us. Her body is tense under my arms, watching and waiting for something to happen.

We make our way to the dirty platform. There's a woman singing in the middle platform, separating the trains coming and going. She's strumming an acoustic guitar playing a sweet melody that floats off the walls and touches your soul. People walk past, ignoring her or dropping change in the guitar case, but she doesn't make eye contact as she keeps playing, her head down and her beautiful voice drifts our way.

Vibrations echo in the tunnel and the wind picks up speed, ruffling Ashley's hair around her face. I watch her checking out the people around us. The train comes in and screeches to a halt. The doors open and we get on as other people get off. Taking a seat in the back of the car, I pull Ashley down next to me and hold her close. Ashton,

Redline, and Christian all surround us standing up, hanging on the bar above their heads.

"So, what's the plan once we get to the apartment?" Ashley asks.

"We're going to get settled in and then Redline, Christian and I will scout the neighborhood. See what we can come up with." Ashton answers, looking around to determine if anyone's eavesdropping.

"What are we supposed to do and are you bringing Mia with you?" Ashley asks.

"You're going to stay low and out of sight and no Mia's staying right where she's at." Christian answers. "I'm going to visit her after our scouting mission and see how she's holding up, then get our SUV and bring it back with all of our stuff."

"I hate being out of the loop," Ashley huffs.

"I can think of ways to keep us busy," I whisper. Ashton grunts and Redline rolls his eyes.

"And that's why we're leaving. The tension in the air is unbearable." Christian states with a smirk.

"Has anyone heard anything about Xavier and Izzy? After hearing your story, Nolan, I'm really worried about them." Ashley says.

"So far, no harm has come to them," Ashton responds.

"How do you know?" she asks, raising an eyebrow.

"Because I have eyes and ears all over this city. Marks and Ramirez flew in an hour ago and they're scouting the area. They've made it into the apartment building where Xavier and Izzy are and planted cameras outside the door and some surveillance equipment around the building. They can't get in though. It's heavily armed with an alarm system and there's always someone guarding the inside of the door. So, we have to tread carefully." Ashton tells us.

"But they've actually seen them?" she asks hopefully.

"Yes. They caught Xavier on camera. He's OK. Only a few bruises, but we need to get inside and get them out. Once Switch realizes we're here, I don't think it'll stay that way." Ashton responds. There's more he isn't telling us. I can see it in his eyes.

The train lurches around the bend and Redline loses his footing. He stumbles forward before straightening.

"Those curves suck," he grumbles.

"Redline, how much do you know about fighting?" I ask.

"I'm surprisingly good. Never really tested myself, but I've never lost a fight before either."

"How many fights have you been in?" I ask.

"Oh, I'd say at least two." Ashley snorts and Redline narrows his eyes at her. "Hey, I did pretty well holding my own." he protests.

"Yeah you did, Redline. It's just weird. I'm not used to you fighting. You're more like a lover not a fighter, but it's what you want to do. Just please be careful." Ashley concedes.

"I will. Thank you, Ashley."

Our train slows down and lurches to a stop. Ashley and I stand up and Christian and Ashton are the first ones at the doors. Redline is standing behind us, blocking the other passengers. We shove our way through the doors, past all the New Yorkers, and up the concrete steps, emerging onto a busy sidewalk in the heart of Manhattan. I keep my eyes on Ashton's feet, not raising my head to look around. The scent of exhaust fumes and Italian food fill my nose and my stomach growls loudly. Ashley has her hand in mine and she lets out a small giggle.

"Are you hungry?" she teases.

"For more than food," I growl, draping my arm around her and dragging her close to my chest.

The sun is setting, and the spring air has turned chilly. Ashley wraps her arms around my waist and snuggles closer. Goosebumps break out across her skin and I rub her arms to keep her warm.

"Dang, I should've grabbed a hoodie from my bag before we left," she grumbles.

"I'll keep you warm," I whisper in her ear. She hums her approval, vibrating my chest, and it sends a blast of lust flowing through my veins. "The things you make me feel." I pull her closer and wrap my arms around her tighter.

"That's perfect." She approves.

"Not much further guys," Ashton says over his shoulder.

I sneak a glance at our surroundings and stumble to a halt. My heart beats hard against my chest and it's not because of the beautiful blonde wrapped around me. My body is trembling, and my ears are ringing. Memories are trying to surface, painful and powerful memories. There's a huge brown brick building looming in front of me.

This is where it all began.

"Nolan, are you OK?" Ashley asks. She rests her hands on my thumping heart. "Nolan, talk to me." She pleads.

"I...shit...," Stumbling through my words, I take a deep breath and try again. "This is where it all began." I finally whisper. "Xavier and Izzy are in that building and I can't do a fucking thing about it." Anger replaces the fear as I stare at the apartment building. My hands shake and it's not from the cold.

Ashton slowly walks up next to me with his hand out in surrender. There must be something I'm relaying because he only does that when the demon is trying to take over. I've had it under control for years, except when Ashley's life was on the line and her asshole ex tried to kill her. I clench and unclench my fists. My body's thrumming with rage and the monster I keep under a strict lock and key is trying to surface. I fight it back to maintain control but I'm failing.

"Nolan," Ashley's voice penetrates through the bloodlust trying to take over. Her soft hands caress my face gently. "Come back to me. I need you here, with me." She whispers against my lips. I wrap my arms around her and yank her against me. I don't want to hurt her, but I have no control right now.

"Back away," my voice is low and deadly, but my hands grip her hips tighter.

"No," she responds firmly. "I'm not letting you go."

"I don't want to hurt you, but I have no control." I grit out through clenched teeth. The demon is banging against my insides, wanting out. It demands to shatter everything in its path. It needs blood and revenge.

"Yes, you do. Nolan, look at me," she says pulling my face away from the apartment and towards hers, looking at me in the eyes. "You have control. It doesn't own you. You own it. Lock it up and come back to me." I pull her closer trying to fight it. Trying to lock it away. "Ashton, back away, I've got this," she asserts, not breaking eye contact with me.

My eyes leave hers and fixate on the three men surrounding us. Revenge vibrates my bones and I'm close to losing it, losing all control and submitting to the demon. They're closer than they need to be to my woman holding onto me. Black dots appear on the edges of my vision and I take a deep breath, not taking my eyes off them. They're extremely close and I will wipe out every last person who tries to come near the woman I'm hanging onto for life. I will snap their necks and burn their bodies if they try to touch either of us. Strawberries assault my nose and Ashley keeps talking trying to bring me back, but I can't hear her. My heart is beating rapidly, and I watch the three men back away.

"That's it, now come back to me," Ashley says in my ear, breaking through the ringing. "I'm here with you. No one else. It's just the two of us." She pulls my head back towards hers, forcing me to stare into her light brown eyes. She smiles, and it lights up the world around me.

The demon I battle with recognizes her and settles down. I'm now in more control as it let's go of the bloodlust.

"Keep watching me, no one or anything else." She says, keeping eye contact. The noises from the bustling city come back into my ears, louder than they were before. She did it, she brought me back from the evil attempting to take over. I thought I had that side under control, but I don't and that scares the hell out of me. There's no telling what I'll do when I lose control, I'm a danger to everyone around me.

"Thank you," I slam my lips onto hers, kissing her with such passion it takes my breath away. I pull apart from our kiss and keep my eyes locked on hers. We're moving again, she's walking backward, not breaking eye contact or letting me go. Her soft hands are under my hoodie, caressing my skin, my scars. A shudder runs through my body from her touch.

"We're almost there." She says, only talking to me. No one else. She knows what I need at this moment and that's her full attention. "Are you under control now?"

"Yes, thank you." I kiss her gently on the lips and she sighs into my mouth. "Please don't do that again. I could have hurt you and then I would've really lost it."

"No, you won't. He recognizes me, knows I'm not a threat. I'm not afraid, Nolan. I battle with the same thing every day. I wonder every day if the pain I've endured through my life is worth looking for the light or if I should succumb to the darkness. There are days where I think it's not worth fighting. It's easier to not give a shit. Then I look at my family and it makes me want to fight it, be a better person." Ashley rests her fingers on my jaw and rubs it gently. I sigh and close my eyes.

"Are we good now?" A deep voice asks from behind me. I snap my head towards the voice and Ashton backs up a little. I blink twice and take another deep breath, more in control now.

"Yes, we're good," I answer. Regret fills me thinking about killing him a moment ago.

"Don't say it," Ashton says. "No regrets. I knew what I was getting into and I know what you battle with. We all have our own demons trying to control us."

"Are you good?" Ashley asks, dragging my eyes back to her light ones. "I need to turn around and walk inside, but I can do it backward if you're not fully in control."

I close my eyes and tilt my head back. I search inside me, finding peace for the moment. I tilt my head back down finding light brown eyes, watching me.

"Yes. I'm in control. We're good."

She gives me another smile that lights up my world and turns around. She pulls my hands around her waist and locks our fingers together, so my front is against her back. We walk slowly into the building and towards the elevators. Marks and Ramirez are waiting for us next to the mailboxes. When they see us, they push off the wall and head in our direction. My heart thumps hard again from their approach and my hands tighten around Ashley, believing they are a threat to her.

"Stay back," Ashton warns them. They both halt their movements and study me questioningly. "Now isn't a good time. Follow behind Redline, slowly."

They do what Ashton says and I relax a little. The elevator doors ding open and Ashley and I step in. We turn around together and Christian hands Ashley a key. A snarl leaves my lips from how close he is. Maybe I don't have total control yet. Christian throws his hands up in surrender, not making eye contact with me. Smart man.

"He's just giving me a key to our own place," Ashley scolds. She shows me the key and I relax a little. The elevator doors close, shutting us out from them. My lips dart across Ashley's neck and she shudders from my touch.

"That feels good," she says, tilting her neck to give me better access. My tongue snakes out licking the side of her neck, tasting her. Blood is thrumming through my veins full of want and desire to have this woman. She pushes her ass against my hardness and a groan escapes my lips. My blood pressure rises, the higher we ascend.

By the time the doors open, the sexual tension is so high, I don't know if I can move. Ashley keeps me against her and we walk down the hallway. She stops at a door and I'm too busy kissing and sucking on the side of her neck to pay attention to where we are. The need to be buried inside her is overtaking my other senses.

She finally has the door unlocked and we stumble inside. My hands are caressing her skin under her shirt. She releases a moan of approval at my assault that vibrates through my body. I slam the door shut with my foot and my mouth is upon hers, taking her breath away. Picking her up, she wraps her legs around my waist.

"Fuck, I need you," I groan.

Ashley pulls back a little and I stare into her eyes filled with lust, love, and need. The demon is battling to break free and mark her as ours. Her back hits the wall, and I pin her against it with my hips. I rip her shirt over her head and toss it somewhere behind me. I remove her bra and her full breast spill free of the confinements. I bury my face in her chest and Ashley lets out a moan, it vibrates straight into my body. I can't wait any longer. I've had enough foreplay for now. Tugging her away from the wall, she still has her legs locked around my waist, and I blindly walk down a small hallway and into a bedroom. Ashley's full lips are sucking on the side of my neck, trusting me to take her away from all the pain and worry, even if it's short-lived.

I enter the bedroom and toss her down onto the queen size bed. She bounces for a moment before righting herself. I rip my shirt over my head and crawl my way to her, stalking my prey. My blood is pumping hard through my veins as my lips descend upon her half-naked body. I kiss my way from her full breasts, down her flat stomach, to the top of her jeans. Ashley's hands are in my hair, tugging it from the roots, creating a pleasuring pain as I pop the button open and slide the zipper down. I yank her jeans and panties down her golden kissed legs and toss them behind me. I lick and nibble a path up each leg. Ashley lets out a low moan and her body is withering under my touch.

"Quit teasing me," she says passionately.

I remove my jeans and boxers quickly while Ashley catches her breath. She watches me crawl my way up her satiated body, licking and biting as I go. She grabs my face and looks me directly in the eyes.

"Nolan, I love everything about you. All your scars, all you battle with, your past, your present and your future. There's nothing that will take you away from me and I will fight for you every day. Don't lose focus of that. I'm here and I always will be."

"I love you too, Ashley. Thank you for being in my life and helping me battle with my past. I don't know where I'd be right now if you didn't pull me back. I do know where I want to be though," I wiggle my eyebrows up and down and press against her. She lets out a half giggle, half moan.

"What the hell are you waiting for?" she groans.

"I'm going to take you hard and fast. It's been building for a while and he's ready to explode."

Ashley presses her lips hard against mine and opens her mouth to allow me access. My blood pumps furiously in my veins, my heart is beating hard against my chest. I close my eyes, trying to control my urges. My hips move to the rhythm of her hand and I'm on the edge of losing it, to succumb to the evil lurking inside me. I remove her hand and bring it up above her head locking our fingers together. I stare into Ashley's eyes and try to control myself.

"With as pleasurable as that was, now's not the time to test my control. I've been wanting you since I left L.A., and today's events have brought the demon to the surface. I can't control the rage battling inside of me and if you keep teasing me, I'll end up hurting you. Pain does not equal pleasure in my world and I don't want any of my past to touch you. I want you to feel loved and cherished, not used and abused, so please let me do this my way so I can control myself better."

"I'm all yours, ready and willing. If you need hard and fast or slow and gentle. I get it, I really do. I'm not holding anything back. My love for you is stronger than anything thrown at us, so when you're ready, so am I." Ashley brings her lips up to my ear and nibbles on the outer edge, sending a shiver down my spine. "Whatever you need, Nolan, I'm here and ready."

With those words, I plunge into her. It satiates the rage battling inside of me for the moment. Moans of pleasure rip from our throats as we move together as one. We're skin to skin, my heart is beating hard against my chest. Ashley slender form shudders under my hands. The smell of sex and sweat is heavy in the air around us. Ashley moans my name and my eyes snap up. I almost lose it watching her pleasure herself. Trailing my thumb across her hip, she moans louder under my touch.

Unable to control myself any longer, I let go. I let go of the pain and the past haunting me. I let go of everything trying to bring me down. I'm here in this moment with this beautiful woman who's touched my heart, my mind, and my soul. Who's accepted me for who I am, not what she wants me to be. With her by my side, I can do anything, be anything.

"I'm coming," I grunt.

"So am I, Nolan." Ashley pleads, breathlessly.

A moan rips from Ashley's lips as she tightens around me, matching me thrust for thrust. Fire burns down my spine, dark spots cloud my vision of the beauty under me, succumbing to the pleasure I'm giving her. We both dive off the edge with groans filling the room, our breathing is rapid, and my heart is hammering in my chest.

Rolling my hips slowly, I lean down and kiss her with such passion, I don't remember my own name. Aftershocks wrack our bodies when I pull my lips from her and bury my face in her hair.

"It gets better every time we're together," Ashley's breathless voice mumbles against my shoulder.

I pick my head up and stare into her honey-colored eyes. Her cheeks are flushed, sweat is on her brow and her chest is rising and falling in rapid succession.

"Yes, it does. No matter what happens, you'll always be my safe haven. The one I can turn to and trust with my whole being. That means a lot to me, Ash." I swallow hard and push her sweaty hair out of her face. She grips my face with her slender fingers.

"Me too, Nolan. I love being your safe haven." She replies. My stomach growls, breaking our little bubble. "I think someone's worked up and appetite." She giggles. I kiss her lips gently.

"I wonder how? It's not like I did anything strenuous, I think he did all the work." I wiggle my eyebrows at her and she burst out laughing. "I want you again."

We make love one more time. This time it's slow and gentle and I bring us both to another mind-blowing orgasm. Touching each other on a higher level than ever before, I realize that without her, I'd be giving into the urges of bloodlust and revenge in a heartbeat. She completes every part of me and keeps me grounded.

Chapter 13

Christian

Watching someone who I've grown to care about and call family, fall apart before my eyes is heartbreaking. I wish there was more I could do for Nolan, but this battle he must conquer on his own. All I can do is help him when he needs it. I'll help train Redline and get Xavier and Izzy back as quickly as possible. Once our family is back together, then I can face my own issues. Although pressing for me to handle them now, these guys come first.

The elevator doors close with a silent whoosh and Ashton glances over in my direction, his similar eyes boring into mine. Ever since he's come back from Iraq, our relationship's been strained. We're not as close as we used to be. There were times growing up when we were inseparable, doing everything together, now we can't be in the same room without tension brewing between us. I know he's been through a lot overseas; I get that, but I miss having my brother, my best friend by my side.

"Come on, we have work to do," Ashton grunts out.

He turns on his heels and walks away. I hurry my steps so we're walking side by side. Redline, Marks, and Ramirez are behind us as we exit the apartment building. We turn left down the busy street, passing throngs of people going about their day, unaware of the torture and evil lurking around them.

Night has fallen onto this glorious city and dangerous people are coming out. We walk down an alley and Ashton stops when we're away from the crowd. He turns toward Marks and Ramirez. We both cross our arms over our chests and raise a brow.

"That's fucking creepy," Redline shudders.

Ashton speaks first, "Marks tell me what you know."

"Ramirez and I were able to get inside like I texted you. It's bad, Ashton. I didn't want to say anything in front of Nolan, seeing how quick he was to lose his head. Will he be all right?"

"Yes, he'll figure out a way to control the urges and when he does, Switch better watch his back. He'll be out for blood and will destroy anyone who stands in his way." Ashton answers. He knows the most about Nolan and his mindset since they've worked together for years.

"He better get it under control and fast," Ramirez responds. They share a look that pisses me off.

"Out with it," I growl.

"Here, it's better to show you," Marks hands Ashton his phone. Ashton hits play on the video Marks took. I lean over him and watch.

"Who the fuck is that?" I ask when the video stops.

"No fucking way," Ashton grumbles. "I thought he was dead."

"So did we," Marks responds.

Redline hasn't seen the video yet and waits impatiently, his fingers thrum against his jeans. "Can someone tell me what the fuck is going on?"

"We need to figure out a new game plan. You can't go in anymore." Ashton answers looking from the phone to Redline.

"What? Why not?" Ashton hands him the phone and hits play on the video. When the guy they all thought dead fills the screen, Ashton hits pause.

"That's why," he explains.

Redline's face pales and his hands shake, "When we received word through the street after they took Ashley, no one said anything about him not being there. I had no idea."

"Who the fuck is it?" I ask again. I'm irritated from being left out.

"We need to get back to Nolan and Ashley. They have to know." Ashton says, ignoring my question.

"Ashton," I growl. His head whips in my direction. "Who. The. Fuck. Is. It?"

"I'll explain in a little while. Right now, we need to get back to Nolan." He holds the phone up waving it, "This right here changes everything. How are you at fighting?"

"I'm a cop, I can handle it." I glare, crossing my arms. I'm really pissed he isn't answering me.

"I don't need you to be a cop right now," he growls, annoyed. "I need you to be an unsympathetic, selfish fighter. Can you do that?"

"You of all people know I can. We might have drifted apart, but we grew up together. You know what I'm capable of." I'm beyond pissed right now. My brother doesn't have confidence in me.

"I know you've turned into a black and white guy. Not the guy I grew up with. I don't even see him in you anymore. The one who used to cause trouble and not have a fucking care in the world that guy is long gone. You've turned into Mr. McGee or some shit," Ashton paces back and forth in the dark alley. "Going into an underground fighting ring is different from anything you've done. You'll be forced to do some shady shit, something you must learn to keep locked away when we're done. There are things you'll have to do to prove yourself to them and you won't like who they'll try to change you into, but you need to hang onto the good in your life."

My mind wanders back to Mia. She's the light in my world of darkness. Her smile and carefree attitude keeps me sane. Keeps the evil in my line of work in perspective.

"Can I see Mia before I need to go in?" I ask.

"Of course, you can but you can't tell her anything. She'll want to be here and The Plaza is the safest place for her to be." Ashton answers.

I'm dumbfounded by his attitude. He doesn't think I can handle whatever they throw at me. Well, I will prove him wrong. Prove I'm not the straight shooter he assumes I turned into.

"Let's do this," I answer, sure and confident. We walk out of the alley and head back to the apartment building. Our plans have changed dramatically, and I hope Nolan can handle what we must tell him. If he loses his head again, we're all in trouble.

Chapter 14

Nolan

Ashley's in the shower and I'm lying naked on the bed we just made love in three times already. I'm sated and at peace for once since being here. Thinking about joining her, but there's a knock on the door putting a stop to that thought. Three loud raps fill the apartment. I climb off the bed and throw my jeans on. Forgoing a shirt, I stride to the door and use the peephole to see who's on the other side. Ashton's massive build takes up the view and I slide the chain and unlock the deadbolt, letting him and the rest of my guys in.

Marks and Ramirez come in last and their eyes widen in shock when they see my chest, but neither say a word. There is no straightforward way to tell someone what I've gone through, so I figure I'll just show them. The tension is thick in here and by the expression on Ashton and Christian's face, something major just happened.

"Problem?" I ask raising an eyebrow.

"Not at all," Ramirez speaks first, swallowing hard.

"Nope, all good," Marks responds, avoiding eye contact with me.

I resist the urge to roll my eyes when Ashley appears from the bedroom dressed in a pair of light blue jeans and a black hoodie. Her blonde hair is still wet and pulled up into a ponytail.

"What's going on?" she asks, noticing the tension.

Christian paces back and forth in the small living room. He runs shaky hands through his brown hair. He passes from the small leather couch to the T.V. stand and back. His shoes squeak on the hardwood flooring.

"Both of you need to sit down for this," Ashton responds. There's an edge to his voice I've heard before and whatever he will tell us won't be good.

I cross the living room and take a seat on the small leather couch. Christian stops pacing long enough to peek through the blinds into the city outside. I can't hear the traffic being this high up, but the lights from the skyscrapers are filtering in, making Christian's stress lines on his forehead deeper. Ashley sits down next to me and grabs my hand. She leans into my side and rests her head on my shoulder.

"I have something I need to show you and you have to promise not to go crazy and do something fucking stupid," Ashton says. Marks hands him his phone and he clicks a button on it. "Do you promise not to go off the rails?"

"I'll try not to, but I can't promise I won't," I answer honestly.

"Ashley, what about you?" Ashton asks.

"Will you just spit it out," she answers, agitated.

Ashton hands us Marks' phone and I hit play on the video. The black screen fills with an image of Izzy tied to a chair. Her hair is snarly, her clothes are filthy, and her head is bowed down, her chin resting on her chest. The video pans away to Xavier handcuffed to a radiator. He has a cloth wrapped around his head, covering his mouth and his ice blue eyes are watching someone in the shadows. He's pinning them with a murderous glare. I've seen that expression on him before and the last person who did this to them ended up dead. Xavier rattles his hands, trying to bust through the handcuffs when the mysterious figure appears from the shadows. Xavier's breathing heavy as he watches the figure move closer to Izzy, helpless to stop him. He shouts through the cloth, fear passes in his eyes.

The screen pans out and all we can see is the figure's back as he leans over Izzy's unconscious form. He grips her chin and forces her head up. It rolls to the side before she comes to and fights to make him release her chin. He let's go with a maniac laugh and turns around. The video freezes on his face.

"No, no, no," Ashley sobs against my chest. "This can't be happening, not again."

I have no words of comfort for her. The man staring into the camera is made of her worst nightmares and now he'll be the star of Izzy's too. My hand tightens around the phone as I stare at the image of the monster I thought I killed back in L.A. I should have snapped his neck when I had the chance. His brown shaggy hair hangs down into his face now, his nose is crooked and he's missing two front teeth. The sneer on his lips lights up his eyes as he watches Izzy struggle against her ropes.

"Ash, you need to call Rush. Get him out here A.S.A.P." I calmly inform her. I'm not calm though. I want to break something, crack heads, shed some blood. The evil is pounding against my soul, trying to break free. Closing my eyes, I channel all the strength I can to keep my head cool and figure out a way to get Izzy and Xavier.

"Will someone please tell me who that fucker is," Christian demands. He's still standing next to the window clenching his fists at his sides.

"Shaun Reiser, my psycho ex. He tried to kill Rush and me." Ashley whispers from my side. She still hasn't called Rush. I don't think she wants to leave my side. I think she wants to stay against me, too scared to leave. This woman is one of the strongest I know, but one look at this monster has her retreating.

"Ash, call Rush, please." I plead with her.

She snaps her honey brown eyes to mine and nods her head. She removes Marks' phone from my grip with shaky fingers and dials his number. I can hear ringing on the other end. Ashley tightens her grip around my waist with her other arm and won't let go. I won't make her either. She needs someone to hang onto until she finds her way back and defeats this asshole once and for all.

The phone picks up after three rings and I can hear Rush's gruff voice on the other end.

"Hello?" he answers.

"Rush, It's me, Ashley. I need you out here now. Something has changed, and you need to be here." she responds with a shaky voice.

"Tell him I'll have the jet out there in three hours," Ashton says pulling out his phone and sending a text.

"Nolan's jet will be there in three hours. Be on it and get here. Tell the rest of the crew they need to stay there and keep their ears to the ground." Ashley relays to him.

"Krimson, what's going on?"

"Shaun," she responds.

"Fuck!" Rush growls through the phone. "I'll be there."

The line disconnects, and Ashley drops the phone onto her lap. "Now what? We can't just sit here with our thumbs up our assess and let him destroy those two." The fire I've been waiting for is in her voice.

"We have a plan but with these things changing, Redline can't go in. Shaun will recognize him at once." Ashton says.

"Who's will take his place?" I ask.

Christian pushes off the window, "I am."

I shake my head, "No, I can't let you do that. You don't realize what these guys are capable of, Christian, you can't."

"What the hell are we supposed to do then? I can't just sit here. I can handle it, Nolan. I want to do this."

"No, absolutely not. I can't let you get this involved. I need to fight. I need to get back in." Everyone talks over each other. They're arguing back and forth.

Ashley stands up and whistles loudly, making everyone shut up and swing their eyes in her direction.

"I have an idea. Shut up and listen." She shifts to my direction. "You train Redline in the gym, teach him what he needs to know." She gestures towards Christian. "You be his coach in the ring. If Reiser asks, Redline was sick of us. He wanted out and is looking for revenge against Nolan and me. Reiser will believe it. The last thing he knew was that Redline was feeling like an outcast and we play off that. Rush, Ashton, Marks, Ramirez, and I will set up surveillance and keep an eye on Izzy and Xavier. Follow Switch and Wrath around the city. See where they're set up at and if we find a way in before Redline has to fight, we'll do it."

"That might work," Ashton says, deep in thought. "Let's get started."

My stomach growls loudly, breaking the tension in the room. "I need to eat first. We were going to grab something before you came." I stand up from the couch and hear a loud gasp behind me. I turn around and Marks' expression is horrific.

Ashley narrows her eyes and stalks over to him. She's standing toe to toe with him and the look she gives him would make any grown man grovel. "He's still your boss. Remember that. If I ever see or hear you talk about his scars, I will end you and you won't know it happened." Her chest is heaving up and down. She's pissed, and it turns me on.

I walk up behind her and wrap my arms around her waist. "Come with me," I whisper in her ear and pull her away from Marks. He's still speechless, his mouth is hanging open and his eyes are so wide they might bug out of his head. Ramirez keeps his mouth shut and his face passive.

We walk into the bedroom and I close the door behind me. My lips are upon hers before she apologizes. I don't want apologies or sympathies. I want her lips on mine and to swallow her moans. She parts her lips and I plunge my tongue into her hot, wet mouth. She moans against my assault and tightens her grip around my neck. I yank her soft curves against my body, picking her up. I need to be buried inside of her again. A want like no other consumes me as I swallow her moans and groans. Ashley wraps her legs around my waist, a whimper escapes from the back of her throat. Walking to the bed, I break the scorching hot kiss and gently toss her down. I unzip and peel her jeans down her slender legs.

Knowing we're pressed for time, I skip the foreplay and unbutton and unzip my jeans, dropping them to the bedroom floor with my boxers. Ashley grabs the back of my head and pulls me up to her lips. She spreads her legs apart and I nestle between them.

"Don't make me wait, Nolan," she growls while nibbling the outer edge of my ear.

"Fuck," I groan against Ashley's lips.

Staring into Ashley's eyes, I continue my punishing pace. A moan rips from her throat and her nails dig into my back, bringing pain with pleasure while she's lost in her own orgasm. Fire burns down my spine as I find my release.

"Holy shit," Ashley pants. "Talk about hot sex. I figured it would take me a while after the last three times."

I arch an eyebrow at her, "Are you doubting my skills in the bedroom?" She giggles against my lips and gives me a slow lingering kiss. I break apart from her lips, "We have work to do."

"Hmm… I don't think I can right now, go ahead without me." She stretches her arms above the bed and arches her body.

"No way, woman. Get your fine ass up and feed me." I answer, pulling her up from the bed. She throws a smirk in my direction and saunters off to the bathroom.

I grab my boxers and jeans and put them back on along with a black t-shirt, hoodie and baseball hat. Sitting on the bed, I put on my socks and boots. Emotions clog my throat, everything is catching up to me. My best friend kidnapped and being tortured, the look of fear on Izzy's face in the video, Switch threatening my family. Wrath taunting me in my sleep, which Ashley has no idea about, the little boy from the street. It's all overwhelming me and tears burn the back of my eyes. I fight them back and clear my throat. Taking a deep breath, I keep everything tucked deep down and open the bedroom door. Redline is standing at the window, his tanned skin and lip ring glowing against the skyline peeking through the blinds. Ashton's massive body is sitting on a bar stool at the island between the kitchen and living room. He's texting someone on his phone. Marks and Christian are missing.

"Where's Christian?" I ask Ashton.

He looks up from his phone with a scowl on his face. "He took Ramirez and Marks to go see Mia." There's an edge to his tone.

"What's up?" I ask, taking a seat on the other bar stool.

Ashton grunts then replies, "Christian, he thinks he can do this, be this involved and not be affected by the outcome. He doesn't know what he's signing up for. I'd rather have him away from here and stay on the good side of things, not be involved at all."

"Then let's keep him in the dark about most of this and get Redline trained to fight. We can adjust our plans. Instead of Christian being in The Circle with him, you do it. Switch shouldn't know what you look like. We'll keep him on surveillance with Ashley. She'll keep him in line from doing anything stupid." Ashley comes out of the bedroom and walks over to me. She rests her palm on the massive scar under my t-shirt, caressing the marking gently with her fingertips.

"That's a clever idea. With Christian being a cop, he can't toe the line. If he does what we have to do, he'll lose his job." Ashton agrees. My stomach growls again and Ashley laughs.

"Come on big boy, let's get you fed." She walks over to Redline who's still standing at the window, their voices are hushed and he nods his head. They walk towards the door and I narrow my eyes at him. Ashley might trust him, but I don't know if I do yet. He really fucked up in L.A. She says they're back on track of where they should be, but I find it hard to believe he doesn't think he's in love with her. Something or someone made him think that and it's my job to figure out who and why.

"Are you coming or what?" Ashley asks raising an eyebrow. I saunter over to her and wrap my arm around her shoulder. She shudders from my touch as my nose skims the outer edge of her ear.

"I already did several times and so did you," I wiggle my eyebrows.

"You're incorrigible," she responds and swats my stomach, making me lose my breath.

"OK, OK, you don't need to get violent." I tease. Ashton pushes past us with a grunt, opens the door and leaves the apartment first, scanning the hallways left and right before we appear.

Once we're down onto the dark street, all playfulness escapes and seriousness settles in. I scan each sidewalk, car, and person passing by us. My grip around Ashley's shoulder tightens and I pull her closer to me. All these people surrounding us are making me paranoid. I can sense the darkness trying to take over and I channel my strength to hold it off. Instead of heading towards the brownstone looming to the right of us, we walk across the street in the opposite direction. My stomach drops when thoughts of what Izzy and Xavier are going through overwhelms me again.

"They're going to be OK Nolan, I just know it," Ashley reassures me. "Where do you want to eat?"

"I know this great mom and pop pizza shop down towards Times Square. We need to jump on the trains to get there." I answer, grateful for the distraction.

Ashley tightens her arm around my waist, "Tell me something about living here. The best part of the City."

We push through the throngs of people staying close to each other. Ashton is in the front, clearing a path for us while Redline is behind us. We still haven't heard from Christian, Marks or Ramirez yet, but if anything were wrong, they'd let us know. It's better for Christian this way. Ashton's right, he's not cut out for this. He's the strait-laced cop who toes the line when needed, but this won't be towing the line, this will cross it into the black abyss. I don't know if I'll come out unmarked and I know damn well he won't either.

"The best part about living here is the distinct cultures," I answer Ashley. "Anywhere you go, you can find several types of people. It was my favorite thing to do when I needed to escape the reality of my world. I'd sit for hours in Times Square and just watch. I'd create different scenarios in my head on what they're thinking and doing."

We walk down the dark entrance to the subway station. I hold on to her even tighter when we come out of the dimly light tunnel onto the platform. Learning your way around these trains takes a lot of time, but I've done this so many times, I can manage it in my sleep.

We're standing on the platform and a sharp breeze blows through the tunnels. There's a train coming in and the hair on the back of my neck stands on end. There's someone following us. I whip my head around, looking for the threat. I know it's there. Scanning each person waiting alongside us, no one appears to be out of place. Most of them have their earbuds in and are scrolling through their phones. Others are clutching their bags tight to their bodies, hanging on for life. They know what happens at night, the dangers lurking around the corner.

"Nolan, what's wrong?" Ashley asks. Her body is tense under my arm and she's scanning the area too. Ashton has his hand resting on his side piece tucked under his shirt. He feels it too. The sense of something dangerous heading our way.

"I'm not sure," I answer. I know someone is here, watching and waiting, but where the fuck are they? It's really starting to piss me off. Redline is standing to the left of us on the dirty platform and Ashton is to the right.

They're both scanning the surrounding area, getting the same feeling I am.

A tingling sensation floats over the back of my neck, creating chills to wrack my body, tiny icicles drift down my spine. I swat at the back of my neck and shake my head. Turning around slowly, something catches my eye in the dark shadows behind us.

A light giggle whispers in my ear and I whip my head around again. No one is around us, no one is here making those noises.

"What the actual fuck?" I whisper. The train's headlight is blinding me as it turns the bend and comes barreling into the station. Everything happens in slow motion but I'm powerless to stop it. Tiny hands shove me hard from behind. Ashley's grip around my waist loosens and I'm plummeting head first towards the tracks with thousands of volts of electricity thrumming through it. I can't stop myself from my head dive and I close my eyes, reflecting on everything in my past. Good, bad and ugly. The last image running through my head is Ashley's beautiful face, honey eyes, and blonde hair. I wish I had more time, more everything with her.

Now it's too late.

Chapter 15

Ashley

Horrified by the events that are happening, I watch helplessly as Nolan falls head first toward the tracks. I can't stop him, I can't help him, I can only watch. My hands slip from around his waist and I can't grab his massive body.

Thank God Ashton's quick. He grabs Nolan by his hood and yanks him back at the last second. They both fall into me and we tumble onto the concrete. Taking the brunt of their weight, I smack my head on the dirty tiles. My vision blurs and the air's knocked out of my lungs. Ashton is on top of us and climbs off first. My head is pounding and my ears are ringing when Nolan rolls off me and lands by my side. I try to move but I can't. I'm still trying to catch my breath and a sharp pain radiates through my back and neck.

Nolan is leaning over me, but I can't hear him through the ringing in my ears. People are circling around us, closing us in. Ashton is trying to keep them back. Fuck! I can't breathe, I can't see, I can't speak. Panic is setting in. Nolan grabs my shoulders and pulls me up gently. I'm cradled in his arms and I can feel his chest vibrate under my ringing ears.

"Redline, where's Redline?" I croak out. I look around, but my neck hurts, and I can only move it a few inches back and forth. I can't find Redline. The ringing in my ears slowly fades and voices are shouting all around us, hurting my head even more.

"Ash, are you OK?" Nolan asks.

"Yeah, I'm fine now," I inhale a deep breath, my stomach is rolling. "My neck and back hurt and my head is pounding. I can't see Redline. Where's Redline?" I sit up and pull away from the comfort of Nolan's hard chest. Redline isn't anywhere around. "What the hell happened?"

"Someone tried to push me in front of the train. I felt a pair of hands shove me hard and I lost my footing. If it weren't for Ashton, I'd be dead and now Redline is missing."

"Guys come on we have to get out of here." Ashton grunts. His body is rigid and tense. He's watching everyone down here.

An uneasiness settles in my bones as realization settles in the pit of my stomach. "They took him," I whisper.

"Who?" Nolan asks.

"Redline. Shoving you was a distraction. Switch took him when we were trying to save you. Fuck! This is all my fault." Tears burn the back of my eyelids and my head is pounding even harder. I can't handle all these noises and people. I need to get out of here, now.

Standing up on shaky legs, I peer around. No one is looking directly at us, but they're discreetly watching out of the corner of their eyes. I walk away from the scene as quickly as my sore body will allow. Nolan and Ashton are right behind me. Redline is missing and I need to find out why and what happened.

Once we reach the top of the stairs from the dark subway station below us and onto the sidewalk, I turn to Ashton. "Can you pull up the footage from down there?"

"Yes. Once we get back to the apartment, I'll pull it up. I'm going to call Marks and Ramirez, get them on this."

"No," Nolan blurts. "If we call them, they'll bring Christian. He can't get involved either. We need to keep this between us. Rush will be here in a few hours. We'll go back to the apartment, pull up the footage and figure out who took him and who tried to kill me."

Nolan is acting like himself again and that's a relief. I know battling these demons are hard, and he's lost his way. I hope he can keep this mindset and be the leader I know he is. Wrapping my arms around his waist I rest my head on Nolan's chest. He holds onto me and rubs my back soothingly. My head is still pounding but being outside again is helping a little.

We walk quietly back toward the apartment building and grab some Chinese on the way. We should have just stopped here first instead of traipsing all over the city, then Redline would still be with us. Nolan and I wait outside in a dark alley under Ashton's insistence we stay hidden while he got our food. Standing arm and arm in the dark alley, neither of us knows what to say. I realize this is my fault for thinking Switch wouldn't touch us, not yet, but it is my fault.

"Ash," Nolan quietly says pulling me from my self-loathing. "This isn't your fault." He pulls my chin up so I'm looking at him in his whiskey-colored eyes. "It's mine. I thought I was untouchable. I thought Switch wouldn't fuck with me. Stop blaming yourself, please."

"It is my fault, Nolan. Redline is my responsibility, and I let them take him. There's something we're missing."

Ashton exits the Chinese restaurant and walks into the dark alley. "Let's get back to the apartment and pull up the footage, then figure out why they want Redline. Nolan, we've got to get you in The Circle fast. Do you still have your contacts?"

Nolan's grip on my shoulders tightens, and he nods his head. "Yeah, let's go." We walk out of the alley and into the apartment building. Nolan avoids looking down the street, but his shoulders are stiff and tension is radiating off him in waves. He's trying to keep his demon locked away. I've seen that look before. Grabbing his hand, I pull him against me and wrap my arms around his waist.

"I've got you," I whisper into his chest. He swallows hard and I hear his heart beating fast against his chest. His grip tightens around my shoulders as I repeat myself. "I've got you, Nolan. I'm not going anywhere. We can do this together."

Walking across the marble foyer, our shoes squeak on the polished flooring. I didn't take the time to look around when we first arrived or when we left. The lobby of the apartment building is very formal. There's a security guard posted at the entrance to protect the residents. A cluster of mailboxes to the left, elevators directly in front of us and a set of stairs to the right. Ashton hits the button to the elevator and a few seconds later it dings open. We walk in and my feet are resting on plush brown and black carpet. The doors close and I breathe a sigh of relief even if it's for just a few moments. A little reprieve and I can get my head back on straight and take care of business.

The elevator doors ding open and we step out into the hallway. Ashton goes first and walks down the long hallway. He pulls a set of keys out of his pocket and has the Chinese food in his other hand. He unlocks the door and we enter. Setting the bags of food on the island, Ashton walks to the window and looks into the dark night. Nolan disappears into the bedroom and comes back out a few minutes later with his laptop in his hands. He hands it off to Ashton and walks into the kitchen. Ashton fires up the laptop as Nolan and I pull out the food. No words are needed at this time. We all know what we must do. We carry the food into the living room and I grab the sweet and sour chicken. Nolan takes the mushroom chicken and leaves Ashton with the orange chicken. I settle into the recliner, taking small bites, watching Nolan and Ashton work. They're both perched on the edge of the couch with the laptop resting on the coffee table.

"Pull up the footage from the train station. Run facial recognition on everyone down there while we were. We'll also run the program Marks made where it tells us how many times each person appears on camera. Then we can find who took Redline." Nolan says between bites of food.

Ashton's fingers fly over the keyboard and then sits back. He releases a deep breath and eats his own food while the programs run. We sit here in compatible silence, each of us reflecting on the day's actions. We all blame ourselves for Redline's disappearance, Nolan's tense situation and Izzy and Xavier's kidnapping.

Nolan's phone buzzes the same time the laptop dings. He pulls it out of his pocket, reading the incoming text, and his face turns pale at the same time Ashton lets out a string of curses. Nolan grips his phone tight enough to hear it crack as the light fades from his eyes being replaced by anger and vengeance. I've seen that look before. He's fading fast to the evil and he can't stop it. I jump up from the recliner, spilling my food all over the floor and pull his phone from his hands before he can break it.

"No Ashley, don't!" Nolan barks out. Too late I already see the text and then my eyes fly to the laptop perched on the coffee table. My world turns upside down when I look at who's on the screen.

Austin.

Chapter 16

Nolan

I've lost all control. I can't move, I can't speak, I can barely breathe while the evil lurking inside is pounding away at my body, demanding to break free when Ashley grabs my phone. I try to stop her from seeing what Switch sent, but I can't. I can't do a fucking thing when I'm subdued in this catatonic state. I watch her face the moment her world turns upside down, powerless to stop it. Her eyes connect with mine and the concern for me overshadows the fear etched into her beautiful features.

Her brother, the one that went missing for years, was the one who took Redline. He did it so fast and in the shadows that if we didn't run these programs, we would have missed everything. He wasn't alone.

Ashton replays the video and we wait anxiously. The hands that pushed me belonged to a woman dressed in a ball cap, black hoodie, and black jeans. Pieces of blonde hair are falling out of the ball cap and she turns her face toward the cameras on purpose. Bruises and blood mark her face, a face I've known for years. She mouths something toward the camera, bolts out of the tunnel right behind Austin, dragging Redline away.

"Replay the last scene," Ashley growls.

Ashton quickly backs up the video feed and hits play. We watch her push me from behind and turn towards the camera. In the background I see myself slipping from Ashley's hold and Ashton yanking me back as we tumble into Ashley. My heart is beating hard against my chest and my fist my hands at my sides. My ears are ringing from the rage brewing below the surface. Gentle hands are caressing my shoulders, helping me subdue the demon ready to break free and wreak havoc on anyone crossing my path.

"There," Ashley sobs, pointing at the screen. "Right there. Look at her face and hands. She's cuffed and beaten. Oh my God, no! What have they done to you, Izzy?"

Ashley's tears tumble down her cheeks and sobs quietly while comforting me. She's close to losing it. I close my eyes and try to channel all the rage and hate back inside. I'm not ready to unleash just yet. I need to control this before I can do anything else. I've done it before, I can do it again.

"Ash," I whisper. She shifts her eyes toward me, they're swollen with tears. "We'll get them back. She didn't have a choice, we can see that. Let's focus on what we can do and not what has already happened. You're exhausted, I'm emotionally drained and Rush will be here in a couple of hours. Let's try to get some sleep and start fresh when he gets here. Ashton, call Christian and tell him to stay with Mia tonight. If we put off him coming over, we can keep him out of this."

"On it," Ashton responds pulling out his phone.

I take Ashley's hand and tug her toward the bedroom, "Come on, let's reset and rest." She follows, her feet barely keeping up with my slow pace. She enters the room in front of me, her shoulders are shaking and she's trying to hold in her sobs.

I close the door and approach her from behind. She's standing in the center of the room, trying to compose herself. I rub her back in a soothing motion. Kissing the side of Ashley's neck, I raise her hoodie and shirt up over her head and toss them on the ground. Her warm, delicate skin is trembling under my hands. I remove my shirt, so we're skin against skin. The contact soothes her inner turmoil and we stand here for several minutes, not moving, not saying a word. I'm holding her together and she's keeping me sane. We're made for each other, one's yin to the other's yang, and the more we suffer these heartbreaking moments, the more I realize we need each other.

Splaying my hands across her stomach, I lean down and nuzzle the side of Ashley's neck, inhaling her strawberry essence. Her quiet sobs have subsided for now and I know it's because of my touch.

"Let's get some sleep and figure out where to go from here in the morning. They're making her do their bidding. That alone tells me Switch is scared."

She shifts in my arms and rests her head on my chest. "Why would Austin be involved?" Her voice is muffled and vibrating against my heart.

"That's what we'll find out in the morning," I answer. I pull Ashley's head from my chest and gently kiss her on her lips. Forehead against forehead I whisper, "We will figure this out. Remember it's what I do." She gives me a small smile and nods her head at my famous line.

"I know, and I trust you, Nolan, impeccably." Tears spring to her eyes again and she wipes them away. We remove the rest of our clothes and lay down on the bed. Ashley snuggles against my chest. Her breathing evens out in just a matter of moments, she's sound asleep. I close my eyes and follow along.

There's a faint rumble coming through the walls of the bedroom that startle me awake. I listen and hear it again, followed by hushed whispers and a male voice. My muscles tense and I'm on high alert. Someone's in the apartment, sneaking around. I slowly remove Ashley from my chest and quietly get up from the bed. The mattress creaks under my weight and I freeze. Listening intently, whoever is in the other room stops moving, I can hear heavy breathing right outside the bedroom door. I quickly stand up, grab my nine-millimeter off the nightstand and tiptoe to the door. With my hand on the knob, I take a deep breath and throw the door open, holding my gun up, eye level with the intruder. My finger ready to squeeze the hairpin trigger.

"Holy shit fucker! Put that thing away," Rush responds, holding his hands up in the air. I breathe a sigh of relief when I see his face.

"Rush, I almost killed you. Why are you sneaking around?" I ask. Ashley stirs on the bed behind me. I lower my nine-mil and step out of the bedroom, closing the door behind me.

"I was going to take a shower and shit before you guys got up. Ashton told me it was fine if I didn't wake you up. My plane landed about forty-five minutes ago and I came straight here." His black eyes meet mine. He's just as worried as I am with all the bullshit going around. "How's she doing?" he asks.

"She's OK. It was pretty rough on her watching Izzy on the camera's, but she'll be fine once we get into action. I'm setting up a fight tonight in The Circle and need you there for support. It's good to see you again, fucker."

"It's good to see you too. L.A. hasn't been the same without you there." He slaps me on the back and walks past. "I'm getting in the shower, we'll discuss what's going down tonight after I get out." I grin, and relief flows through my body. We have another ally with us, ready to fight and take Switch down.

Opening the bedroom door, I walk to the bed and kneel, gently shaking Ashley awake. She stirs under my hands, not opening her eyes. She's awake, but she doesn't want to get up yet. I know how to fix this. Something we both need after last night. I lean down and nibble on the side of her neck, my hands tracing down her chest and cupping her full breast. She arches her back under my touch and releases a moan that has my body responding. Need roaring through my veins.

I carefully climb onto the bed and pin her down with my body, my dick responding as she widens her legs and makes room for my bulky frame. Her eyes are still closed, but she's smiling. I kiss a path from the bottom of her ear, down her neck and toward her breast. She groans and lifts her hips, her fingernails dig into my back pulling me closer.

"I need this," she pants. Sitting up I remove my boxers and strip her panties down her slender, sun-kissed legs. "Come here," she groans out.

I kiss my way up her body. Ashley grabs my face and kisses me hard. Our tongues tangle together in a song and dance tempo, I'm seeking and she's offering. Slowly I inch inside her and a gasp rips from her throat. Our bodies are bonded together as one. One love, one beat, one soul. She's panting against my lips, arching her back.

Rolling over I pull her with me so she's straddling me. "Ride me," I grunt. Ashley sits up, and it's the most erotic sight I've ever seen. Sweat is beading on her forehead as she rocks her hips back and forth. Fire races through my spine while she rocks faster and faster, chasing her own release.

"Shit, I'm going to come," I groan. She moves faster, a whimper escaping her throat. My fingers dig into her hips and I can't hold back any longer. My name rips from Ashley's throat as she finds her release, panting hard. I follow into the bliss, her name rips from my throat and spots don my vision. She collapses on top of me, our bodies slick with sweat. I caress her back with long strokes and she shudders under my touch.

"We need to get up and get shit around for tonight," I mumble, thoroughly satisfied and content.

"What's going to happen?"

"I'm going in The Circle and I would like you there with me. Watch my back. Rush will be there as well." I trace shapes on her back as I talk.

"What about Ashton and the rest of your team?"

"Ashton and the rest of my team will set up a perimeter around the apartment building Switch has Izzy and Xavier in. If I know Switch, he'll catch wind at the last minute I'm in The Circle and will leave them alone. If that happens, Ashton and the rest of my team will extract them."

"All right let's get moving then. We have a lot of planning to do before tonight," Ashley responds. There's a catch in her voice, something is bothering her.

"What is it, Ash?" I ask.

"Nothing."

"Don't tell me nothing, I know better than that."

She hesitates before answering, "Why did they want Redline and what's going to happen to Austin? He's still my brother and there has to be a reason why he's here. Over the past few months, he hasn't acted out or anything. He fit right in with the rest of us, this doesn't make any sense." She sits up and climbs off me, pacing the small bedroom.

"I'll have Ashton dig into his past and see if Switch has something on him that forced him to come along. If not, I can't guarantee his safety." I stand up and stop directly in front of her, grabbing her shoulders. This will break her heart, but I don't want secrets between us. "If he's betrayed you, here on his own free will and has been playing you this whole time, I will take him down, no hesitation."

"It's part of the game, I know. I hope that's not the case." She walks into the attached bathroom and shuts the door. Something's got to give. I knock on the door, "Ash, I promise we'll explore all options before we do anything." Resting my head on the door, I wait for her to answer.

She turns the shower on before answering, "I know, Nolan, I just wish it wasn't like this."

"Me too, Ash, me too." I walk across the room and put on my blue jeans and a black T-shirt on. I strap my nine-mil to my side and walk out the door into the living room. Ashton is sitting on the couch with the laptop doing a search. He's staring out the window into the bright sunny day, lost in his own thoughts. Entering the kitchen, I start a pot of coffee and drum my fingers on the counter. Thinking back to all the events that have developed, I'm absorbed in my own head. The note, Izzy and Xavier missing, the phone call from Switch, arriving in New York City, going to The Circle alone, the girl, Ashley showing up, my demon fighting to be freed, all of it. It all repeats in my head over and over and it's driving me crazy. There's something we're missing, some piece of the puzzle we're not seeing.

"Hey man, you good?" Rush asks, snapping me out of my mind.

"Yeah, I'm good. I'm just trying to figure all of this out. Why, after all these years, come after me now? It's not like I took anything important with me when I left." I wrack my knuckles on the counter, trying to put the pieces together. Ashton, Rush, and Ashley are standing around me now, watching and waiting for me to say something else. "When I left, there was nothing of importance I took with me. I just don't get it." Pacing the tiny kitchen and the three pairs of eyes on me is making me feel trapped, caged in like an animal. I've got to get out of here. I need to get out of here.

    I yank open the apartment door and head toward the stairs leading up to the rooftop. I need some air and open space. My ears are ringing and my heart is beating hard against my chest. The demon is begging to break free and wreak havoc on everything and everyone around me. I don't want to fight it, I want to set it free and destroy everything around me. It might be the only way to save Izzy and Xavier. I won't be the same after this, none of us will be.

Chapter 17

Ashley

Nolan takes off from the apartment barefoot and he doesn't stop when I call out his name. I've been watching the struggle in his eyes. The fight he's been putting up against his own head. If this goes on for much longer, I'm going to lose him, and I can't lose him. Without him in my life nothing makes sense.

I pour myself and Nolan a cup of coffee and turn toward Rush. "I'm happy you're here. It's not the best circumstances, but shit keeps changing. We need to stay ahead the best we can. I'm going to talk to Nolan and I want you to watch the video from last night. Ashton has it." I turn toward Ashton, "Can you get Rush all caught up to speed with what has happened and what we are dealing with now? I need to check on Nolan."

"We've got this part covered." Ashton agrees.

"Oh, one more thing. Run a background and full scan on Austin Jonathan Force. Dig deep and find his connection to all of this. He should never have been here. There's something we're not seeing, and he was missing for several years of my life. See if you can find anything on that time he was gone."

"Wait," Rush says, crossing his arms over his chest. "Why Austin? What the hell is going on?"

I turn around with my hand still on the doorknob, "Austin is here, and he helped kidnap Redline last night. You'll see it all on the footage." I open the door and slam it shut behind me, trying to balance two coffee cups at the same time. It's quiet out in the hallway and my feet sink into the plush carpet. Looking right toward the elevators, I spot a shadow in the corner. The person's head pulls back quickly around the bend. I turn left and head toward the stairs that lead to the roof. Climbing the stairs, the hair on the back of my neck rise and I quickly turn around. No one is there, but it feels like there are eyes on me.

I push the heavy metal door open with my hip and the bright sunlight blinds me for a second. After my eyes adjust to the bright sun, I spot Nolan pacing back and forth, his feet are red from the cold and he appears to be lost in his own head. His body is tense, and his hands are shaking. Approaching him carefully, I set the cups down on the iron table.

"Nolan," I speak, gaining his attention. His eyes pin me to my spot and I can't move. Gone is the carefree guy I've grown to love. In his place is the cold hard killer he's afraid of letting loose.

"Leave," he grunts through clenched teeth.

"I'm not going anywhere." There's a slight shake in my voice and his lips snarl in a menacing grin. I just fucked up. His demon prays on the weak and I made myself sound like it. Straightening my spine, I release my authority. "Nolan, get the fuck over yourself. I'm not going anywhere." I hide my shaking hands and school my features, facing him head on.

"I said leave," his tone is low and deadly. He paces around me, watching and waiting for a shake or anything for him to rip apart.

"No," I answer firmly, following him with narrow eyes. "I'm not leaving and you're not giving up. Get the fuck over yourself, get control and drink some coffee. We have a lot of shit to handle in the little bit of time we have left before you enter The Circle."

Nolan stalks up behind me, and I don't move a muscle. He wants to test me, and I'll welcome whatever he throws at me. His hands grip my waist, his fingers digging into my hips. Yanking my back against his hard chest, I let him handle me however he needs to. His lips trail up to the side of my neck and I tip my head to the side, giving him room. I close my eyes and inhale his woodsy scent wrapping around me. The wind is lightly blowing, and goosebumps break out across my skin from his hot breath and the cool air. The sensation is intoxicating.

"I'm no good for you, Ash. I can't control this anymore." Nolan whispers in my ear.

Taking a chance, I turn around and his hands grip my ass, pulling me closer to him. I look him directly in the eyes and gently cup his face with my fingers, his stubble rough under my hands. "Yes, you can. You are my perfect match, Nolan. Always have been, always will be. Pull yourself together and fight this. I need you to get Izzy and Xavier back. I can't do it without you."

Nolan closes his eyes and inhales a deep breath. I lightly kiss him on his cheek, his stubble tickling my lips. "You can do this, I'm here to help. You're not alone anymore," I whisper in his ear.

His fingers loosen their grip on my ass and Nolan nuzzles my neck, his hot breath fanning across my skin. He breathes deeply and rests his head against mine. "I'm losing control and I can't stop it."

"Yes, you can. You've done it before, you can do it again. We'll do it together," I encourage him. We stand here for a moment, Nolan trying to regain the upper hand and pull himself together. I'm trying to stay strong and not make him snap. "Come on, let's drink our coffee and put together a plan, please."

He releases his tight grip on me and picks up his mug, the turmoil he's suffering is written all over his face. Nolan scrunches his nose and a wrinkle forms in the center of his forehead. I rub my fingers over the crease, not taking my eyes off him. His face relaxes from my touch and he gazes out into the city skyline. Closing his eyes, he releases a deep breath. "Thank you, Ashley. What we're going to walk into tonight will not be roses and sunshine. It will be dark and deadly. My body will respond to the scene and there will be no mercy."

"I know," I reply taking a drink of my coffee. The bittersweet taste coating my tongue and throat. Looking out over the skyline, I'm left breathless at the beauty of New York City. The buildings are glistening from the bright sun, hiding the evil that lurks below. I can faintly hear the horns from the cars several stories below and the sirens from police cars. Turning toward Nolan, he's looking out over the city, lost in his own mind, only this time he's here with me not battling for control. I rest my cold hand on his warm arm and he turns in my direction. "I'm prepared for it and ready to face this head on. I hate sitting idle and now that Rush is here, we can get on with it and get Izzy, Xavier, and Redline back."

We finish our coffee in silence and head back inside. The hair on the back of my neck standing on end again and I falter a little on the steps. Righting my stumble, I scan the stairs below us. It's a dark descent into the hallway and a creepy sensation washes over me. Nolan is right behind me, his hands are holding my hips, keeping me balanced.

"Ash, what is it?" he asks.

"It feels like someone is watching us. I had the same reaction coming up here, and I brushed it off, but twice in a row is not a coincidence. Someone's here." I whisper and stop walking. We both quiet our breathing and listen carefully. There's a faint ticking of the heater and soft footsteps scurrying away. A giggle breaks the quietness. Nolan releases my hips, and he's moving fast down the stairwell and around the corner before I even realize he's gone.

"Nolan, wait!" I shout, but it's too late. He's out of my site in a flash. I hurry down the stairs and around the dreaded corner. Nolan is nowhere around. I sprint down the hallway toward the elevators just as Rush and Ashton open the apartment door.

"Ash, what's going on?" Rush barks.

"Someone was here, now Nolan's gone," I answer over my shoulder. I hear the door shut behind me when I skid around another corner. Empty. I push open another stairwell door leading down to the lobby and quickly make my way down to the next landing, Rush, and Ashton are hot on my heels. I keep going down as fast as I can, my legs are burning, and my feet are slapping the floor, but I push forward, desperate to get to Nolan. We reach the bottom quickly.

I try to open the door, but Ashton pulls me back. "I'll go first, then you follow." He draws his .45 caliber from his side and pushes me back against the wall.

"Fucking move it would you," I growl, highly irritated he's taking his time. He pins me with a glare that has me keeping my mouth shut for a moment. If he doesn't move his ass, I'm going to bust through without him. The longer we wait in here, the farther away Nolan is. I can feel it in my soul he won't be in the lobby that he's disappeared.

Ashton pushes the door open and disappears. I follow right behind him and almost collide with his muscular back. He holsters his gun and turns around, shaking his head. I whip my head in every direction and panic sets in.

Nolan is gone. He's nowhere in the lobby. Men and women are coming and going, starting their day or finishing it up. I quickly make my way across the marble floor and shove open the outside door. I stumble onto the sidewalk from my fast pace and the bright sun blinds me for a moment. Squinting my eyes, I look left and then right. Nothing. He's not here.

"Fuck," Ashton growls right behind me. "Where the hell did he go? Son of a bitch."

Tears well up in my eyes and I push my emotions deep down, not letting the sadness overtake me. Walking back inside the building, we're all quiet when we enter the elevator and exit on our floor. I open the door first and Nolan's scent lingers in my nose. Stifling a sob, I plop down onto the couch and release a breath.

Ashton sits down in the chair next to the window and Rush sits down next to me. He wraps his arms around my shoulders and tries to soothe my aching heart.

"Ashley," Ashton says quietly. "Tell us exactly what happened."

I stare into his eyes and retell everything that happened. He nods a few times and pulls out his phone from his pocket. He's typing away while I'm talking. When I finish his phone buzzes with a text. His brow furrow's, creating a deep crease in his forehead.

"What are we going to do now?" I ask.

"Where's Nolan's phone?" Ashton asks.

"His phone?" I return, confused.

"Yes, his phone. Where is it?"

"I don't know. I figured he had it on him. Why? What's going on?" I ask.

"He doesn't have it on him. The GPS app isn't on either. That tells me he either shut it off or someone shut it off."

"Can you track his last location?" Rush asks.

"I tried but it's showing it's here."

"What the hell does his phone have to do with anything?" I'm beyond pissed now. I want to get him back, not look for a damn phone.

Ashton releases a deep breath, "Before he left Michigan, he received a phone call from Switch. Telling him he has Izzy and Xavier. Maybe if we find the phone, we can find more clues to where he might be."

"But we know Switch has Izzy and Xavier in the apartment building down the street. What the fuck else would we find on it?"

"There's got to be something on it, come on help me find it," Ashton says standing up. He walks into the kitchen and starts looking. Rush gets up to help.

I draw my shaking legs up and go into the bedroom. Grief surrounds me when I walk in and can smell him everywhere in the small room. I wipe the tears from my eyes and start looking. A few minutes later I find his phone under the bed. He must have knocked it off the stand this morning when he got up. I hit the side button and a lock screen appears. It's a picture of us together out in L.A. on the beach. We're both smiling, gazing into each other's eyes, portraying the love we share. Rush walks into the room and finds me crumbled on the floor, tears spilling from my eyes. I wipe them away and hand him the phone.

"Iverson, she found it," Rush shouts. Ashton walks into the room, takes the phone from Rush's hands and walks back out. Rush sits on the floor next to me and holds me tight, trying to comfort me. "Ash, you've got to pull it together, please. Don't disappear on me now. We all need you to find your inner strength and help us. Izzy, Xavier, Redline, Austin, and Nolan. They all need you to be strong and get them out of there, find a way to get them out. You can do it and I'm here to help."

I wipe my nose and clean my face with the sleeve of my hoodie. Rush's black eyes are watching me, waiting for me to do something. Finally, it clicks and excitement strums through my body.

"I know what I have to do. I know how to get them back. Come on." I stand up without waiting for a reply from Rush and hurry into the living room. "Ashton, I know what I have to do. Give me Nolan's phone."

Ashton looks up at me from the couch. He has his laptop open on the coffee table and it's running a program while hooked up to the phone. Numbers and letters are swirling around on the screen. It beeps, and he disconnects Nolan's phone, handing it to me. Ashton was breaking in to access Nolan's information. I click on his contact Icon and scroll until I find what I'm looking for. I click on the message Icon under the contact and send a quick message. I see he did the same thing a few hours ago, while he was supposed to be sleeping. He already had it set up for him, now I did it for me.

"Ash, what are you doing?" Rush asks trying to peek over my shoulder.

"There, done. Do what you need to do now, Ashton." I reply ignoring Rush.

"Krimson," Rush growls. He's pissed. He only uses my street name when he's talking to someone or irritated with me. "What the hell did you just do?"

"I'm getting our friends back," I answer over my shoulder as I walk toward the bedroom to get ready.

"God damn it, Krimson. What the hell did you do?" Rush pleads.

I stop at the door and turn around facing him. "I did the only thing I can do. I'm fighting in The Circle tonight."

Chapter 18

Nolan

Darkness. That's all I see surrounding me is darkness. I fade in and out of consciousness several times.

Voices. Muffled, hate- filled voices assault my ears when I slip in and out of consciousness.

Pain. White hot pain pierces my body. My arms and legs are numb from the burn of the ropes and I fall in and out of consciousness.

Confusion. Waking up in total darkness blurs my mind, my aching body, and my tortured soul.

Where am I? What happened? Why are my hands tied? Why can't I move? These questions assault my mind as I fade in and out of consciousness, again.

Dreams. I dream about better times, happier days filled with love and laughter. Ashley is the star of my dreams. The first time I heard her voice, the first time I saw her. These memories flip through my mind like a movie playing on repeat. They can torture my body, but they can't touch my mind as I slip back into unconsciousness.

****

"Nolan," Xavier stops me from walking toward my Dodge Ram pickup. His jeans are covered in grease and his blue eyes are etched with worry. We've been working on their race cars non-stop. They have a couple of days before their big race and both of them are trying to deal with Izzy's dad still in a coma after his accident. Not to mention there's someone out here trying to hurt them. "I need a favor. With our big race coming up, I want to do something for Izzy. Something to put a smile on her face. I have a cell number for her friend she lived with out in California. Will you call her and see if she'll come out to support Izzy? She hasn't said it, but I know she misses her."

"Of course, I will." Xavier hands me a piece of paper and I put it in my pocket. I need to get back to my office, but I must play it cool. Xavier doesn't know what I do for a living and it needs to stay that way, his life could be in more danger if he finds out.

"Thanks, bro, I owe you one," he replies with a smile. His blue eyes are shining in the sunlight and he walks back into his garage with some stress lifted off his shoulders.

I climb in my pickup and pull out my phone from my pocket. I dial my right-hand man, Ashton Iverson. He picks up on the second ring.

"Boss, what's up?"

"Iverson, can you track a number for me? Xavier said he wants to have Izzy's friend from California out here, but I want a full background check on her to make sure she's legit. They don't know the whole situation of these people. Her names Ashley Force and I have her cell number if you need it." I rattle off her cell phone number.

"Give me a second and I'll have the information." I can hear him moving around on the other end. The telltale sound of a laptop comes through the line and listen as he hits the keys. "Got it. She's legit. Studies at Otis College of Art Designs in Los Angeles, California. Born and raised in the area and has been everything Izzy has said about her. She's got the green light."

"Thanks, bro."

"Anytime."

We end the call and I start my black Dodge Ram. I pull out of Xavier's driveway, the exhaust growls when I touch the gas and head toward my office in town. I park my pickup in front of the immaculate building and pull out my phone again. I dial the number Xavier gave me with unsteady fingers. What the hell is wrong with me? I've never been this nervous before. The phone rings several times before a charming melodic voice comes on the line.

"Hey! This is Ash, I can't answer your call right now. I'm either livin' it up or in class. Either way, leave a message and I'll call you back!" The phone beeps for me to leave a message.

"Ashley, you don't know who this is, but I'm a friend of Izabella's. Please call me back as soon as you can. Thanks." I hang up the phone and twist it between my thumb and fingers. I climb out of my pickup and head inside.

The sunlight spilling into the lobby is bright against the marble floors as I make my way toward the set of elevators on the opposite side. The security guard to my left nods his head when he sees me. I nod back, push the up button and wait for the elevator to descend. The doors whoosh open and I step inside. I watch my reflection in the floor to ceiling mirrors and the cart carries me up to the top floor. Thanking my grandfather for this opportunity to have a different life, I step out of the elevator and walk down the hallway and into my office. Everything is where I left it this morning.

My massive red oak desk is neat and tidy, and my large leather chair is pushed in. I pull it out and swing around, staring out the enormous bay windows. My phone vibrates from my desk and I answer it without checking to see who it is.

"Ryan here."

"Nolan? It's Izzy's friend Ashley." Her sweet melodic tone draws me in and I'm stunned. I've never

heard a voice like hers. It's like an angel is talking to me
"Are you there?" she asks softly.

"Sorry, yes I'm here," I respond. My tongue is tied, I can't find the words I wanted to say.

She giggles on the other end and my heart skips a beat. What the fuck is wrong with me? "You said you wanted me to call you, so what did you need? Is Izzy OK?"

Clearing my throat and composing myself I finally respond. "Yes, Izzy is as OK as she can be. Her dad's still in a coma but that's not why I called." There's silence on the other end.

"So, why did you call?" she questions.

"They have a big race coming up on Saturday, and I wanted to know if you could come out here to support her." My words rush out, and I'll be surprised if she understood me. I've never and I mean never had a reaction to a woman like this before. Must be from the lack of women around here. My heart is hammering in my chest and my palms are so sweaty, I almost dropped the phone.

"Yes, I can be there. I can't leave until Friday night though. Is everything else all right with her?" Ashley answers concern etched in her voice.

"Yes. She's fine, just worrying about her dad. He's still in a coma and the doctors don't know when he'll wake up. She's been a beast on the track and making all of us proud."

"That's great to hear." Ashley grows quiet, she wants to say something, but I don't know if she will. I should put her out of her misery, but I don't want to finish this conversation and hang up just yet. Talking to her is like a breath of fresh air and I've been drowning way too long. "How's Xavier treating her?" She finally asks. Ah, there it is.

"He's treating her the way he should have all those years ago. He's an idiot and knows he is lucky to have a second chance with her. She's the sweetest person I know and loves with her whole heart for life." My grip tightens on the phone and rage consumes me with the thought of anything happening to either of them. My ears start ringing and my hands start to shake. The demon is waiting in the recess of my mind to take over and destroy anyone who dares to hurt them.

"Nolan, are you OK?" Ashley's voice breaks through the ringing and for some reason, it calms me down. That's never happened before. It's usually hard for me to snap out of it. "Do you need my help with anything?"

"What? No, I'm OK." I shake my head. "Do you need me to pick you up at the airport? Let me know when you get in and I can be there." I hear male voices in the background and her walking away, closing a door. Figures she'd have a man. A woman with that sweet-sounding voice can't be single.

"No, I'll be getting in really late. Just text me the address where Izzy will be, and I'll be there Saturday morning." I can hear a door in the background open and loud voices fill the line.

"Hey Krimson, we gotta go." A male voice announces in the background. She mumbles something to them, then comes back on the line.

"Listen, I hate to cut this short, but I've got to go. I have some stuff I need to take care of before I head out there. Thank you for calling me, Nolan. I'll meet you in a couple of days."

I love the way my name rolls off her tongue. "No problem. Thanks for coming out on such short notice."

"Any time. I told her all she needs to do is call me and I'll be there in a heartbeat. I really have to go. Just text me the address." Ashley says.

"I will, and I'll see you in a few days."

"Thank you, bye," she responds. I don't want to hang up, but the voices in the background are getting louder.

"Bye." I answer, and the line goes silent. I stare at my phone for a few minutes until a loud knock on my door pulls me out of my head. Ashton's massive build comes strolling in without a care in the world. He stops walking when he looks at my expression.

Cocking an eyebrow in my directions he asks, "Do I need to come back? You look like you want to have a moment to yourself."

"What?" I ask shaking my head and dropping my phone onto the desk. "No, I'm good. I was talking to Izzy's friend Ashley. She'll be here late Friday night. Can you put Ramirez on her when she lands to keep her safe? I don't want these assholes near her."

"You got it boss," Ashton answers and turns to leave. "Oh, I have a new client who will be here in an hour. Can you sit in?"

"Sure."

"Thanks, boss." Ashton leaves my office and quietly closes the door.

I turn around and face the bay windows. Thinking back to the conversation with Ashley, my jeans become tight, her sweet voice echoing in my head. What the hell is wrong with me? I know it's been a while, but fuck, this is crazy. I've never even met her, why would my body respond this way?

Then it dawns on me like a slap in the face. She controlled the rage brewing under my skin. No one has ever pulled me from my dark and deadly secret before. I *respond to her. I wonder how I will react seeing her in person.*

****

White hot pain penetrates my chest and I slowly open my eyes. Blinking a few times, I can finally see where I'm at. Fuck! This isn't good. Not good at all. What are they planning to do to me now? I've already been tortured and beat beyond submission. They have my life on their hands right now. I'm powerless to stop them.

Chapter 19

Ashley

Rush quirks an eyebrow at me and his mouth is hanging open. He opens and closes his mouth a few times before he finally finds his voice.

"You're doing what?" he asks, exasperation is clear in his tone.

"Going into The Circle tonight. When I win, I'll draw that bitch Wrath out and take her on too. I've got a plan, Rush. Trust me." Venom seeps from my voice and Rush is smart enough to keep his mouth shut. I'm not changing my mind. They're going to wish they've never fucked with me.

Walking into the bedroom, I quickly change into a pair of jeans, a black hoodie and slip my racing boots on. Nolan's phone vibrates in my pocket and I check the messages. It's a confirmation text for tonight with an address below. Once I'm dressed, I leave the comfort of the room and walk to the door.

"Where are you going now?" Rush asks.

"Going to scope the place out. You coming or staying?"

Both Ashton and Rush follow me out the door. I knew Rush won't leave me to wander the city streets by myself. We make our way out of the apartment building and walk down to the subway station. Once we're down waiting for the trains, a sense of foreboding settles in my bones. This asshole will pay for the trouble he's caused. I have no doubt about it. Once I get Nolan back, we will take Switch down and make him wish he never crossed us.

The wind picks up and I step to the edge of the platform. Rush and Ashton are standing behind me scanning everyone who steps near us. The brakes from the train make a squealing noise as it stops. The doors open and the three of us step inside. I walk to the back of the train and take a seat on the hard-plastic bench. Rush follows, and Ashton stands guard in front of us.

"Did Ashton get you all up to speed?" I ask.

"Yeah." Rush nods his head, his black hair with blonde highlights fall towards his eyes. He pushes it back and looks at me with concern. "Are you sure you want to do this?"

"More than anything. I need to do this for Nolan, Izzy, and Xavier. Redline was going to go in, but now he can't. They need to be stopped and I'm not backing down." My hands are shaking again from the anger seething in my body. I clench my hands into fists and take a deep breath. I need to have more control and not let my emotions overpower me.

"We're here," Ashton grunts.

The train slows down and the three of us stand up and walk toward the doors. I'm in between Ashton and Rush this time. The doors whoosh open and we step out onto the platform. There are people all around us waiting for other trains or making their way out of the underground city. I look around and spot a young girl and a little boy sitting on a bench. She's scolding him, while he cries in his little hands. She pulls her blonde hair into a ponytail and there are big hoop earrings dangling from her ears. Her hazel eyes meet mine for a moment before she turns her attention to the little boy. She whispers something to him and he pulls his little hands away from his face. His eyes meet mine. Similar features I've adored just a few hours before staring back at me. Before I decided to approach them, a swarm of people passes between us. I shove my way through the crowd, my heart beating hard in my chest. There's no way. This can't be happening. Rush is shouting my name, but I ignore him.

Finally able to break free from the crowd, the teenager and the little boy are gone. Disappeared. Nowhere in sight. Rush and Ashton approach me. I spin around pinning Ashton with a deadly glare.

"What the fuck is going on?" I demand.

"What are you talking about?" Ashton asks. He's withholding something. I can see it in his eyes. "Come on we need to get out of here."

"Ashton Iverson, so help me God, you better explain yourself now. Who the fuck was that? I know you know." I growl.

"Not here. There's so much in play right now, I can't explain it here. Come on. Let's scope this place out and I'll tell you." Ashton answers.

"You better explain everything. This shit doesn't work if you keep things to yourself. I'm so pissed right now I could throttle you."

"Good, keep that feeling. You're going to need it tonight," he responds.

We walk toward the tunnel exit and into the street. The sun is hiding behind some dark clouds and the wind picks up, creating a shiver to wrack my body. We walk in silence down an empty side street. The massive buildings are blocking the wind and I glance around. There's a large bald man standing in front of a discreet brown brick building, smoking a cigarette. His eyes meet mine from across the street for a moment and I break eye contact. Walking between Rush and Ashton, I peek around Ashton's massive form to get a better glimpse of the building. The man is following us with his eyes as we walk around the corner and stop.

"The guy out front is a guard. We might need a password to enter the building." Ashton says.

"I have it. They sent it to Nolan's phone when confirming the fight. Come on. It's getting close to time and I need to focus on what I have to do inside and change my clothes." Feeling like this was a wasted trip, we head back to our apartment building. No one saying a word.

Once we get inside, I go into the bedroom and shut the door. I pull out Nolan's phone and turn it on. I scroll through his pictures of the two of us and a tear falls down my cheek. I don't bother to wipe it away. Why are these people so adamant about getting to Nolan? What did he do to make them want to hurt Izzy and Xavier? Why are they tearing apart my family? I've never even met these people before.

A loud knock on the door startles me from my questioning. I get up from the bed and pocket Nolan's phone. Opening the door, I'm face to face with Ashton.

"We need to talk." He grumbles. I follow him into the living room where the laptop is still on and a picture of a little boy fills the screen.

"That's the boy from the subway station," I say, shocked.

Rush comes up behind me and studies the picture too. A small gasp flows from his lips. The little boy staring back at us is a spitting image of Nolan. From the brown hair to the whiskey-colored eyes and crooked smile, this has to be Nolan's kid. My heart drops to my toes staring at the screen. Is Nolan really missing or did he go back to whoever this kid's mother is and make us think they took him? Is this why he wanted to come back and not tell me? These questions plague my mind as I stare off into space. The seed of doubt for how much Nolan loves me and how much I don't know about him takes over and I become furious. Angry at Nolan, angry at Switch, angry at this unknown woman who's trapped my man in her sticky web of lies and deceit.

"Ash," Rush says gently, rubbing my arms. "Stop. You know Nolan. You know he loves you and if he knew, you know he would have said something."

"Are you sure Rush? What if all of this was a lie? What if he's out fucking this other woman as we speak, laughing at the way I'm worried about him?" Tears are threatening to spill down my cheeks and my stomach is churning. I'm going to be sick. I run into the bathroom and dry heave into the toilet. Once I stop retching, I lean back against the wall, wiping my mouth with toilet paper. Sobbing, I lay on the floor, curling up into a ball. How could I have been so stupid and let someone like Nolan into my life? Into my heart? Everyone I've ever loved leaves me and why should he be any different? I was just a means to pass the time until he could come back here and be with this woman.

The bathroom door cracks open and Rush sticks his head inside. He sees me on the floor, a crumbled mess and immediately comes to my side. At least he's never left me. No matter how hard things get, Rush is always there for me. My heart shatters into a million pieces, I cling to Rush and cry. He strokes his hands down my silky hair, soothing the inner turmoil running through my head.

"Ash, please. You know Nolan isn't like that. He's not going to leave you. I strongly believe they took him and we need to get him back. He loves you." Rush's strong rich voice quiets my sobs.

Sniffling against his hoodie, I look out into the bedroom. Our bed is still disheveled from this morning's fun we had. Every caress, every touch, every look is etched into my mind. "How do you know this? How can you know he isn't laughing at us right now? Everyone I've loved leaves me. How can you know he won't?"

"I know because I see the both of you. I see the way he watches you move. I see the way his eyes light up when you walk into a room. I see the way he needs to touch you when you're near, the way he reaches for you when you walk by. I see it all and I see both of you are made for each other. Trust me, I've never lied about something like this before. I've never seen the dynamics you two have for each other with anyone else." He raises my chin to stare into his black eyes. "You've found your other half. Now, get off your ass and fight for him."

Staring into Rush's black eyes, I get what he gets. I see what he sees. "Thank you, Rush. God, I feel like such a baby. My emotions are all over the place. What do we do now?"

Ashton walks into the bathroom and a frown crosses his face when he sees Rush's arms around me, comforting me. He crosses his arms over his chest and lets out a grunt of disapproval. That has me on edge and my temper flares. I stand up and wipe the stray tears trailing down my cheeks. Approaching Ashton, he quirks an eyebrow at me. "You got something to say?" I demand.

"Are you two about done with your circle jerk time? My partner is missing, and you're snuggled up to him, instead of doing something about it." He points his finger at Rush and a look of disgust passes across his face. He doesn't get the bond we have and thinks we're fucking around. That pisses me off.

Without thinking, I slap Ashton hard across the face and point my finger in his line of sight, making myself very clear. "Fuck you, Ashton. You want to point fingers at someone, point them at yourself. You've withheld vital information from us and you want to berate me? Fuck off." I seethe through clenched teeth. "If this is anyone's fault, it's yours. You have no idea what the fuck I've been through. So, I suggest you back the fuck off and do your job. Find me this kid and the bitch Wrath."

I walk out of the bathroom with fire in my blood. I'm going to burn this city to the ground and get my man back. One way or another, I will bring them all down and they won't know what happened.

Chapter 20

Ashley

We arrive back at the building where the underground fight is located. The bald man from earlier is still standing at the door, acting intimidating. He doesn't scare me one bit. I walk up to him with Rush and Ashton right behind me, flanking me.

"Can I help you?" he asks, crossing his arms over his massive biceps.

"Looking for Amber," I state, glaring right back at him. His lips curl into a menacing grin and I stand my ground, not backing down.

"They'll let anyone in won't they," he responds, shaking his head. "Hope you know what you're getting into sweet thang."

"What the fuck is that suppose to mean?" I ask.

"First time here?" he asks ignoring my question.

I can hear Ashton take a deep breath behind me. After the blowup at the apartment, he told me everything he knows and we're in a good place. My fears have been pushed away and I know without a shadow of a doubt, Nolan didn't leave me by choice. Which is why I'm here now.

Footsteps crunch against the sidewalk from behind us, but I don't turn around to see who it is. I keep my eyes on this guy blocking my way into getting my man back. His glare leaves mine and glances at the people behind us. His eyes grow wide and he swallows hard.

"Is there a problem here?" the guy behind me asks. I turn my attention from the bald guy and spot a tall, black man scowling at the guard. A thin goatee covers his chiseled face, and he's wearing a yellow bandana around his head, covering his buzz cut hair. He's dressed in all black, from his hoodie to his boots. His light brown eyes are cold and deadly as he stares at the doorman. The four men behind him are all dressed in black, wearing their own yellow bandanas, standing tall and glaring at the guard.

"No problems, Ace," the man says with a tremble in his voice.

Ace swings his deadly eyes in my direction and a smile curves his full lips. "Krimson, welcome to The Circle." Confusion etched on my face, Ace releases a rough chuckle and approaches me. The smell of his cologne is strong. "Come on, you're going to need me inside. I've been watching for Mayhem to arrive. Where is he?"

Unable to form words, I keep my mouth shut and follow Ace inside. He throws his arm around my shoulder and mumbles low enough for only me to understand. "Keep quiet and play along. Nolan's life depends on it."

Ashton grunts behind us and Ace removes his arm from around my shoulders. Rush is walking next to Ashton; he's clenching his hands at his sides and he's glaring at Ace. Ace's four men are behind Ashton and Rush. No one says another word as we walk down a dirty hallway. Vibrations below us are rumbling the floor as we walk. The air smells like sweat and copper, causing my stomach to churn. I bite back the vomit threatening to make an appearance when Ace opens a heavy metal door at the end of the hallway. Chants and music fill the stairwell, the adrenaline down below seeps into my body and I feel my fight or flight instincts kick in. Ace leans in next to me so we're eye to eye.

"Shit you've never seen before is down there. Keep your game face on and don't show emotion no matter what you see."

"Why are you helping me and who are you?" I ask.

Ace releases a chuckle from deep in his throat. His cold brown eyes turn soft for a moment when he looks me over. "Names Ace and I'm the leader of The Black Heart Crew. I want to help Nolan because what The Corridore Rosso's have done to him is unjust. We have a code we live by and those fuckers don't. They think they own this city, but they've fucked with the wrong people. I'm out for revenge. Once this is taken care of, I'll go my way and

Nolan will go his. He's a badass fucker I don't ever want to cross. He needs us to help him, so here I am." He stretches his muscular arms out wide. "Come on Krimson, let's get the show started."

We descend the dark stairwell. My hands are gripping the metal railing as we go down, afraid if I let go, I'll lose my footing and tumble to the bottom because my legs are shaking badly. The further down we walk, the louder the crowd gets. Once we reach the bottom, I glance around. Concrete floors, walls, and ceiling are what's holding everyone inside. Bodies are crushed together, sweat pouring off them in waves. Shouting, screaming the smell of blood is so much thicker down here, I feel like I'm going to suffocate. Ace gently grabs my elbow and steers me toward the back of the crowd, down a dark hallway. The craziness of the crowd is shut out when we file in a small room and Ace's men shut the door. There's nothing in here but a single metal folding chair, a fluorescent hanging light, and boxes in the corner piled up to the ceiling.

"Holy shit," are the first words out of my mouth and I release a shaky breath.

Ace raises an eyebrow at me and smirks. "Told you it's a different world down here. Those people out there," he gestures to the closed door. "Are blood thirsty. If you don't put on a good show and shed someone else's blood, they will eat you alive. Can you handle this?"

I look into Ace's light brown eyes and he's serious. Can I do this? Can I give these people the show they want?

Rush speaks up first, "Krimson, you can do this." His tone is strong. "Think of what these fuckers are doing to Izzy, the torture they're putting that sweet innocent girl through. What they made her do in the subway. Think of Xavier that video feed we watched while they taunted him. Redline, who knows what they've done to him. And most importantly think of what they're doing to Nolan. You've seen the scars, you know of his past. What are they doing to him right now? Use that as fuel, go out there and kick some ass. We have faith you can do this."

Listening to Rush talk sparks a fire in my veins. He's right, of course. The bruising on Izzy face flashes in my mind. My anger starts brewing under the surface. The torture on Xavier's face while they taunted him flashes in my mind. The rage I keep locked up comes roaring back. My hands begin to shake with adrenaline.

Nolan. What they did to him in the past comes rearing its ugly head at me. The scars that mar his body, the nightmares he has when he sleeps and lets his guard down. The hopelessness he feels from these people are fueling me to fight. To hear the sickening crunch of bones as my fists are pounding into my opponent.

"That a girl. You're ready," Ace's smooth voice says next to me. My eyes narrow at him as he picks up my hands and tapes them from my knuckles to my wrists. He chuckles softly, "This is to protect your wrists. So, you don't break anything."

Once he's finished, I remove my hoodie and jeans. Underneath is a pair of black and red shorts and matching sports bra. He rubs oil over my skin and I pull my hair up in a tight ponytail, then braid the end and wrap it around the elastic. That way my opponent can't yank my hair and distract me. The chants from the crowd beyond the door are growing louder, anxious for the next fight.

Ace settles his hands on my shoulders, "Come on you're up. Give them a show and I'll guarantee Wrath will come running. You know what to do," he says. His massive black hands knead my shoulders, loosening up my tense muscles. He nods and one of his guys opens the door and the crowd's anticipation buzzes inside the tiny space. One by one we file out of the room. Three of Ace's men takes the lead, then Ashton, who surprisingly hasn't said a word, followed by Rush, then me. Ace is behind me, his hand resting on the small of my back, guiding me and his other man is behind him, bringing up the rear, watching our backs as we walk to the edge of the crowd.

The blood thirsty animals part for us and The Circle opens in front of me. It isn't anything special like I expected. A blue tarp covers the surface, fastened down to the concrete floor. There's blood on it already from the fights before me. Nothing is holding the crowd back from entering The Circle. They form a tight ring around the two fighters and that's it.

Shit, how are we supposed to control the crowd when nothing is separating me from them? Ace must have sensed my distraught because he nudges me and nods his head. I peel my eyes away from The Circle and look into the crowd. There are several other dark skin men standing at the edges, wearing yellow bandanas around their heads or biceps, separating me from the crowd. Satisfied they have it under control, I step away from my entourage and enter The Circle. The crowd grows quiet, waiting for me to do or say something. I narrow my eyes and scan around me, waiting for my opponent. I'm ready to get this shit over with and get Nolan back. A man dressed in dark blue jeans and a green t-shirt steps forward into The Circle with me. His light blonde hair is cut short and his cloudy blue eyes scan the crowd. A sneer curves his full lips and he holds his hands up in the air and the crowd stays silent. I don't like this.

"Ladies and gentlemen, we have a new fighter among us. At five feet nine inches tall, weighing in at one hundred and forty-five pounds. All the way for Los Angeles, California, please give a big Circle welcome to Krimson." The crowd stares at me and cheers my street name. Confused at how they know all this information about me, I glance at Rush. He whispers something to Ace and Ace nods his head at me. He mouths the words, *roll with it* and I scan the crowd around me. I lift my arms up over my head and their chants get louder and louder, fueling me on.

"Krimson! Krimson! Krimson!" The rush from the crowd is sparking my adrenaline and I'm ready. Rolling my neck around, my muscles are loose, and the nerves are gone.

The announcer holds his hand up again, and the crowd quiets down. The anticipation for what comes next is buzzing around me. "Krimson's opponent is a New York City native. You all know her from her previous fight the other night, which she lost to our champ, Wrath."

I drown out everything else he says when I spot a small woman in the crowd. She's sneering at me with her arms crossed over her chest. Her blonde hair is tight against her head in a ponytail and her hazel eyes are shooting daggers in my direction. She cracks her neck from side to side, not taking her eyes off me. I glare at her right back. I want her in here with me, so I can beat her ass. Rage and hate fill my body and I'm ready to pound the shit out of everyone. A sneer passes my lips, and the woman smirks at me. She turns her back and disappears into the crowd. Once she's out of my sight, the roar of the crowd penetrates my ears and I turn my head toward my opponent who's finally graced me with her presence. That pisses me off and I reach deep inside to wake the monster

I locked up after I killed those two men who fucked with Rush.

My opponent is my height and weight. She's sporting fresh bruises on her pale face and her hands are shaking. Her black hair is braided down each side of her head and she's wearing dark blue shorts and matching sports bra. I zone in on her nervousness and use that to my advantage. The announcer leaves The Circle and we walk around each other. My fists are up to protect my face and body. She's unsure what she should do. She acts like she doesn't want to be here. I move in and throw an uppercut, knocking her in the chin. My hand vibrates from the contact. Showing no emotion, I strike again and the buzz of the crowd fades as I concentrate on my opponent. This time a jab to the side of her head, leaving her stunned. She drops her arms. Big mistake. I throw an elbow and it connects with her nose. Blood drips down, and she attempts to shake off the hit.

This is too easy. I zone in on her body and deliver blow after blow on her torso and arms, tiring her out from defending herself. The crowd around us is screaming my name fueling me on even more. My breathing is heavy when I land hit after hit on this poor unsuspecting woman. She doesn't even get a chance to hit me back. She's doubled over as I deliver the last punch. A blow straight to her face knocks her out cold, her blood coating my knuckles as her nose shatters under my fists, and she drops to the ground, not moving.

My heart is beating hard against my chest and my hands are shaking with adrenaline. The announcer steps into The Circle and holds my bloody hand up above my head, announcing me the winner. The crowd is going nuts from my win and I'm ready to take anyone on. He holds up his hands after he drops mine and the crowd quiets down.

"Ladies and gentlemen. We have a winner for this round. Krimson!" The crowd chants my name and I feel like I'm on top of the world. I look toward Rush and all the blood drains from my face when I spot someone standing in the back of the crowd. His whiskey-colored eyes are narrowed in my direction and he's pissed. I've seen that look before. Bruises cover his face and he's limping toward me, pushing his way into the crowd. Ace grabs Nolan by the shoulders and he whips around so fast, Ace doesn't see it coming. With a clenched fist, Nolan rears back, ready to strike.

"NO!" I scream. I push my way into the crowd and place myself between Nolan and Ace. He's so far gone, I'm afraid I can't reach him. There's a blank, deadly look in his eyes as he watches Ace. I rest my bloody hands on Nolan's shoulders and force him to look at me. Nothing, no recognition, no life. Nothing.

"Nolan," I reach up and gently touch a fresh bruise on his face. He closes his eyes at the contact and I release a deep breath. "I'm here. It's me, Ashley. What did they do to you? Fight your way back to me, please." I look behind him at the woman who was glaring at me earlier and another man with dark skin and black hair are trying to make their way to us, but Ace's men have them stopped, surrounding them.

I turn to Rush and Ace. "We need to get out of here, now." I grab Nolan's hand and rest it on my hip. He tightens his hold on me, his fingers digging into my flesh, but I bite back the whimper that wants to pass through my lips. I need to get him out of here and deal with the outcome later. Ace nods his dark head and I follow him through the crowd and up a back stairwell I didn't notice before. Moving as quickly as we can up dark metal stairs, Ace and Rush in front of us leading the way. Nolan and I are in the middle and Ashton is behind us. Ace's men are still downstairs, keeping the woman and the other guy surrounded. Why did they have him there? What was their plan? Did they think they could break him? Did they succeed in breaking him and sent him to kill us?

These questions are running through my head as our feet pound up the stairs. Ace and Rush drop their shoulders and barge into a heavy metal door at the same time. The door gives away from their force and they stumble out into the night, disappearing from my line of sight. Rush pops his head back in and motions for us to follow. One by one, we're out of the dark stairwell and quickly walking down an alley filled with dumpsters and smells of human and food waste. Rats scurry past us as we walk further down.

Nolan's grip is still biting into my flesh and he hasn't said a word. I'm afraid of what I'll find in his eyes when we stop. He had no life in them down there at The Circle, no spark of recognition. For all he thinks we're going to do the same things to him that those guys have done. I've got to get through to him and I can't do it with all these men around us. The last time he lost himself, he almost killed Ashton.

We're near the end of the alley and the city noises come roaring back in full swing. Even at night, this city never sleeps. Traffic horns and headlights are blaring ahead of us and there are swarms of people all over the sidewalk. I feel Nolan's grip tighten even harder on my hips and I stop walking. Ashton keeps a wide berth and leans against the building opposite from us, keeping his hands up in a defensive stance. Rush and Ace are at the end of the alley. The streetlights are casting an eerie glow around them, hiding their faces in shadows. When they turn around towards us, Ace takes a few steps in our direction and Nolan releases a low growl from deep in his throat.

"Don't come any closer," I tell Ace. He stops walking in our direction and stares at Nolan. His brown eyes are bugging out of his head and his breath catches in his throat. I can hear his gasp from here. "Go around the corner, both of you and wait. You can't be near him right now."

"Ash," Rush starts. Nolan growls again and Rush stops talking, staring at him.

"Rush trust me. Only I can reach him and you're not helping. This state he's in, I've been there with him. He needs me and I'm not leaving him. You have to go, please. We'll come out soon." I plead. I can do this. I've done it before, I can do it again.

Rush walks backward towards the busy street and Ace follows. Both watching us as they leave our sight. I release a deep breath and turn around facing Nolan. Ashton hasn't moved a muscle since we stopped, and I ignore him as I focus on the man in front of me. I rest my palm over Nolan's rapidly beating heart and he drops his head to look at what I'm doing.

"Nolan," I whisper. His eyes drift from my hand resting on his heart, up my arm and finally stop when he reaches my eyes. "Come back to me, please. I need you here." My voice is strong, but I'm shaking inside. Tears slip from my eyes and a heavy feeling deep in the pit of my stomach is rearing its way up and I pray I'm not too late.

That I can reach this beautiful, broken man and bring him out of his mind and back to me.

Chapter 21

Nolan

I have no idea why Wrath and Switch took me to The Circle tonight. Maybe they thought they could control me in that setting like they used to in the past? But as my fingers dig in Ashley's hips, keeping me in the present, I know I've made the right decision. I almost turned back toward Wrath and left with her, but my girl saved me again. Her gentle touch brought me back to her, and she didn't give up. She kept the demon tamped down. I'm slowly regaining control of myself, but I still feel threatened with all these men around what's mine and a low growl escapes my throat. Ashley turns toward me, resting her hand against my chest and I recognize what she's touching as her angelic voice floats through the city night and straight to my heart.

"Nolan," she whispers. I trail my eyes up from her bloody palm wrapped in tape, gently caressing my scars through my hoodie, up her slender, sun-kissed arm until I look into her soft brown eyes. "Come back to me, please. I need you here." Her body is trembling with fear. The evil lurking below wants to surface and taunt her fear, but my head realizes she isn't afraid of me, she's afraid it's too late to reach me.

I open and close my mouth several times, trying to find the words I need to say. Nothing seems sufficient enough for what she's done for me, to me. So, I do the only thing I can at the moment. I close the distance between us and rest my forehead against hers. She's my lifeline, the air I breathe. Without her, I would be lost in a sea of darkness. I need to feel her soft curves in my hands, touch her heart, taste her. Ashley wraps a slender arm around my neck, her other hand still resting against my beating heart and her lips finally meet mine. A surge of protectiveness wraps around my mind as her soft kiss penetrates through my body. My lips trembling against hers, I inhale her strawberry scent, but it's tainted with blood. Realizing she must be freezing in the little shorts and sports bra she has on, I pull back and remove the sweatshirt I'm wearing, oblivious to what Switch has done to my body while I was unconscious. A loud gasp flows from her lips and I frown.

"Nolan, what did they do to you?" Her sweet voice is full of concern as her eyes scan my bare chest. Fresh bruising and dried blood is still coating my skin.

"It's OK, Ash," I finally say. I haven't spoken in what seems like days and my voice is raspy. I hand her my hoodie and she shakes her head at me. "You're freezing, you need it."

"Thank you, Nolan. Rush has my clothes. Can I have him come back and give me my stuff?"

I glance up and look around. We're in a dark alley and the bustle of the city night is ahead of us. I don't see Rush anywhere. I close my eyes and channel the inner strength she gives me. Having myself under control, I give her a slight nod. I sense someone moving from the brick building to the right of me and my eyes snap open, narrowing in their direction. Ashton steps out of the shadows with his hands raised. I recognize the gesture and release a breath I didn't realize I was holding.

"Ashton," I say. He stares at me, concern etched across his face. "Thank you for taking care of her." He flinches at my words and Ashley stiffens under my hands. Something happened between them while I was gone.

"I'll go get Rush and Ace," he grumbles, ignoring my thanks and walks quickly toward the end of the alley. I look at Ashley and she shakes her head.

"It's a long story, I'll explain later. Is it OK if Ace comes too? He saved my ass down there tonight. If it weren't for him, I wouldn't have survived."

"Yes," I answer.

The shuffling of feet down the alley coming toward us gets louder and I tighten my grip on Ashley. She rests her head against my chest and I stifle a groan. My body is aching all over, but I push the pain away and revel in the feel of her against my bruised and beaten skin. I didn't think it would happen again, I didn't think I'd get to hold her against me, ever again. I didn't think I'd get to see her sweet smile, her beautiful face, have her body wrapped around mine. An urge to get her alone fills my mind and she giggles. It's music to my ears.

"Nolan," she whispers against my bare chest. "I've missed you and I love you." She tightens her hold around my waist, neither one of us want to let go. My heart beats hard against my chest when she says those words. How could she love me after everything she's been through? Everything I've put her through? But she does and it's clear in her voice and her touch.

"Nolan, bro. Are you OK?" Rush asks when he's close enough.

"I will be," I answer, not letting Ashley go just yet. A shiver wracks her body and I feel like a selfish bastard for not letting her get more clothes on. I take the hoodie Rush is offering with one hand and give it to Ashley. She reluctantly lets me go long enough to put it on, while I put mine back on, covering the bruises.

We stay wrapped around each other for several more moments before Ace speaks. "We need to get out of here. I have a place we can go to for now. Nolan, I want to help. Will you finally let me help take these bastards down?" I nod my head. "Thank you," he responds.

We follow Ace out into the bustle of the city. The bright lights and loud noises have my senses on high alert as Ace hails a taxi. I look at the man who saved my woman. His arm muscles ripple under his black hoodie and his full lips are thin as his eyes dart around, looking for a threat. I'm thankful he was there looking out for her. A taxi stops in front of us and we all pile in. Ace takes the front seat, while Ashton, Rush and I squeeze our big bodies into the back. Ashley sits on my lap, her arms wrapped around my neck, her head resting against my chest. I tune everything and everyone out, focusing on Ashley's soft body resting against mine. I rub my hands up and down her back as the taxi takes off at breakneck speed, swerving in and out of traffic. The tension in the cab is unbearable and I feel like I'm going to lose my mind. Twenty minutes later, the driver pulls up to a brownstone and Ace pays him. We all get out and Ashley doesn't let me go. She has her arms around my waist, her head resting against my chest while we wait to see where Ace is taking us.

He approaches us, and I see him in a different way. Before it was our gang against his, now it's us against them. His brown eyes look tired and stressed, his stance is stiff and unsure. The hair on the back of my neck stands on end, my senses on high alert. He's hesitating for some reason.

"Ace," I say getting his attention. "What's going on? Why are we here? Where are we?" I rapid fire questions at him.

He hesitates before answering, "This is my home. My mom and kid are inside."

My jaw drops, and my eyes grow wide. I had no idea he had a family and now I understand his hesitancy in letting us in. We're not exactly innocent citizens.

"It's OK, we won't harm them in any way," I promise him. "I understand if you don't want to let us in. We can go back to the apartment."

"No, it's not that at all. My mom understands this life. Hell, she was raised in it. It's just, my kid doesn't. I haven't let that part of me touch her and it never will if I have my way. She's my angel in this dark world," Ace says with a hint of anger in his voice.

"How old is she?" Ashley asks.

"Four," Ace answers with a smile. "And she tests my patience every minute of every day." There's pride in his voice. "Come on, let's go inside. Get you two cleaned up and then we'll go over a game plan." He turns on his heels and walks up the concrete steps to the beautiful brownstone in front of us. He inserts a key into several locks running down the solid oak door and pushes the door open. "She might be sleeping so try to stay quiet."

We follow him inside and stay as quiet as possible. I haven't let Ashley go the whole time. She's tucked under my arm, her fingers splayed across my chest. Feeling safe for the first time in a couple of days, I relax against her grip and want nothing more than to bury my face in her bare breasts, lick and suck every inch of her body, bury myself so deep inside of her, that I don't know where I start and she stops. My breathing picks up and Ashley gently slaps my chest.

"Not now," she whispers against my chest.

"Hmm, kind of hard not to think about that right now with your body pressed against mine," I whisper in her ear. She lets out a soft giggle and it's music to my ears. I didn't think I'd get to hear that giggle ever again.

Ace turns toward us and narrows his eyes. "Remember, my kid is sleeping in here. I'm going to put you two far, far away from her."

We walk out of the foyer and into a living room. Ace turns on a light and the brightness hurts my eyes. There's hardwood flooring throughout the house with a plush maroon carpet in the living room. A brown couch and matching chair with a big screen T.V. are against the wall. Heavy maroon curtains cover the windows, blocking the street lights outside. A noise from behind me makes me jump and I turn around, holding Ashley behind me.

A skinny, older woman with dark skin, black hair streaked with grey, and light brown eyes comes out of the kitchen with a smile on her plump lips when she sees Ace. She's wearing dark jeans and a blue sweater. "Oh, good you're home. Angel is sleeping in her room. She tried to wait up for you, but I read her a story and put in a movie. She's been asleep for an hour. Are you in for the night or do you need me to stick around?"

I shift from foot to foot, feeling like an idiot for my actions. The woman's eyes land on me and a gasp leave her lips. "Ace, can I talk to you alone?" she asks, not breaking eye contact with me. Ace puts his arm around her slender shoulders and they walk out of the living room and into another room. I don't like this at all.

"Nolan," Ashton says bringing my attention to him. "We need to talk about what happened."

"Not now," I respond through gritted teeth.

"When? We need to do it soon."

"When you tell me what happened between you and Ashley," I respond. Ashley's body turns stiff.

"We had a misunderstanding," Ashton replies and Ashley snorts behind me.

"A misunderstanding? Is that what you're calling it?" she says stepping out from behind me, exasperated. Her honey eyes meet mine. "He accused me of cheating on you with Rush, of all people and I let him have it. He obviously doesn't trust me and needs to deal with his own issues before he comes at me." There's fire in her eyes and she's pissed. Rush tenses next to her and nods his head in agreement.

"What?" My eyes land on Ashton and he sits on the couch running his hands through his hair. He sits back and nods his head. Fury fills my veins and my hands start to tremble with rage. My right-hand man accusing my woman of cheating. "What the hell is wrong with you?" I growl.

"I don't know. I know she wouldn't cheat on you." He looks at me with trepidation in his eyes. "I just thought the worst when I saw the two of them together. They have a tight bond and I just don't know." He blows out a deep breath and runs his hands down his face. "My head is all fucked up right now."

Ashley sits next to him; her eyes are full of pity. She rubs his shoulder gently, "Does this have anything to do with Natalia?"

His eyes fly in her direction and he slowly nods his head. "She won't talk to me and I don't know why. I've done everything right. Gave her space when she needed it, listened to her, been there for her after everything went down and she still shuts me out. What did I do wrong?" He's torn up about this and it's causing him to lose focus on what we have to do.

"Ashton, you didn't do anything wrong. Give her time, she's just as fucked as you are and doesn't know how to handle it. Everything will work out the way it's supposed to. Right now, we need to get this shit taken care of and then we'll figure that out."

"Thanks, Ash. And again, I'm really sorry for the way I've been acting. It's not like me to let this shit bother me."

"It's fine, but next time you want to come at me, make sure you're ready." She responds with a giggle.

"Yeah, no shit. You handed me my ass." Ashton teases back. He looks at Rush, "Rush, I'm really sorry. You don't know how much of an ass I feel like right now."

"No worries. Just don't let it happen again. Ash and I have been through so much in our lives, we have a tight bond. To some, it looks like more, but trust me, it's not." Rush smiles to himself. There's a glint in his eyes and Ashley notices it.

"Rush? You didn't." Ashley groans exasperated.

"I don't know what you're talking about?" he answers with a smirk. Now I'm confused.

"She's the doctor. What the hell are you thinking?" Ashley scolds.

"Hey, I've got to do something. Being around you two made me lose my head." Rush winks and shrugs his shoulders.

"What the hell, Rush. If something goes wrong, we have to find a new doctor to stitch you up." Ashley grumbles. I'm still at a loss for words, I have no idea what they are talking about.

"Nah, it's all good," Rush grins from ear to ear. Ashley lets out a groan and sinks into the couch covering her face with her bloody, taped hands.

"Ash," I say, breaking up their conversation. Her honey colored eyes land on me and a flare of lust penetrate my body. "Come here."

She stands up and walks over to me. I lift her hands and begin taking the tape off her knuckles, gently. Ace walks back into the room and there's a fire in his eyes. He's pissed about something. I watch as he paces the room back and forth, running his hands through his short black hair.

"Is everything OK?" Ashley asks.

He stops pacing back and forth and releases a deep breath. His eyes land on me, "Yeah, apparently my mother knows who you are and wants to help, too. I talked her out of it and told her I need her here to take care of Angel. This is the safest place for both of them."

"How does she know who I am?" I ask, worried.

"She knew your mother. Remember she's been in this world her whole life and she didn't like what your mom did to you and wants to whoop her ass."

"Holy shit. I just, I can't right now." The news Ace just dropped on me takes my breath away and I feel like I'm going to pass out. My breathing is rapid, and my heart is beating hard against my chest. I stop unwrapping Ashley's hand and try to steady myself. No one is supposed to know what that woman did to me. No one is supposed to understand how wrong it was to leave a seventeen-year-old out in the cold, to fend for themselves and let them get involved with a gang to pay for her drugs. The abuse she put me through after Switch would beat me into submission.

Ashley's gentle hand rests on my stubbled cheeks and she pulls my face to hers. "Come on, let's go shower and get our head back together." There's a tear trailing down her cheek and I wipe it away with the pad of my thumb.

"This way guys." Ace gestures to us and we follow him, arm in arm. None of us saying a word as we walk up a huge oak staircase and down a long hallway. There are three doors on each side, all of them are shut. He opens the last door on the right, flipping a light switch next to the door. "Take whatever time you need. There are clothes that should fit in the dresser. Don't worry, Angel is downstairs in her room."

Ashley walks in first and I follow behind. I'm still stunned by Ace's confession. I shut the door behind me and lean against it. Ashley stops in the middle of the room and looks around. There's a queen size bed covered with a black and white comforter underneath a window covered with chestnut brown curtains. An oak dresser with a large mirror sits to the right of the bed and two open doors on the opposite side. One leads to a walk-in closet and the other to a bathroom. The room is carpeted the same color as the curtains. A black leather chair sits in the corner with a thick blanket draped over the back.

I close my eyes and lean my head back, trying to push the memories of the last couple of days away. Gentle hands caress my shoulders and arms. Ashley still hasn't seen the worst of what they did to me and I'm afraid to show her, knowing it will set her off and she'll turn dark and kill them. She gently runs her hands down my chest to the hem of my hoodie and lifts it up over my head. A groan escapes my throat as her full lips gently kiss a trail up my torso, her teeth gently scraping along the way. She doesn't say a word and doesn't need to. Lust floods my body and I need to get inside of her now. No slow and gently this time. I need to feel her body against mine to shake away the rage brewing under the surface.

I reach my arms around her waist and lift her up. Ashley wraps her legs around my waist as I walk into the bathroom. I set Ashley on the counter and remove her hoodie, revealing her sports bra stained with drops of blood. I remove her bra exposing her sun-kissed breasts, her nipples are hard pleading for attention. Ashley grabs my hips and pulls me against her. My lips trail kisses from one full breast to another and a moan escapes her lips, her hips grinding against me as her nails dig into my hair.

"Nolan, I don't want to wait any longer. I need you inside of me now," she sighs against my ear, sending shivers down my spine. I caress her sun-kissed skin with my lips and tongue, working my way up to her full pink lips. Our bodies are pressed together tightly as my lips descend upon hers, capturing her moans and groans. My hands grip the sides of her face and our tongues battle back and forth, demanding and seeking a connection only we can get from each other.

With a growl, I pull Ashley off the countertop and yank her shorts down her slender legs and toss them aside. I remove the rest of my clothes and start the shower. Turning back toward Ashley, her eyes are hooded with desire and she's nibbling on her bottom lip, turning me on even more. She's leaning against the counter waiting for me to take her. Her hand catches my attention as she plays with the hem of her black panties, teasing me with what waits underneath. I saunter over to her, watching her. I run a palm down her toned stomach and inside her panties.

I trail kisses up her body and kiss her with pent-up passion I've had since watching her fight in the ring. Ashley hooks her legs around my waist and pulls me against her. A deep moan escapes my throat as our tongues battle and our kiss heats up. Steam fills the bathroom from the shower, making our bodies slick with sweat. A primal instinct takes over and I break our kiss then turn Ashley around so she's facing the mirror. I step up behind her, wipe away the steam and look at our reflection in the mirror. Her eyes are dark with desire, matching mine. I trail my eyes down her slender body and she's watching me, watch her.

I run my hand down her spine and meet her eyes in the mirror. "So beautiful," I whisper. "So ready," I kiss her shoulder. "So mine."

As our bodies connect, we both groan at the same time, watching each other in the mirror. I move with a slow pace, building her up. Ashley sucks in a deep breath as I move faster. We don't take our eyes off each other and a fire burns down my spine. I grip her hip hard with my other hand, leaning over her, craving skin on skin contact. Moans, groans and the smell of sex fill the air around us and we both seek our orgasm. I need her heaving chest against mine, her heartbeat against me, her lips on mine. I crave to be as close to her as possible. I sit on the edge of the tub and Ashley straddles my waist.

"Fuck, Ash, I can't hold off any longer," I grunt and grit my teeth. Her arms lock around my neck, pulling me closer. A moan escapes my lips as our bodies connect on another level.

"Keep going," she moans, and my lips capture hers. Our tongues are in sync with our bodies. Fire races through my spine again and I can't stop my pending orgasm this time. Breathing heavy, we both stay still for a moment until we have our bearings and our breathing evens out.

Without saying another word, we both step into the shower. I wash away the blood from her fight earlier, watching the water turn clean. Ashley does the same to me. She gently washes away the blood marring my body and reveals the bruising left behind. We both clean each other and touch each other's souls.

By the time we're both clean, we're ready to face this issue head on and get Izzy, Xavier, and Redline back. We're ready to fight for our family and our loved ones. We're ready to grasp our demons and use them to our advantage. We're ready to take down anyone who stands in our way, no matter what it takes.

Chapter 22

Xavier

Drip, drip, drip.

I'm going nuts hearing the sink drip repeatedly. Handcuffed to the register in the corner of the room, a sense of helplessness fills my body. My arms and shoulders are stiff and sore from being suspended, and my legs are numb from sitting here for so long, not being able to move. I lift my pounding head from the wall and peer around the moonlit room. I can see Izzy tied to a chair, her chin is resting against her chest. Her breathing is even, and there's a rag covering her beautiful mouth. She's been beaten several times by the chick they call Wrath and I've had to watch, helpless to do anything. I've tried to get them to channel their anger toward me, but they love taunting and teasing Izzy. At least they haven't punched her stomach and for that I'm grateful.

They've fed us enough to keep us alive with stale crackers, bread, and water. A large man with a brown buzz cut and honey colored eyes have been in charge when Wrath and the other guy with deadly black eyes aren't here. He doesn't act like he wants to be here, but they have something on him. They keep tormenting him with something about a kidnapping and he does what they say. He won't touch either of us though. The two have tried several times to get him too, but he refuses. If anything, he's saved Izzy from Wrath several times. The times Wrath has beat Izzy is because that guy wasn't here.

There was one time a couple of days ago where Wrath untied Izzy from the chair and made her leave with her and the other guy. A few hours later, Izzy came back with tears in her green eyes and she shut down. She won't speak or look at me. I feel like a failure for letting her get hurt. I've got to find a way to get out of here soon before I lose Izzy for good.

Loud footsteps stomp down the hallway and loud voices follow. I lean my pounding head against the wall and prepare myself for what waits on the other side.

"How could this happen?" Wrath shouts from the other side of the door. Izzy picks her head up, and a whimper escapes through the rag covering her mouth. I'm trying to get Izzy to look in my direction, but she won't. "You're a fucking idiot, Switch. We had him in our control and you let him get away. Now he's back with her and we're fucked." Locks turn on the door and it slams open.

"I didn't let shit happen, Wrath. Watch your tone with me. I'm still in charge here." The guy with cold, black eyes replies as they step into the apartment building. Finally learning his name, Switch, I open my eyes a little and watch them enter.

Switch turns on a light and I try not to wince as the brightness fills the room. He walks to the kitchen and grabs a beer out of the refrigerator and takes a long pull from the bottle. He sets his bottle down on the counter and crosses his arms over his chest, watching Wrath pace back and forth. Something happened tonight, and she's pissed. Her fists are clenching at her sides and rage is rolling off her body in waves.

"Fuck!" Wrath shouts and stomps off into the bedroom, slamming the door behind her. Switch follows her with his eyes and takes a deep breath. He picks up the bottle and finishes the beer before tossing it into the sink. He glares in my direction and then Izzy's. My body tightens with tension with the way he's leering at her. Fuck no, he isn't touching her. I rattle my handcuffs drawing his attention back to me and a deadly glint is in his eyes.

"You got something to say?" Switch asks. I don't answer and glare right back at him. "Don't worry. It'll be all over soon." He says and walks out of the kitchen toward Izzy. He squats down in front of her and raises her chin so she's looking into his eyes and removes the rag from her mouth. "Are you hungry?"

She tries to pull her chin out of his grasp, but he tightens his hold. "I asked if you're hungry," he spits out through gritted teeth. Izzy shakes her head, and he trails a finger down her cheek, wiping away a tear. Rage fills my body and I try to get up but fail from my weakened state.

"Motherfucker. Don't. Touch. Her." I spit out.

Switch spins around on his heels so he's facing me, "What are you going to do about it?"

"I'll fucking kill you," I answer, low and deadly.

He barks out a laugh and stands up, "Just like Nolan said? Well, I hate to tell you Xavier, but Nolan can't touch me, and neither can you." He walks out of the room and into the bedroom Wrath went into.

It's just Izzy and me in the room. She's whimpering behind her snarled blonde hair. "Izzy, please look at me." She shakes her head, keeping it down. "Nothing you have done is your fault. I'm going to get us out of here. Please, have faith we will get out."

"I can't, X. I've done something I'm not proud of and I almost cost Nolan his life," she cries.

"Tell me what happened. We can get through this," I plead.

"I," she starts and then stops. Her face twists with pain and a low groan escape her cracked lips. "Shit, X, help me." She whispers. She curls her chest down toward her legs and whimpers.

"B, take deep breaths and stay with me, please," I beg. "Tell me what happened."

Izzy takes a deep breath and sits back up. Her green eyes are full of unshed tears. "They made me push him, so they could grab Redline. If it weren't for Ashton, he would have died. I was so close to escaping. I could smell freedom all around me, but I couldn't escape X, I won't leave you." She cries quietly.

"B, if you ever get the chance to escape again, take it. Don't stay for me." She shakes her head back and forth violently. "Yes, B. I can handle what they do to me, but I can't handle what they'd do to you. If you ever get the chance again, take it, please. This isn't your fault. You did nothing wrong." Tears are burning my eyes and my lungs are burning. I'm trying to stay strong for her, but I'm close to breaking down, giving in.

"I'm just as bad as they are. I didn't have to push him in front of that train. I could have said no, but I didn't. I did what they told me to do." Izzy sobs. Fuck, I wish I could hold her. I flex my fingers several times, wishing I could run them through her hair. She's so close, yet so far away.

"B, you have more than yourself to look out for now. You have to do what is best for all of us. If escaping and leaving me here is what you must do, then do it. I won't fault you or be angry. I swear B, you've got to get out of here if you ever have the chance too, again." Emotions clog my throat and I fight back tears threatening to spill. "Promise me, B. Promise you'll take the next opportunity."

Izzy finally looks me in the eyes and nods her head. "I promise," she whispers.

"I love you so much, B," I choke out, keeping eye contact.

"I love you too, X," her voice is full of sadness, hurt and anger. "I promise."

The bedroom door yanks open, interrupting our conversation, and Wrath stalks out with Switch hot on her heels. She stomps over to Izzy and unties her feet. "If you try anything, bitch. I will drag you back here, torture lover boy, slowly kill him, and make you watch. Got it?" Wrath spits out. Izzy's wide eyes fly toward me and nods her head.

"Yes," Izzy whispers. I mouth *I love you, promise me,* to Izzy and she nods her head slightly, not taking her eyes off me. She mouths *I love you,* back and Wrath stands up, interrupting our silent conversation. She yanks Izzy up from the chair, throws a zip-up hoodie over her shoulders and ties her hands in front of her.

"We're going on a little trip. Don't try anything or his pain will be front and center in your mind for the rest of your life." Wrath grits out through clenched teeth.

"Ok," Izzy says quietly. Tears are glistening in her eyes and she connects with mine again. I nod my head and she does it back. Relief fills me knowing she will escape when the opportunity arises. Switch shuts off the light, plunging me into darkness yet again and the three walk out the apartment door. I lean my head against the wall and let my tears fall. I'm not a praying man, but right now I pray to God he lets Izzy escape and get help. Propped against the wall with the constant drip from the kitchen faucet soothing me to sleep this time.

Chapter 23

Nolan

A heavy thump jolts me awake and I stand up quickly. Looking around the unfamiliar room, I blink a few times trying to figure out where I am. Moonlight is filtering in through a slit in the dark curtains and memories of the last couple of hours come flooding back in full swing.

I see Ashley curled up on the king-sized bed and relief fills my body that she's OK, she's right here. A whimper escapes her lips and she throws her arm over on my side of the bed, seeking me out. Her eyelids flutter open and she sits up. Rubbing the sleep from her eyes, Ashley stands up and walks over to me in the middle of the room. She wraps her arms around my waist and holds onto me tight.

"What are you doing up already?" She asks. Her voice vibrates against my bare chest.

"I heard a thump downstairs and it woke me up," I answer.

"Well, since we're up, let's talk to Rush and Ashton and come up with a plan. I have a feeling if we wait any longer, something bad will happen to Izzy, Xavier, Redline, and Austin." Ashley's still holding out hope for her brother. I pray it doesn't come back and bite us in the ass.

I pull her head away from my chest and stare into her honey brown eyes. I lean in and kiss her passionately. The last couple of days pour from my lips to hers and she whimpers. I tighten my grip around her waist and hold her against me. I never want to lose this feeling, her body flush against mine, the passion I feel from the bottom of my toes to the top of my head. I don't ever want to lose this.

I pull away from her soft lips and let her go. I grab a clean shirt, hoodie, and jeans from the dresser and put them on. Ashley does the same and we go downstairs, hand in hand. Ace, Ashton, and Rush are sitting in the living room. They're all drinking beer in the quiet room and the tension between the three of them is thick. Rush's head snaps up in our direction and a smirk appears on his face when he sees the two of us. Ashton swings his head in our direction and gives us a brief nod. Ace doesn't say a word either as we sit on the couch.

Ashton is the first to speak, "Nolan, I hate to do this to you right now, but I need to know what happened and where you were when they took you." Ashley's body tenses next to me and her grip on my hand tightens. "It's inevitable. I need to know so we can put together a plan with the rest of our team. They need to get involved at this point. We can't do this alone, Nolan. They took you in broad daylight. There's got to be more than Switch and Wrath involved."

"There is," Ace says, quietly. All of us look in his direction, but he keeps his eyes locked on me. "You know who's all involved, and we need all the help we can get."

"Who is it, Nolan?" Ashley asks me.

"Back when I was associated with the Corridore Rosso's, they were looking to expand their reach down the east coast. I stopped them at every turn and they never knew. After I left, I kept tabs on Switch and his father Marcus Angelo. Marcus has connections all over the U.S. I didn't realize back then how deep his reach went." I hesitate to continue.

"Where did it lead, Nolan?" Ashley asks. I close my eyes and gather the strength I need to tell her the next part. It's going to spin her entire world upside down and she's going to lose it.

"What I'm going to tell you, I need you to believe I had no idea until they took me. I overheard Switch and Marcus talking when they assumed I was unconscious after they tortured me. Marcus was gloating about having the furthest reach in all the gangs. That reach," I take a deep breath before continuing. "He has pull with the Tres Seis Gang. More specifically, Diablo."

Rush stands up quickly, "What! No fucking way. That can't be. How did we not know about this Ash?" He starts pacing back and forth across the living room. "That's impossible. Tell him that's impossible."

Ashley is very still, not saying a word. Her hand holding mine grows slack, and she's staring off in the distance, lost in a memory and I can't help her. Rush stalks toward us, his tall frame hovering over her small one, there's fire in his dark eyes and his nostrils are flaring. His aggressive stance has the hair on the back of my neck standing on end and my heart beats hard against my chest. If he doesn't back off, I won't be able to control myself. I step forward in front of Ashley, a menacing glare focused on him. "Rush, I will only tell you this once," I respond in a low and deadly voice. "Back the fuck away before I lose my shit and you'll regret it."

Rush's black eyes grow wide and he steps back. Ashley tightens her grip on my hand and gives it a squeeze. I turn around and look at her. She has tears trailing down her cheeks and I wipe them away with the pads of my thumbs. "I thought this was over. I thought we could get out and do our business." Her voice cracks on the last part. "I guess not. We're not here for this. We're here for you," she adds, her honey colored eyes boring into mine. "Forget about what's going on out there. My crew will deal with it. We need to focus on here and you, not across the country. If Diablo is a threat, we will handle it when the time is right." She shifts her body so she's looking at Rush. "Call Quickshift and have him keep an eye on Diablo. There's nothing we can do right now. If you ever come at me like that again, you will regret it."

"I'm sorry Ashley. It won't happen again. I'll call him right now," Rush responds pulling out his phone and sends a text to Quickshift.

"Nolan," Ashley says quietly. "We need to know what happened while they had you. I've seen the marks, now we need the story and why. Why did they bring you there?"

I sit down on the couch next to Ashton and rest my head in my hands. "I don't know why they took me to The Circle. Maybe they thought they beat me into submission like Switch has done in the past. I'm stronger than I used to be and could fight them. I played the part, but they couldn't touch my mind. It's not going to be pretty or fun, I'll guarantee you that."

Ashley perches her ass on the edge of the couch, next to me and rests her hand on my shoulder, offering comfort. "We can handle it. We just need to know so we can help you."

"When I went down the hallway, that little boy was running around the corner and down the stairwell. I could hear his little feet slapping against the concrete. I don't know what it is about him that draws me to him, but it does. He looks so familiar. I ran through the lobby and onto the street. I looked in both directions, but he wasn't anywhere in sight. It's like he's a figment of my imagination. Like he doesn't really exist, and my mind keeps on having him pop up. Anyway, I was turning to go back into the building when a blonde ponytail caught my attention turning down the alley. I ran over to the ally entrance and there was no one there. I walked down toward the dumpsters, the hair on the back of my neck stood on end and my gut was telling me to turn around, but if he was down there being hurt or worse, I'd never forgive myself. I reached the first dumpster when I sensed someone behind me. I turned around and Wrath was standing there."

******

The sun is shining brightly, high in the sky, warming up The City. Once I reached a dumpster to my left, the hair on the back of my neck is standing on end and I sense someone behind me. I turn around and Wrath is standing there, an evil smirk on her face. She crosses her arms over a red hoodie she's wearing, and she has a red bandana wrapped around her left jean covered leg. She's sporting fresh bruises on her scarred knuckles and her long blonde hair is pulled up in a high ponytail. There are scars on her face, one above her left eyebrow and another across her chin. Her hips are slightly wider, and she could be a beautiful woman, but the hate on her face right now is making her ugly. Her hazel eyes are pinning me to the spot, trying to take control of my mind, like she could when we were kids. I'm not a kid and she can't control me anymore. Once she realizes I'm not falling for her tricks, the smirk disappears, and she speaks.

"Mayhem, what a pleasant surprise. I've noticed you've seen my sister around." Wrath sneers, licking her lips. I don't bother to answer her. She knows what she's been trying to do and it's not worth my time. I don't take my eyes off her, but my other senses are on high alert. Familiar footsteps approach me from behind, coming at me fast. I don't dare take my eyes off Wrath. I slowly move so my back is against the building and I can see everything around me without moving. Switch appears and stands next to Wrath. The same hate filled smirk is on his face.

"I'll take it from here, Wrath. Go back to the apartment and check on our guests," Switch commands. He's talking about Izzy and Xavier and my heart beats hard in my chest. Hate and rage flow to the surface and my hands begin to shake. I look between the two of them and see the hesitation in her eyes, but she doesn't dare go against his demands. Spinning on her heels, Wrath huffs out a mumble under her breath and walks away.

Two other men approach us, ready to strike at a moment's notice. I recognize one of them from back when I used to run with Switch, but his name slips my mind. He was a lower rank and not worth my time. He's always been jealous of my progress in the gang and has been itching to take me down. He's wearing a black t-shirt and blue jeans with a red bandana wrapped around his dark hair. His green eyes are boring into me, waiting for the command to attack. The second man is wearing the exact same thing, but he has blonde hair and blue eyes. He looks unsure of what they're going to do.

Sick of waiting for them to make their move, I cross my arms over my chest and lean up against the building. "Is there something you want?" I ask, goading Switch.

"I want what you took all those years ago," Switch answers.

"I don't know what you're talking about. I got out and left you high and dry. The only thing I took was my life back."

"No, you took something that belongs to me. I want it back," Switch demands. He looks to the two guys and nods his head. They slowly approach me and green eyes is excited. I can't take them all down right now. I need to get inside to Izzy and Xavier. I hold my hands up in surrender when the two guys stand in front of me. I'm not going to put up a fight.

They yank my arms down and zip tie my hands behind my back. One pats me down for weapons and the other hangs onto my hands. Switch is enjoying watching me submit, but the difference between this time and last is that I'm doing this willingly now. He doesn't know that he's *too conceited to see the difference and that will be his destruction.*

Barefoot and tied up, we walk down the alley in the opposite direction I entered. A black SUV is waiting for us and I'm shoved inside. They throw a black sack over my head and the driver takes off, throwing me back into the seat. The base of the music is vibrating my back as they crank it up loud, muddling my senses. My shoulders stretch from my weight pulling on them and I shift slightly to relieve the pressure. I can't see anything as we take turn after turn and ride for what feels like hours. With my sense scrambled between the loud music, the crazy driving and the sack over my head, I have no idea where we are when we finally stop. Strong hands yank on my arms and pull me out of the SUV. I try listening to the noises around me, but my ears are still ringing from the music and I can't hear anything, only feel. My feet are cold on the concrete as I'm lead down a set of steps. I can feel the dank air penetrate my skin the further we walk, and the temperature drops a few degrees.

Someone clips the zip ties and hooks heavy chains around my wrists. The weight of the chains is familiar as they pull them until my hands are above my head, my feet barely touching the ground. They remove the black sack from my head and I blink several times, trying to adjust to the harsh spotlight shining down on me.

I detect a shadow in the corner of the basement watching and waiting. I can't see who it is, but the humming of electricity running in the ceiling above my head brings back memories that set me free. Memories of the last time they had me here. This isn't where I wanted to go, where I wanted to be.

Hours upon hours of torture Switch, Wrath, and Marcus inflicted upon me for nothing. My body has shut down, but my mind is still going. I'm plotting the way I will perpetrate the same torture to them. They won't have a quick and painless death. No. I will make them suffer at my hands every minute of every day they do this to me. Switch and Wrath will wish they never laid a hand or a whip on me.

Once I regain consciousness for the sixth time, they uncuff me from the beams and I fall to the cold concrete with a thud, unable to stop myself. My arms and legs are numb from being suspended for so long and my body is bruised from the beatings they delivered repeatedly. Some of my ribs are cracked and my face feels like it's on fire. Switch grabs me by my armpits and hoists me up with the help of two other men I don't recognize. He plops me down in a cold, metal chair and paces back and forth. The two men walk out of the room and leave us alone.

"Well, Nolan, I see you've learned a few things while you were away," he scoffs. I laugh, unable to stop myself. I've lost my damn mind. The movement brings pain to my already beaten body, but I can't help it. They have no idea what I've taught myself after the last time they inflicted this type of torture and it almost cost me my life.

"What do you want Switch?" I ask between bouts of laughter.

"I want to know what the fuck you did to my gang, you ass fuck," he growls.

"What I did to your fucked up little family? I didn't do anything, you sick fuck." I snap. Switch backhands me across the face and my mouth fills with blood. I spit the copper out onto Switches shoes and meet his black eyes. "Go ahead, give me your worst."

His nostrils flare and his eyes narrow in my direction. He turns on his heels and stomps out of the room. The heavy metal door slams behind him, locking me in the dingy and dirty basement, alone. Fatigue overtakes me, and I fall asleep bounded in the metal chair.

****

"When I came too, they stuck a needle in my arm and the drug they injected shut my mind down and I had no control over my body. I was under their command for a limited time. With my massive body weight, the drug didn't last as long as they expected and I played it off. I acted like I was still under their full control, so Switch and Wrath took me to The Circle. I think they wanted to make me fight again, but then I saw you," I look up at Ashley and grab her hand. "My angel in a dark world. The drug was still in my system, but I had a reason to fight again. I had control of the hate and rage burning through my veins. You all know the rest."

"I knew something was wrong when I saw you," Ashley responds. Tears trickle down her cheeks and her eyes are red from crying. "I wanted to bring you back."

"You did, Ash, you did," I whisper as I rest my forehead against hers, breathing her scent in. Her arms wrap around my neck and she hangs onto me tightly. Ashton shifts next to me and stands up, pacing the living room. His phone rings and he answers it.

"Iverson here," he says into the phone. "What do you mean? When?" He stops pacing and stands right in front of me. "Yes, he's right here." He hands me the phone. "Marks wants to talk to you."

I remove the phone from Ashton's outstretched hand with unsteady fingers and put it up to my ear. "Marks, what's going on?"

"Boss, thank God you're OK. Listen, they just left the building with Izzy. I don't know where they're taking her, but Xavier is there alone. Now's our chance to get him out."

"We're on our way," I answer and hang up the phone. I find Ace standing in the doorway. "I need a couple of fast cars. Can you help?"

"In the garage," Ace responds.

"Come on, let's lock and load. Xavier is alone right now. They took Izzy somewhere and now's our chance to get at least one of them back."

We all stand quickly and run to the garage attached to Ace's brownstone. He flips on a switch and the fluorescent lights come alive, shining on the three cars he has stored in here. All the hoods are up like on a showroom floor. One is a shiny purple Dodge Charger SRT Hellcat with a 6.2-liter super charge V-8 engine. The second car is a sleek grey Ford Mustang Shelby GT 500 super snake with a 5.4-liter V-8 engine. Ashley squeals like a little girl when she spots this car. Her body is throbbing with excitement. I know what car she wants to take. The third car is dark blue Dodge Viper GTS with a 6.2-liter V-8 engine.

"Ace, I'm speechless," I finally say, salivating over these magnificent beasts.

He grins and runs a finger down the Dodge Charger SRT Hellcat. "This one is my baby. Be gentle with her."

"Aren't you coming with us?" I ask.

He raises a dark eyebrow and gives me a duh look. "Of course."

"Nolan," Ashton says from behind me. "We need weapons."

"I got that covered too." Ace says and walks to the back wall. He hits a switch and the fake wall drops, revealing an arsenal of weapons. "Take what you need." He grabs two black Smith and Wesson .40 caliber guns. He cocks one back and chambers a round, tucking it into the waistband of his jeans. He hands the other one to me and I do the same. Ashley is staring at all the guns and ammo and picks up a 9 mil. She cocks it back and straps it to her thigh, giving me a wink.

I pick out a sleek .45 caliber and chamber a round. I strap that one to my other hip. Once we've all picked our weapons, Ace hits a switch again and the wall rises, hiding his weapons.

"We're locked and loaded, let's roll," I say with a cocky attitude. Finally able to do something other than play on the defense against these ass fuckers, I'm ready. Ready to get Xavier back and find out where they took Izzy. I'm ready to end this for the last time. If we shed a little blood, it doesn't matter anymore. I'm done being their sheep, being herded by their command.

Chapter 24

Nolan

Ashley and I are in the Shelby GT 500 Super Snake. She's driving and handling the beast like a pro, weaving in and out of traffic. The engine vibrates under her command. Ashton is in the Dodge Viper GTS and Rush and Ace are in the Dodge Charger Hellcat. If things go bad, at least we have these fast cars to escape in. I glance out the window and the moon is peeking through the clouds, bringing a slight chill to the air.

Ashley shifts gears and weaves again, passing people left and right. Headlights directly behind us, tell me Ace and Ashton are right on our tail as we fly through the streets of Manhattan.

"Nolan are you with me?" Ashley asks.

"Yes," I answer with a raised brow.

"There's something you're not telling me. You've left out some details back at Ace's house. Now it's just the two of us and your chance to come out with it." She sneaks a glance in my direction and smirks. My face must have shown my thoughts. "Thought so."

"I overheard Marcus, Switch, and Wrath when they assumed I was unconscious. Wrath was yelling at them, begging them not to use someone named Sherwood as bait. She acted like she honestly cared for whoever it is." Ashley swallows hard and I realize she's hiding something. "Ashley, what is it?"

"I don't know how to explain this, but I'm just going to rip the band-aid off. Brace yourself because you're going to be pissed." She takes a deep breath and continues. "Sherwood is her ten-year-old son."

The world falls away at my feet. My stomach is churning and I'm going to be sick. "What?" I whisper. "She has a son?"

"I just found out and haven't had time to tell you. That little boy you've been chasing around the city is Wrath's son." Ashley rests her palm on my thigh and gives it a gentle squeeze. Images of the little boy with similar brown eyes and light brown hair flash in my mind. His little hand reaching for me after being dragged away by Wrath's sister. He was trying to get my attention and I ignored his pleas. Breathing deeply, I control my mind and push it down.

"Nolan are you all right?" Ashley quietly asks.

"I'm good," I answer, clearing my head. "I'll deal with that later. Right now, I want to get Xavier back and find out where they took Izzy."

"Good because we're a few minutes away and I need you at one hundred percent," Ashley says. I cover my hand with hers and give it a gentle squeeze. We're in this together, no matter what happens, the two of us will get through this and come out on the other side. I must believe that, or all of this is for nothing.

Ashley steers the car to a curb right in front of the apartment building where it all started. I fight to keep the rage and hate tamped down looking at the place. Memories of a past I don't want to remember flip through my mind. I get out of the car and stare up at the building. My eyes narrow on a single window I remember exceptionally well crawling out of many times. The fire escape is rusted, and the black paint is peeling withstanding the weather. Ashley stands next to me, shoulder to shoulder. She's ready to do whatever is necessary inside this building with me, by my side. Ashton gets out of the car and stands next to my other side, he's ready to go. Ace stands next to him and Rush is next to Ashley.

Shadows move from the side of the building and approach us quickly. Marks, Ramirez, Harris, and Christian come into the light flickering down from the street lamp. They're all here with me, too. A sense of belonging rushes my body and a weight has lifted off my shoulders. My team is back together and I'm proud of the way they stayed by my side even though I've pushed them away.

"Boss," Harris speaks, breaking me out of my moment. "You ready?"

"I'm ready. This is what we do. No matter what happens inside this building, you get Xavier out. I will not guarantee I won't lose my head, but I need you all to promise me you'll put his safety first and get him out. Then we'll scour this city for Izzy. I won't stop until she's back and neither should any of you. Same with Redline, he's missing too. If we can get them all back in one piece, safely, I'll consider it a job well done."

We're ready, we're a team and we're going in. Marks, Harris, and Ramirez draw their guns and lead the way up the concrete step toward the building, followed by Rush and Ace, then Ashley and me. Bringing up the rear is Ashton and Christian. We quietly make our way inside, moving like a well-trained machine. Each of our movements are coordinated with each other and no one makes a sound. No heavy breathing or clomping footsteps. Once we're inside the building, we walk down a long, dirty hallway toward the rickety old elevator. We bypass the elevator and opt for the stairwell. It's going to be a long trek to the apartment, but we can handle it.

Several minutes later we reach the point of no return. Standing outside the door that'll lead us to Xavier, we all check our weapons, making sure they're ready and I give Harris a slight nod.

"Ok, listen up," Harris whispers. "There's a camera outside this door, pointing right at us as soon as we step into the hallway. If they have anyone set up around the apartment, it will alert them. We need to go in fast and fiercely. Everyone ready?"

"Oh, I'm ready. Let's do this." I respond. My heart is beating hard in my chest and adrenaline floods my body. I close my eyes and steady my breathing, calming my heart rate down. I must maintain control before we go in. Opening my eyes, everyone is watching me, waiting to see which side of me emerges. I've tamped the beast down and sealed it off. I'm in control, not the other way around. I narrow my eyes on the door and give the go ahead.

"On the count of three," Marks quietly says. He holds up a hand, "One." He rests one hand on the door, ready to push it open. "Two," he makes eyes contact with each of us. "Three." He shoves the heavy metal door open.

We rush down the dirty hallway fast and low, guns drawn, fingers on the trigger ready to take anyone down. No one comes out of the other apartment doors. We reach the door of my teenage years and I try the knob. It's not locked and swings open with an eerie screech. Harris turns on the light switch and fills the room with a soft glow.

Memories of my mother getting high and doped up flow into my mind as I stare into the small living room. The many backhands and punches I took growing up, trying to get her to stop. The many boyfriends or dealers, it's all too much and I bend over, gagging and coughing.

Ashley's gentle hands rest on my back and her soft voice breaks through the dreadful memories. "Nolan, I'm here, stay with me. You're safe. You're not a teenager anymore. She can't hurt you again. You're strong, independent and don't need her approval, her fucked up ways. I've got you, we all do."

Standing up tall, I take another look around. Christian and Ashton have Xavier uncuffed from the radiator and are helping him up. He's worn down, beaten, and his bright blue eyes are dull. He's feeling helpless and I need to push him past this. I walk toward him, my best friend, my brother. Xavier watches me approach and swallows hard.

"They took her, Nolan. We have to get her back," he pleads.

"We will. I won't stop until Izzy is back with us and safe," I reassure. "Xavier, I'm sorry they dragged you into the middle of my mess. Now you're hurt and Izzy's missing." My voice cracks on the last part and I push my emotions down deeply. I need to focus, not get caught up in the pity party. There'll be time for that later. Staring at Xavier I ask him the hardest question I don't want an answer to, but I need to know. "Did anyone hurt her or you?"

He shakes his head as Christian hands him a water from the refrigerator. He takes a long drink and answers. "Just knocked us around and starved me. They fed Izzy occasionally. Anytime that fuckhead, Switch, had a hair up his ass, a tall man with short blonde hair stopped him. There was one time he told Switch he'd fucking kill him if he laid an inappropriate hand on her. I don't know who he was, but he saved her quite a few times." Tears are falling down Xavier's face.

"Does he look like this?" Ashley asks, holding out her phone. Xavier takes it with trembling hands and stares at the picture. His eyes flash to hers and his bottom lip quivers as he nods his head. Ashley breaks eye contact and takes her phone back. I get a glimpse of the picture on her phone. It's a selfie she took of her and Austin. "That's why he's here. He must have caught word from Diablo about what's happening and came here to protect them."

"Who is it?" Xavier asks.

"My brother I thought was dead. I'll explain later. Right now, we need to get out of here and find Izzy. If he isn't with her, there's no telling what they'll do to her." Ashley says.

The rest of my team is searching the apartment and Marks comes back with a notepad in his hands. "Boss, I found this. You're going to want to read it." He hands me the notebook and I open it up. Inside is details of each operation Switch, Marcus, and Wrath have going on. Names, numbers, and addresses. There's one that stands out to me and I close the notebook.

"Come on, I know what they're doing and where they took Izzy. We've got to hurry though. According to this, a shipment of guns are coming into The Graveyard on Staten Island tonight."

"Are you sure?" Ace asks. "That place isn't ideal for a large ship. Any coming in will sink. It's too shallow to maneuver a vessel that big."

"Not if you have a small boat and know the path. When I was in their gang, we did many drops there." I respond.

"What are we waiting for? Come on let's go," Christian speaks up.

"Is Mia still here?" I ask.

"Yeah, she's back at the hotel waiting for a report from us. It wasn't easy getting her to remain behind. Her crazy started to show," Christian answers.

"OK call her on the way to The Graveyard and tell her to stay inside the room. Don't answer the door, don't call room service. I don't like her being there alone. Something in my gut feels off."

"I can stay with her if you want," Harris offers.

"Would you? I know you want in on the action, but I think we can all do our jobs better if I had reassurance someone was there with her." I respond.

"Of course. I don't have an issue protecting Mia. Whatever makes it easier, I'll do it," Harris says.

Christian is pacing back and forth. His hands are clenching and unclenching into fists. He's torn about what to do. "My cop instincts are saying go with you, but the boyfriend side is telling me to go to Mia. What do I do?"

"Christian, I understand where you're coming from. You need to do what you need to do. That's your decision. It's a tough one but make it fast. We need to get moving and get out of here." I tell him.

"Since the drop is tonight, why don't we all go to the hotel, shower, reload with our weapons, then go?" Ashley suggests.

"That's a good idea. Come on, let's get out of here and get back to the hotel for a quick bite and regroup." I agree.

We all file out of the apartment and quietly walk down the hallway, watching and waiting for an attack. This felt way too easy like they wanted us to get Xavier. The hair on the back of my neck stands on end and something is off. Once we reach the stairwell, I stop Ramirez. "Do you still have eyes on this place?"

"Yes, boss. We never took them down. What's up?" he answers.

"Something seems off, this was too easy. For as long as they had them why would they leave him alone when they knew I was here?"

"Maybe they have what they want or they thought you were under their control. Or they're getting too cocky, thinking they're untouchable. Either way, it helped us and we have one back. I'll keep the cameras up and monitor them when we get back to the hotel." Ramirez counters.

"Let's do that. Keep an eye on this place. It feels abandoned like they had no intention to come back. But I want to be on the safe side and know if someone comes back." I agree.

"I'll set up a trigger to warn me if someone comes into the apartment. If I set it up here, it'll constantly go off because of the other residence, but I can set one up at the door. If anyone approaches or enters the apartment, I'll get a warning. How does that sound?"

"That works. Take Marks and meet us back at the hotel when you're done." I order. "Oh, and Ramirez."

"Yes, boss?" He questions.

"Watch your back. Come back safe."

"You got it, boss," he salutes me like a smartass. "Marks come on. We have one final job."

Ramirez and Marks disappear back into the apartment hallway and I rush to meet up with the rest of my team. Ashley raises an eyebrow and takes my hand. "Everything all right?"

"Yes, just want reassurance no one will be entering or leaving that apartment without us knowing." I squeeze her hand for support while watching Xavier. The guy has had it rough the last couple of weeks and we need to find Izzy. He's going to torture himself until she's back safely.

We walk out of the apartment building and I breathe a sigh of relief as the breezy night air cools my skin and regenerates my mind. I watch Xavier stand under the street lamp. His eyes are dull and a frown is upon his face. He's stressing about Izzy and I know how he feels. I felt the same way when Shaun took Ashley, so I know what he's going through. Approaching him, I rest a hand on his shoulder, snapping him out of his head. His blue eyes collide with mine and something passes between us. This is the second time someone has kidnapped Izzy, but this is worse than before. "X, I don't know what to say. I feel like everything that's happened to both of you is my fault. Marie, now Switch. It all leads back to me and my haunted past. I won't be mad or upset if you want to blame me for it. I should have come clean, but I thought I left them behind, this life behind."

"Nolan, you've been my best friend for a long time. I really thought I knew you. After this happened, I realized I don't know who you were in the past," I lower my head in shame. My past is ruining a friendship. "But, I know who you are now and that's all that matters. If we get Izzy back safely, nothing else matters. Not what you've done here, not who they made you become. You've been like a brother to me since we were eighteen. I knew there was something in your past you didn't want to share and I'm fine with that. What I'm not fine with is these dumb fuckers messing with the wrong guys." Xavier's response shocks me to my core. I thought for sure he'd be pissed and want to take a swing at me. "But Nolan, when it comes down to it, I want a piece of Switch. I want to inflict the same torture he did to us. I want to watch him beg and plead with tears in his eyes before me. I want pain and punishment." His voice is cold and deadly. He might regret it later, but it's the least I can do.

"You will be there with me when we take him down and you'll be there when we get Izzy back. I won't shut you out of that. Just be careful with what you wish for because sometimes the outcome isn't something you can remove from your head."

"I don't care. I want him gone and that little bitch too. She's horrible and has no remorse for anything. Honestly, watching the two of them, it felt like she was controlling him. Wrath would snap her fingers and Switch would grovel at her feet." Xavier reveals.

My head is spinning with this new knowledge. "Let's get back to the hotel. I have some research I need to do." We all get into the cars we brought. Harris rides with Ashton, Ace and Rush ride together and Xavier rides with us. We leave the SUV that Marks brought behind for them to get back with.

As Ashley drives us into the busy nighttime traffic, thoughts overwhelm my mind. Have I had it wrong the whole time? When I was with them, it was the other way around. Switch snapped and Wrath responded. Have they been playing me this entire time? Has Wrath been the one in control since we were teenagers? If so, why would they role reverse? What does she have on him to give her the power? They didn't talk much, but since the first day I met them, something was off between the two of them and I could never figure out what. I see it now and I will get to the bottom of it.

Chapter 25

Ashley

Driving on a busy street in the dead of night, The Plaza comes into view. The Victorian hotel sits on the corner of 5th Ave and Central Park, giving off a sense of comfort and peace in the middle of a storm, a safe haven for us.

Nolan directs me to a parking garage a few blocks away and we get out of the car. The low fluorescent lights cast shadows over our faces. I stretch my tight muscles as we wait for everyone else to catch up. I watch him and Xavier talk and my heart breaks for those two. They've been through so much in the last year, I pray this won't push them apart. Xavier has lost weight from the kidnapping and I'll bet he's starving. I know he won't eat until we get Izzy back, but I will have to force him. He needs to be strong when we go after her. They give each other a slap on the back, their bro code for everything is good again and Nolan must have said something because Xavier is cracking a small smile. My smartass Nolan keeping things light in the face of danger. I haven't seen that side of him lately and a smile graces my lips witnessing it.

Ace and Ashton park their cars next to us and get out. Nolan approaches me and drapes his arms around my shoulders, pulling me close to him. He kisses the top of my head and I inhale his masculine scent, resting one of my hands on his beating heart and my head on his hard chest. We stay this way for a few precious moments and I revel in the love we have for each other.

"Everyone here?" I ask, not moving from Nolan's hard chest.

"Yes, they're all here," Nolan's strong voice rumbles in my ear. I pull away and we walk, hand in hand down the concrete steps and into the night.

We walk a few blocks and The Plaza comes into view. Traffic is still crazy this time of night and we finally get a break to cross the street. The colossal French doors leading into the hotel are beckoning me to enter and rest for a while. A doorman opens them and we all file inside. The beautiful white and gold marble floors are shining under the warm lighting as we walk across the lobby toward a gold colored elevator encased around white marble. Everything in this hotel screams money and I suddenly feel out of place. After we all pile inside, the doors close and I study each of us in the mirrors.

Something is wearing Ashton down; his shoulders are slumped forward, and his head is bowed. Ace's dark skin is shiny under the lights, but his light brown eyes are clouded over, filled with vengeance as he looks uncomfortable here. Rush is feeling the jet lag from traveling across the country and going on a manhunt. His body is stiff and straight, but his black eyes are tired. Christian is finally feeling the adrenaline wearing off as he leans against the back wall with his arms crossed over his chest and he closes his eyes briefly. Nolan's team member Harris looks like he's still ramped up and ready to go. His towering frame is standing tall and at attention as his black eyes keep scanning each of us, ready for someone to strike. My eyes travel to Xavier. His jet-black hair is filthy from the lack of a shower and his athletic build appears to be shrinking like he's losing the willpower to continue fighting. His piercing blue eyes are dull from the stress of not having Izzy here and he looks like he will pass out any moment.

Then my eyes drift to Nolan. No matter what we're doing or where we are, he still takes my breath away. His whiskey-colored eyes collide with mine in the mirror and he gives me a wink while tightening his hold on my hand. A silent moment passes between the two of us, we've got each other. No matter what happens, he will pull me from the darkness and I'll do the same. We're in this together, for the rest of our lives.

The elevator doors ding open and we step onto an elegant beige carpet littered with gold specks. Christian uses a key card to open the main door of the Grand Penthouse Suite. I walk into a majestic looking foyer and spot Mia sitting on an overstuffed gold covered chair, curled up fast asleep. Her short red and blue hair is messy and sticking up all over the place. Christian quickly strolls across the room and gently shakes her awake. She blinks a few times before her eyes land on Xavier. Tears swell in her brown eyes and she jumps up from the chair and runs to him and wraps her arms around his neck, hugging him tightly. She's crying hard onto his neck and won't let go. Xavier wraps his arms around her waist and hugs her back. Tears are in his eyes. After a few moments, Mia pulls away and searches him for injuries.

"Where are you hurt? What can I get you? Do you need food? A shower?" Mia rapid fires questions at him and doesn't give him a chance to respond. "Come on, let's get you something to eat. I've been going out of my mind worried. Where's Izzy?"

"Mia," Xavier responds, interrupting her rambling. "I'm OK for now, yes I need a shower and some food, but no physical injuries. We don't know where Izzy is yet, but we'll find her."

"Oh, then sit and I'll bring you some food from the kitchen," Mia answers and pulls Xavier to the sofa. She forces him to sit and disappears out of the living room with Christian following behind her.

Xavier gives into Mia's demands and stays on the sofa, his head is bowed, and his hands are clasped in front of him. He's trying to keep it together. Occasionally, I can see his back shake from trying to hold in a sob. Nolan is sitting next to him on the sofa, Ace and Ashton are standing at the floor to ceiling windows overlooking Central Park. They're talking quietly between themselves. Probably coming up with ideas on what to do next to get Izzy back.

Harris is sitting at the dining room table with the laptop fired up looking at the layout for The Graveyard. Rush is pacing back and forth from the foyer to the living room and back again. When he passes by me, I stop him from turning back toward the living room.

"Talk to me, Rush. What's on your mind?" I inquire.

He stops pacing and stands in front of me. "I'm trying to figure out what they want with Redline. Diablo has had issues with him, but why would Switch take him? What is it with him they want?"

"What if I call Diablo and ask him?" I suggest.

"If we do that, we tip our hand knowing he's involved," Rush counters.

"Not if I play dumb. I'll tell them he's missing and wonder if they've seen him."

"That could work," Nolan says from the couch. I didn't realize he was listening. "Go for it, do your thing." He encourages.

I take my phone out of my pocket and dial Diablo's number. It rings several times before he answers. "Krimson, what do I owe the pleasure?" I can hear music and loud voices in the background fading away.

"Diablo, have you seen Redline? He isn't answering his phone and I can't seem to find him." I ask, getting right to the point.

"Redline, hmm," he pauses dramatically, and I roll my eyes. "Can't say that I have. Last I heard he was with you in New York while you chased the demons of your boyfriend's past."

"Well, here's the thing. Something pissed him off, and he hopped on the first plane back to L.A.," the lie rolls off my tongue and guilt surrounds me. "I tried to call him, but he isn't answering. I didn't know if he's sniffing around your bitch, again."

"My bitch as you blatantly call her knows better." Anger radiates through the phone. "Actually, I got rid of her ass a few days ago when she started asking questions she shouldn't be." Shocked, I scramble to find the words to say, but he beats me to it. "Shocking, I know. A man can only take so much bullshit in my line of work and if I can't trust her, she's gone. Now, tell me the real reason you called and don't bullshit me either."

My eyes fly to Rush, and he nods his head. This isn't how I planned the call would go down. Diablo speaks before I can, "Krimson, I was actually expecting you to call before this. I thought you would've figured it out long before now."

"How are you involved with the Corridore Rosso Gang and why?" I ask, getting right to the point. He already knows I know, so there's no point in beating around the bush.

"Honestly, Marcus Angelo and his hotheaded son Switch, approached me years ago when I first took over, before I realized what they were involved in. I've been trying to get out from under his thumb for years, but he doesn't let go very well. Some of his thugs are actually here sniffing around. I've got protection, but your crew doesn't have enough. When you got out of the guns that pissed several people off and they turned their back on your crew. I can offer protection, but it's got to be under my terms. I'll let you think it over and call me back. Don't wait too long, though, or things will get very ugly for you and I'm sure you don't want anything to happen to that fine Latina ass or the nerd. Quickshift has his own connections and can take care of himself, but that won't be enough either. This thing is bigger than us separate, but together, we can bring these fuckers down."

"Why would you help me?" I ask the question rolling around in my head.

"Because I like you and I admire you going somewhat legit. Few people have your vision and I want to help you. I don't need too, but I want to. There's a difference," Diablo's honesty shocks me.

"Let me think it over and call you back," I respond.

"Talk it over with Rush. I know he's next to you. You're predictable and that's got to stop. You've become too comfortable and everyone knows wherever you are, Rush is with you, since the whole Reiser incident. Can't say I blame him since Reiser is missing."

"He isn't missing. He's here and working with Switch," I confess. Diablo release a deep sigh on the other end.

"Do you need protection out there?" he asks.

"No, we have protection covered out here," I answer looking at Ace. He nods his head and sends a quick text. "Diablo protect my crew out there, please. I don't care what your terms are. The safety of my crew is number one. Redline is missing already and I don't want anything to happen to Natalia, Quickshift or Noah. They're my priority."

"On it," Diablo says quickly. "Oh, and Krimson?"

"Yeah?"

"Stay safe. Keep that man of yours safe too. They want him dead. He's good for you. I can hear it in your voice and see it when we last talked face to face. I'm sorry for the way things went down before and you have my support. Just help me get out from under these guys and we'll call ourselves even."

"Thanks, Diablo. I'll do everything in my power to get you out from the Corridore Rosso's."

"I know you will. That's why you're good at what you do and you have my support."

"Take care, Diablo. We'll talk soon." I hang up the phone and my mind is swirling with questions. I don't see Nolan approach me and I don't feel his arms around me. I'm numb. Numb to the emotions, numb to the touch, numb to any kind of feeling. This is bad. Really, really bad. At least Diablo will protect my crew except for one and I have to figure out why they want Redline. What is it about him that they need? He has no family ties out here. His father was the leader of his crew years ago and I've known him his whole life. Nothing is making sense.

"Ash, did you hear me," Nolan asks breaking through my thoughts.

"What?"

"What's going on?" Nolan asks. His voice is my vessel, his body and mind are my harbor. I cling to him and don't let go.

Mia enters the living room with a bunch of food, but I'm not hungry anymore. She sets it down on the coffee table and sits next to Xavier, making him eat. Christian sits in the overstuffed chair. All eyes are on me as I relay the information I have. I'm so lost and in way over my head. Nolan's grip on my waist tightens with every word I speak. Ashton looks torn between jumping on the first plane to L.A. and staying here to protect Nolan. Nolan's team needs him out here, focused, so I send a text to Natalia telling her to call Ashton and ease his mind. Quit playing fucking games with him and get over herself. She likes him and he likes her. His phone lights up and a smile graces his lips as he answers it and heads up the vast staircase to the outside balcony.

"What do we do now?" I ask.

Nolan is the first to answer. He releases my waist and clenches his fists at his sides, something changed, and his voice is deadly when he answers, "We go to The Graveyard and get Izzy back."

"What's The Graveyard?" Mia asks, quoting graveyard with her fingers.

"It's a place where broken ships go to spend their last days," Christian answer from the chair.

"Why would Izzy be there?" Mia asks.

"There's a shipment coming in tonight and that's where Switch and Wrath will be," Christina responds.

"Ok, but how do you know they'll have Izzy there? Seems to me, these guys are smart. Why would they take their captive with them to a drop when it's better to leave her with someone she won't run away from?" Mia questions.

"What do you mean won't run away from?" I ask.

Mia rolls her eyes, "Come on, girl. You guys are thinking about this all wrong. Izzy knows who Redline is right?"

"Of course, she does."

"Then why would they separate them? I'll guarantee they have them together and have someone ruthless and has no remorse keeping an eye on them. They won't take her with them because she's a liability. You've got to stop thinking like yourself and think like them." Mia's eyes settle on Nolan. "You've been on the inside. You know how they work, their actions. Stop thinking like a pansy and think like a gangster. You're trying to play it safe. Stop it. All you do when you do that is waste time. You saved Izzy last time the psycho took her, channel that guy, go in there and do your fucking thing." She stands up and paces back and forth from the windows to the sofa and back, wringing her hands in front of her.

I'm shocked. I never thought of it this way.

"She's right," Nolan says. "We need to quit being worried about what will make me snap. We've been on the defense way too long, it's time to go on the offense and fight fire with fire. Harris, pull up every surveillance footage of the area Izzy and Xavier were in and search for Reiser. Ace, get on the phone and call your guys, have them be on the lookout for this guy," Nolan shows him a picture of Sean. "And this is what Izzy looks like. Send these to your guys so they know."

"Show them a picture of Redline, too," I offer. I send Nolan a picture of Redline and he sends it to Ace.

"On it, I'll have them report every hour. If they're still here in the City, we'll find them." Ace answers.

"Oh, they're still here, I doubt they left. They have nowhere to go."

"Now we're getting somewhere. What's left?" I ask.

Ashton comes back in with a small smile gracing his lips. Natalia and he must have worked through some issues. I raise an eyebrow and Ashton stops walking. He gives me a wink. "What did I miss?"

"Mia is one smart lady," Harris says from his spot at the dining room table, still scanning the footage on the laptop. Mia blushes and sits on Christians lap. He wraps his arms around her and holds her tight, kissing her shoulder.

"X, how long were you alone before we showed up?" Nolan asks him.

Xavier shrugs his shoulders with his head down. He's torn up about this. He suddenly jumps up from the couch and runs up the stairs as fast as his feet and sore body will take him, Nolan quickly follows. I debate following too but decide against it. They need this time together, best friend with best friend. I turn to Harris when the phone on the table rings. Ashton grabs it, "Yeah," he barks into the phone. "Send them up." He hangs up the phone. "Marks and Ramirez are here."

I pace this time, thinking. "Harris let's get a timeline when we think they took Izzy instead of searching through hours of footage. What time did we get to your place, Ace?"

"I'd say around midnight. It took about a half hour to get here from The Circle. So, we left there around eleven thirty." Ace answers.

"Good, but we had the issue with Nolan and that took about fifteen to twenty minutes. So, I'd say we left The Circle around eleven fifteen. How long does it take at a normal pace to walk from The Circle to the apartment we found Xavier in?"

"Around twenty minutes."

"So, I'll go back and watch the footage from eleven fifteen last night to one a.m. and run the program Ashton created for face recognition. That'll speed it up some." Harris turns back to the laptop and begins typing codes in quickly. His fingers fly over the keyboard, then he sits back. His tattooed arms run through his crew cut hair. I creep up behind him and watch with him, over his shoulder. "Jesus woman. You've got to stop being a creepy ninja." He yells. I can't help but giggle.

"Sorry, two sets of eyes are better than one. And I wasn't being quiet, you just weren't paying attention."

Harris swings a chair around for me to sit next to him. We watch the footage together, waiting for something to hit. Nolan and Xavier still aren't back yet and I'm worried. "Hey, Nolan's got this. It's what he does."

"I know, but I still feel helpless. I wish I can do something for him."

"You are doing everything right, Ashley. Once we find Izzy and Redline, we're going to make these fuckers pay. Every last one of them. One thing you can't do is hold Nolan back. If he loses his head, let him. The demon he battles with will take over. There's no doubt about that. What we need to do is let it. He won't be able to control it if we hold him back. I've been working with him for years and in my personal opinion, if we stop it from surfacing, he'll never be fully in control. Let him do his thing and trust that we have him."

"I can't lose him," I voice my concern.

"You won't. It won't be pretty, but we've been with him for years. We've got this under control. He thinks his head is fucked up, but it's not. His instincts will take over and those fuckers will have hell to pay when he gets his hands on them. There will be no stopping him and if you try, it'll only hurt both of you. He must channel his past and use that to his advantage. Sometimes when the past and present collide, you have to sit back and hang on for the ride if you want the future to work out." I can feel Harris's gaze on me and I turn my head to look at him. His black eyes are full of sympathy, but his strong jaw is set hard. I have to trust them to keep Nolan safe. Something that's hard for me to do. Trust someone I don't know. Nolan is confident in his team, so it's time I put my fears aside and have faith in them too.

Chapter 26

Nolan

I follow Xavier up the stairs quickly and find him in the bathroom of one bedroom, throwing up everything he ate. I wait at the open doorway for him to finish. Tears are flowing down his cheeks and snot is running down his nose. He wipes his face with toilet paper and flushes the toilet.

"God, I feel like such a fucking pansy," Xavier grumbles. He washes his hands and splashes chilly water on his face. "I failed her," he whispers, resting his hands on the sink and lowers his head.

"X, you didn't fail her. If anything, this is my fault. I'm the one who should be shouldering the blame, not you."

"You don't get it," he digs his fingers into the marble sink. "I failed to protect her. They just swooped right in and took us and the torture they inflicted on us, I couldn't stop it. I tried, and I failed." Xavier takes a deep, shuddering breath and I walk into the bathroom. I lean against the counter, facing him.

"X listen to me." His eyes finally reach mine and I continue. "This isn't your fault and you didn't fail her. If you believe you did, then now is the time to help. We need to get her back and we will. It's what I do. I've been playing this all wrong as Mia said earlier. I was too worried about my past coming back at me, I didn't see the bigger playing field in front of me. We have The Black Heart Gang on our side. We have Diablo's crew on our side and if Ace reaches out to others, we have them on our side. The only thing Switch has is his gang. If we all pull together and tear this city up looking for Izzy, we will. I won't stop until I find her and bring her home safe." I rest my hand on his shoulder and deliver my next words carefully. "I need your help in doing this. Can you keep it together?"

He nods his head and holds back the tears. "Yes. I can do that." He hesitates before continuing. "The hardest part is after the first time they took her out of that apartment, she couldn't make eye contact with me and she stopped talking. I don't know why. They must have made her do something she feels guilty for."

"How long ago was this?"

"Just a couple of days ago. It was dark outside and they all left for about three hours. When she came back, there were tears streaming down her face and she wouldn't stop sobbing. The only thing she kept saying was, *I'm sorry*. What would she be sorry for?"

My eyes grow wide, my heart is beating hard in my chest and my palms are sweaty. He has no idea they tried to make her kill me. I need to figure out how to say this gently, so he doesn't go into another tailspin. "I know."

"What is it? I've been wracking my brain trying to figure it out."

"X, take a seat." He closes the toilet lid and sits down, watching and waiting. "I know what night you're talking about because we were there, and I didn't know it was her until we watched the surveillance videos. There's no straightforward way to say this." I pause and look away. This will be hard for him.

"What is it, Nolan?"

Taking a deep breath, I continue, "They made Izzy push me toward an oncoming train. If it weren't for Ashton pulling me back at the last second, I would have landed on the tracks and died."

"Oh fuck!" Xavier spins around, lifts the toilet lid quickly and dry heaves. "This can't be happening. Why would they do that?" He lost it again. "Why would they make my beautiful girl do something like that?" he wails.

"Because they're a bunch of twisted fucks who get off on inflicting torture," I answer, sadly.

Xavier dry heaves one more time and leans against the wall. His spirit is broken, and his soul is torn to shreds. He wraps his arms around his raised knees and rests his head between them. I watch his back shake several times. Taking the spot against the wall next to him, I wait it out, the anger and rage will surface soon and together we will take these fuckers down.

After several minutes of his self-loathing, Xavier raises his head and meets my eyes. "You're not angry with her, are you?"

"Not at all," I answer quickly. "There's no doubt she didn't have a choice. When we played the surveillance tapes, she looks directly into the camera and mouths the words, *I'm sorry*, with tears running down her face. I know they didn't give her a choice because they grabbed her tied hands and yanked her away. It happened so fast, we had no idea what was going on and that Redline was missing. So, no I'm not angry with her. I'm angry with myself for putting her in that situation. She's a bright light in a dark world and I never wanted any of my past to touch either of you. But, now that it has, I will do everything in my power to get her back safely and bring her back into the light."

"Nolan, can I ask you a question? You don't have to answer if you don't want to."

"Fire away."

"What did these people do to you?"

I was hoping he never asked, but I knew this was coming. "Do you want the gentle version or the hard one?"

"I just want to know why they are out to get you and what they did to you," Xavier replies.

"There's a reason you've never seen me with my shirt off, no matter how hot it is. I've always said I didn't know how to swim when we'd go to the lake or a pool, but this is the reason why. When I show you this, I don't want sympathy or anything. I've dealt with it and with the help of Ashley, I've learned a life lesson." I take a deep breath and lift my hoodie and t-shirt up over my head. I hear Xavier suck in a deep breath but thankfully, he doesn't say a word.

"This is what happens when they think you crossed them. I did a job for Switch and the junkie got the drop on us. After I killed the junkie and burned the crack house down, he decided I didn't learn my lesson enough and caught me off guard. They strung me up in a basement and tortured me. Let me rephrase that. Switch hung me like a pig in the basement and Wrath did all of these." I point to each jagged scar marring my chest. "I don't know how long I was there for. I kept losing consciousness and when she felt I had enough, they threw me in an alley. Thankfully, I regained consciousness long enough to painfully crawl my way to the street. A passerby found me and called nine-one-one. A few months after I recovered, I left."

"How did you get out?" Xavier asks with a tremble in his voice.

"I want to tell you, but I can't. It's my secret I must keep. Not even Ashley knows. Let's just say I had to bargain with the devil to escape the hell I was in."

"Do you think…" Xavier swallows hard. "Do you think they'll do that to Izzy?"

"No," I answer quickly. "This is a special type of torture they like to inflict upon me. They saved their pent-up anger and aggression for me. That's why I can't let them get me. If they do, I'll be done for. Now we need to play the offense and take these fuckers down."

"Where do you want to start?"

"Are you sure you're ready for this? It's going to get ugly really fast. You've never seen the side of me that will come out. It scares me sometimes." I confess.

"I'm more than ready. I want to get her back quickly. The longer she's with them, the more they're in jeopardy." Xavier answers. "I need a shower. Can you give me twenty?"

"Sure, I have clean clothes for you around here somewhere. I'll go ask Mia where they are and leave them in the bedroom. You're safe now X, I promise you. We have a whole team here who will do anything for you, Izzy, Mia, and Ashley. We got this." I slap him on the back and stand up, putting my t-shirt and hoodie back on. Xavier follows and stretches his arms above his head. He's going to crash soon from the emotions he's endured.

"Thanks, I appreciate it," Xavier gives me a bro hug and I leave the bathroom.

Making my way down the stairs, I contemplate our conversation. I halt at the top of the stairs when something he said occurs. What the actual fuck? Why did he say they're in jeopardy?

I turn back around to ask him, but I hear the shower kick on. I'll have to ask him when he comes out. Both will have a tough time finding their way back to the people they once were, but I will be with them every step of the way. They will never be the same, but they have a choice to grow and conquer this together.

Voices drift up the stairs and I can hear Mia laughing about something. Ashley giggles too and a smile graces my lips. That voice can pick me up when I feel like I'm going to surrender to the darkness. I have the sudden urge to wrap my arms around her and feel her warm, soft body against mine.

Walking down the stairs quickly, I find Ashley sitting next to Harris at the dining room table watching video surveillance tapes, talking quietly to each other. Mia and Christian are curled up in the chair talking to each other. Ashton, Rush, and Ace are standing at the floor to ceiling windows looking out at Central Park. Marks and Ramirez are pacing back and forth, waiting for orders to do the job.

Ashley head snaps up from the laptop and offers me a bright smile. God, I love that woman with my whole being. I make my way toward her and she stands up from her chair, waiting for me to sit down with her.

"Mia, can you find clothes for X and leave them in the first bedroom? He's taking a shower right now."

"Yes, I know right where they are," she gets up and gives Christian a quick kiss before disappearing up the stairs. Christian stands up and heads over to us at the dining room table.

I reach Ashley and pull her into my arms. I kiss the top of her head as she wraps her arms around my waist and rests her head against my beating heart. We stand like this for a few moments before Harris interrupts our little bubble.

"Hey boss, I got something here," he says pointing at the screen. I release my hold on Ashley but keep her next to me. Harris hits the play button and the images come to life on the screen. I watch carefully as I see Izzy exit the house between Wrath and Switch. Wrath as her hand wrapped around Izzy's ropes, dragging her along. Watching her manhandle Izzy is pissing me off. It must be pissing Ashley off too because I can feel the tension radiating from her body. They come to a black car idling in a parking spot out front and Wrath shoves Izzy hard into the back seat. A man wearing a baseball hat, dark hoodie and blue jeans approaches them and climbs into the back seat with her. Someone says something, and he leans his head out the window. Suddenly his hat flies off his head, like someone knocked it off, revealing his face. Ashley sucks in a deep breath and her body trembles. He pulls his head back into the window and the car speeds off.

"Follow that car," Ashley says, trembling.

"I'm on it," Harris reveals. He pulls up several smaller screens and we watch the car drive for a few blocks. It pulls into a parking garage in Midtown and Harris pulls up the information on the garage. "It's at Park Here, Pay Here parking garage in the abandoned part of the business district in Manhattan. It's about twenty blocks from here."

"Yeah, but where did they go from there? Are there any cameras in there?" I ask, excited that we have a lead.

"Let me check," he types codes into the laptop and suddenly the parking garage comes to life. He backtracks to when they pull in.

"Freeze it right there," I rumble. Harris pauses the video when the car enters the garage and the driver grabs a ticket.

"Holy shit. What's he doing?" Ashley asks as she stares at the screen.

"He's keeping her safe. Let's focus on that." I respond when Ashley sees her brother Austin on the screen. His face appears pained and then we watch as he turns his head to the backseat. He says something then drives off. We follow the car up to the top and watch as they get out. Sean yanks Izzy out of the car and she falls to her knees. Austin steps between them and helps Izzy up, gently. He whispers something in her ear and she slightly nods her head while shooting daggers at Sean. Austin gently cups her arm and leads her down the stairwell and out into the street. We follow them on the cameras until they disappear into an abandoned warehouse.

"That's it. That's the end of the footage," Harris says. "The warehouse is an old abandoned machine shop. Squatters and druggies take up residence there. That's where they have Izzy and I'll guarantee your boy Redline is there too."

"Get the address. Ace, can you contact your men and tell them about the shipment coming in tonight? Will they stop the exchange while we go after Izzy?" I ask.

"On it," Ace replies.

Xavier's heavy footsteps stomp down the stairs with Mia in tow. "What did you find?"

"They have Izzy at an old machine shop," I respond.

"So, why are we standing here with our thumbs up our ass, let's go and get my girl."

"We can't go in half-cocked. We will go and get her, but we need to assess everything around us to keep her and us safe. X, let me do my job." I growl. He's going to get her and himself killed if he goes in guns blazing.

"I can't just stand here and let something happen to her," he pleads.

"You aren't, and we won't. We're getting around and now we have a lead we'll get shit done. You go in there in this state of mind won't help her or anyone else."

"But..."

"No, no fucking but's. I've been doing this job for years. If you can't trust me to get this done, then I'll leave your ass here tied up under Mia's watchful eye. You got it?" I roar.

"Yeah, I got it." Xavier sulks.

"Good. Harris, get all the blueprints on the warehouse and see if you can find any live camera feeds. We need to know every entrance, exit, and obstacle inside."

"On it boss." Harris turns back to the laptop and types.

I shift my body so I'm watching Xavier. His eyes are burning into the side of my head and he's pissed. "Look, I get that you want to go in there and tear shit up. So do I. Here's the thing, we need to access everything and everyone inside that building. If we go in now, we will put Izzy in danger. We can't go in half-cocked. It must be thought out, planned and executed to perfection. My team has been doing this for years. Trust me to do my job."

Xavier doesn't want to listen, but he has to. I don't know how else to get my point across and make sure he doesn't go in there without us.

"Xavier," Ashley says gently. His body shifts from an attack stance to alert as she approaches him slowly. "You and I need to have a chat. Come on." She pushes him toward the staircase and he walks with her willingly. She turns around and gives me a wink. "I'll handle this, you stay here and keep working." They walk up the stairs together and disappear out of my site. Mia jumps up and follows them.

Christian, Ashton, Marks, and Ramirez are standing behind me. Each awaiting orders. It feels good to be back in control, back taking action. "Ashton, what's our weapons look like? Are we good to go?"

"Come on Christian let's get them ready," Ashton and Christian leave the room together.

"Got the blueprints, boss," Harris says from the table. I lean over his chair and take in the warehouse layout. The main floor has three huge overhead doors on the east side of the building with two exit points. The west side of the building has a smaller overhead door and one exit point. The north and the south side have two exit points each. They used the south side of the building for storage at one point. The center of the main floor is a huge open space with skylights above. The second level is a catwalk all around the building with several rooms used for office space.

"Here is where we'll enter," I say pointing to the top of the blueprints. "We'll climb up to the roof and go in through the maintenance entrances. That way we can watch from the catwalk and see where they have Izzy and Redline at. We might get lucky and they'll be in one of the rooms, but I doubt it. My guess is that they're going to be in the center of the main floor. We'll be exposed trying to get to them, but that's where Marks, Harris, and Ramirez's skills will come into play. You three will stay up top and pick off anyone trying to sneak up on us. Ashton and Christian will be with me on the ground floor."

"What about Ace, Rush and Xavier?" Marks speaks up.

"Ace, you and Rush good at covering the east side exit points? We'll need to use your cars again. I'll keep Xavier with me."

"Works for me. Can I use any of my guys? They'll kill me if I do this alone."

"Yes, bring in three of your guys. The ones you trust with your life, not some flunky looking for a quick in.

Have them guard the other exits and only act if necessary. Have them meet us on Madison Ave. We go in tonight while Switch and Wrath are busy with the drop. Are your other guys still set up to intercept?"

"Yes, they're all ready to roll."

"Great. Hey, Ace."

"Yeah, Nolan," Ace's light brown eyes watch me carefully.

"Thanks for your help."

"Any time brother," An understanding passes between us. We might not have always been on the same side, but at this moment, we're together and that means something.

"OK team let's get some rest. We're going to have a long night ahead of us," I check the time on the massive clock on the wall. It's already eight a.m. and the sun's rising, promising a new day, casting a red fiery haze through the floor to ceiling windows. I walk up the staircase in search of my girl, leaving the rest of my team to get their heads ready for tonight. Right now, all I want is to feel Ashley's soft curves against my body.

Chapter 27

Nolan

Walking up the staircase, I watch below for a moment. My team, my family is mulling around, trying to relax. Christian and Ashton return with several big black bags and begin checking and rechecking our weapons. Harris, Marks, and Ramirez disappeared into the kitchen and Rush and Ace are talking quietly to each other again. That puts my senses on alert, but I'll deal with that later. Right now, I just want to find my girl.

Satisfied my team will be ready, I turn and walk up another set of stairs that lead onto the rooftop. Sitting in a wrought iron chair with a huge fluffy white cushion, I find Ashley. She has her legs curled underneath her, watching the sun rise over the rooftop. Xavier and Mia are sitting on a matching couch and there's a coffee table separating them. Xavier has his head down, resting his elbows on his knees. Mia is rubbing his back soothingly. Ashley is the first to notice me standing in the doorway and a smile lights her face. She motions for me to come over with a flick of her head and I walk outside.

"How's it going down there?" Ashley asks.

"Good, we're all set for tonight. We need to get some rest and regroup. Ace is bringing in a few of his men and together we'll get Izzy and Redline back. The plan should work as long as everyone does what they're supposed to do." I stare at Xavier as I speak the last part. His head snaps up and there are tears in his eyes again. He wipes them away and an understanding passes between us. "X, I'm sorry I came down hard on you earlier. I can't let you go off and get yourself killed. I need you with me tonight. If we go in right now, it'll only put Izzy in jeopardy. I understand you want action now because you've been idle for so long, but it will come. I promise. You'll be with me on the front line. If we go now, we won't have the element of surprise on our side. We must penetrate the warehouse at the same time the drop goes down. Switch and Wrath will be busy with that and have some half-ass goons watching them. It's our best shot."

"I know, and Ashley is very persuasive. I lost my head for a minute. I promise I won't go off and do something stupid. I'm with you." Xavier stands up and stretches. "I'm going to go and see if I can help with something. Thank you, Nolan, for everything."

"Don't thank me. None of this would have happened to you if you didn't know me. It's my fault you're put in this situation and I promise these fuckers are going to pay."

"It's not your fault. You didn't choose to kidnap us. They did. Let's focus on that and stop feeling guilty for something that's beyond your control." Xavier gives me a bro hug and they head back inside. It's now just Ashley and me up here.

I walk to the edge of the roof and overlook the bustling city below. Ashley approaches me from behind and wraps her arms around my waist, leaning her front to my back. I can feel her soft curves against me and my dick takes notice. Turning around, I pull Ashley into my arms and hold her tight, burying my nose in her hair. Her heart is beating hard against her chest and her breath hitches. She picks her head up from my chest and peers into my eyes. No words are needed between us as my lips descend upon hers in a quick motion.

She parts for my probing tongue and I kiss her with built up passion and tension. She returns the kiss, our tongue's battling back and forth. I squeeze her perfectly round ass and lift her up. I break our passionate kiss and walk with her still wrapped around me to the doors leading outside. I close the door with my foot and offer her a devilish smirk. She knows what I'm about to do and the fire is reflecting from her eyes. Ashley yanks her hoodie and shirt up over her head while trusting me to hang onto her.

"I bet you're soaking wet for me right now," I groan. She arches into my touch and that fuels me on more. I navigate my way back to the couch and lay her down onto it. I watch her lust filled eyes as she squirms under my smoldering gaze. Yanking my hoodie and shirt over my head, I toss them behind me and crawl my way up Ashley's body. I kiss and lick her stomach while my fingers quickly pop the button on her jeans and pull the zipper down slowly, the sound of the teeth pulling apart sets my skin on fire until I have the zipper all the way down. Ashley lifts her hips and helps me pull off her jeans and tiny underwear she insists on wearing. I toss them behind me to the growing pile of clothes. I unzip and remove my jeans and boxers and toss them behind me, too. Ashley's biting her bottom lip, her brown eyes are dark with desire, watching me. My heart beats hard against my chest as I drape my body over hers. She spreads her legs wide for my massive frame. My mouth collides with hers as she arches her back, seeking what I'm offering.

"What do you want Ash?" I ask, my deep tone vibrating against her lips. She can't complete a sentence with as high as I'm bringing her and it turns me on that this strong, independent woman is mush under my hands.

"You, I want you," she groans and digs her nails into my back, pushing me closer to her body. Done with foreplay, I give my girl what she wants. Her breath hitches in her throat and a moan passes through her lips. I can't contain myself as the sweat beads down my back and my blood stokes with fire from what this woman does. The push and pull of our sweaty bodies, the grunts and groans, the smell of sex and the warm spring sun is too much for me to handle. As Ashley finds her release, bucking, squeezing, and moaning my name. I tighten my grip on her hips and find my own release.

Out of breath, I release my death grip on her hips and almost fall off the little couch we're on. Ashley tries to stifle her giggle at the way my body is reacting, and I glare at her, jokingly.

"Watch it, woman, I still have you pinned down." I tease and suck on the side of her neck. Her giggles turn to moans and I feel myself getting hard again. This time around, I'm gentle with her as she scratches her nails up and down my back, urging me to move faster.

We make love until the sun peeks over the rooftop, casting Ashley in a heavenly glow. My angel, the light in a world of darkness. One look from her honey brown eyes and I'm spent. I'll do whatever, whenever she asks. I'm not afraid to admit she's my weakness and strength all in one tiny package.

~~~~~~~~~~~~~~~~~~~~~~~

A few hours later, I'm awakened by a knock on the bedroom door. Sitting up, I look around, trying to figure out how I got here. Memories of the rooftop with Ashley flash in my head and I can't help but smile. After we made love one more time, I carried her quickly into the bedroom and we fell asleep wrapped in each other's arms. Her warm soft body curving around mine, holding onto me as if her life depended on it. I cast a glance at her side of the bed and Ashley isn't here. Panic consumes me. Where did she go? What happened? Another loud knock on the door draws my attention to it and I get up. I hear the shower running in the attached bathroom and stick my head inside the door. Relieved it's Ashley in the shower, I turn back around and throw on a pair of jeans. Leaving them unbuttoned, I yank the door open before the intruder knocks again and come face to face with Ace.

His light brown eyes are accessing me, carefully. I open the door and he walks into the room. His body is ridged, and his eyes are watching everything at once. "Ace is everything all right?" I ask.

"No, it's not. Your boy is going to get us all killed if he doesn't straighten his shit up," Ace growls and sits on the big white chair in the corner of the room.

"What are you talking about?"

"Xavier, he's gonna lose his head and get us all killed. He won't shut up about payback and vengeance. Nolan, I'm telling you man, if you can't get him lassoed in, me and my guys are out. I won't put my men in jeopardy because he can't get his shit together."

"I'll handle it," Ashley says from the bathroom doorway, startling both of us. She's dressed, and her long blonde hair is up in a tight ponytail. She walks across the room and stands in front of Ace. "Don't worry about Xavier, I will handle him and put a tight leash on him. He won't do anything stupid."

"How can you be so sure?" Ace asks, a look of doubt passes his face.

"Because I know how to handle guys like Xavier. I'm not just a pretty face, Ace. I'll guarantee he won't step out of line because if he does, I'll be the one to dish out the consequence. Not you or Nolan or anyone else. I run a tight ship, and no one will double cross me. The last person who tried ended up dead." Ashley tells Ace with a no bullshit attitude. "And that goes for you too, Ace. Don't double cross me or anyone else here." She crosses her arms over her chest and stands tall.

"I'm not planning on it. I have a daughter to think of and if we don't stop these guys, she'll never have a chance at a normal life." He stands up quickly offering me a small nod and leaves the room.

"I don't know what to say," I turn toward Ashley.

"You don't need to say anything, Nolan. I'll keep Xavier in line. Don't worry about him or me. You just go in and do your thing and I'll do mine. We need to convince Mia to stay here though. She was determined to go with us tonight and I don't want her there. I'm worried she'll put herself in danger and what we come across tonight will change her. I can already see it in her eyes. She's struggling and she hasn't even left this hotel room."

"How about we talk to her together with Christian?. You convinced her last time to come here, I'm sure the three of us together can get her to stay here."

"Do you think we should have someone stay with her?"

"I can ask Ace to have one of his men stay. I need all of my men with me tonight for this to go down without any issues."

"Let's ask him first and then talk to Mia."

I rise from the bed and pull Ashley into my arms. Kissing the top of her head, I feel her body relax against mine. "Thank you, Ash, for being my light in all of this."

"I'm no angel Nolan, and you've got to stop treating me like one," she mumbles into my chest. "I've done too many dark things to be considered an angel."

"You're my angel. It doesn't matter about your past. What matters is how you will bend over backward for those you love." I gaze into her eyes, "You have pulled me out of the darkness so many times already. That's an angel to me." My lips descend upon hers before she can rebuttal. We're a frenzy of lips and tongues, battling to pull each other from the ledge. I pull back and release a deep sigh, her flavor still on my lips.

Together we leave the confinement of the bedroom and walk down the stairs. Marks, Ramirez, Harris, Ashton, Mia, and Christian are missing. Xavier is sleeping in the chair and his form is at peace for once. Ace is on the couch nodding off. Rush is standing at the window again, overlooking Central Park. There's tension in his black eyes and he tries to mask his features as we walk over to him.

"Rush, what's wrong?" Ashley asks.

"I'm worried about everything. What if we do stop these guys, but it's not enough?"

"What do you mean?" Ashley gently asks.

"What if their reach is so big that even if we stop them, they have others that take their place and we still can't escape them?"

"Are you worried about your doctor friend?"

"I'm worried about everyone," he responds running his hands through his highlighted hair, blowing out a big breath. "I talked to Noah earlier and he told me Diablo is holding up his end and moved everyone to his place, but after everything, how do we know he isn't setting us up?"

"We have no choice right now but to trust Diablo. He's never wanted me dead, he just wanted Redline to stop sniffing around his girl." Ashley responds.

Rush snorts, "His girl is all sorts of fucked up. She'll spread her legs for anyone who shows her attention. I'm surprised she lasted as long as she did, and he put up with it. Thank God he got rid of her. She gives me the creeps." He shudders at the thought. "She tried hitting on me once and I had to put her in her place. I told Noah to be careful if she does weasel her way back in, he'll be her prime target."

"Noah is smart. He won't fall into her trap, but I see your concern. He's an attractive young man and she'll try to sink her claws into him just to hurt Diablo." I watch as something passes through Ashley's eyes. "Rush, can you call Doc and have her out here by tonight? I know it's late notice, but I'd feel better if we had someone here when we get Izzy back."

"Yeah, I can do that. I'm sure she'll jump on the first plane." He responds wiggling his eyebrows.

"Is there something on your mind?" I ask.

"I'd feel better if we had a doctor we trust to look her over."

"I can send my jet and she'll be here in eight hours. Will that work?"

"Would you?"

"Of course, anything to help ease your mind and there will be fewer questions if she's on a private jet. How about we have Ace's guy and Mia pick her up at the airport?"

"We need to ask him if he can spare someone first," Ashley answers peering past my shoulder to watch Ace sleeping. "If he can do it then, that's a clever idea."

"Let's find out right now." I walk up and shake Ace gently on the shoulder. He sits up quickly, rubbing the sleep from his eyes.

"Bro don't fucking do that. You're lucky I'm a light sleeper and could hear your conversation. Having kids will do that to you." He smirks.

"Then you know what I'm going to ask."

"Yeah I do," he looks over at Xavier sleeping in the chair. "He's at peace right now, but I don't doubt he'll be rearing to go when he wakes up and if he knows he has a doc on hand when we get Izzy back, that'll calm him down some. He keeps mumbling something about keeping them safe. I don't know what that means, but I'll call one of my guys and have him here in a few hours."

"Thanks, man. I owe you."

"Nah, just return the favor if I ever need it." Ace gets up from the couch and walks into the kitchen, making the phone call. He comes back out a few minutes later. "My V.P. King will be here soon. Hey, I need to go see my kid for a little while. I'll be back soon."

"Do you want someone to go with you?" I ask.

"Nah, I've had eyes on this hotel since we got here last night. My guys are waiting and watching for any threat. I've got that covered and so far, they haven't seen anyone coming or going. Once they see me leave, some will follow, the others will stay. I'll be fine." Ace walks out the door and now it's just the three of us and Xavier still sleeping.

Chapter 28

Nolan

Time creeps by as we wait for night to fall. The rest of my team came back and we're all milling around, going over the blueprints, watching the warehouse, checking and rechecking our weapons. We're all on edge, as the time ticks by, ready for everything. Tension is high and tempers are on edge. Ashley's had to talk Xavier off the ledge twice today. He's so high strung, he thinks something will happen. I start to question if bringing him along is a good idea, but then he calms down and I know if I leave him behind, he'll go off the deep end and hurt himself or get himself killed. I understand where he's coming from and can sympathize with him.

Ace and King appeared a few hours ago and intimidating isn't a strong enough word to describe King. He has said little, but his dark eyes watch everything. He's massively built, like an enforcer and not a VP, and detailed tattoo's cover his dark skin. I remember him from The Circle when Ashley was there to fight. He was one guy who blocked Switch from coming after us. After Ace passed out greetings, he stayed in the corner of the room and watched us get ready. He and Ace had a few conversations, and he warmed up to Mia. Unsure of how to handle Mia at first, she broke through his tough guy act and now they're talking to each other. Mia does that to people though. He just hasn't seen her side of crazy yet. That should be fun if she brings it out.

Christian approaches Ashley and me while watching Mia and King talk. His light brown eyes are pinning Mia to her spot. She's watching him, watch her. There's something different about him tonight. A side we don't normally see. He shifts his eyes in our direction, "I don't know about this," he says concern etches in his voice.

"She'll be fine, Christian. Mia knows how to handle herself and if it gets too weird, she'll bring her crazy out." Ashley says.

Christian snorts, "That's what I'm worried about. If she gets too crazy, he won't know what to do with her."

"Doc will know. She'll be arriving soon and can handle Mia's crazy. Trust me. If I thought this was a bad idea I'd stay here with her. We need to stay focused on the main goal." Ashley says as she chambers a round in the .45 Colt and holsters it to her side. Holy shit, that's hot. I shake my head and try to get rid of the dirty thoughts passing through my mind. She gives me a wink as she picks up a .38 Smith and Wesson, checks the rounds and chambers one, strapping it to her ankle. "Now boss," Ashley whispers getting my attention, "You can unstrap me later."

Her teasing tone does things to my body and I will myself to calm down. I shake my head and stand behind her, pulling her back to my front so she can feel what she does to me every second of the day and whisper in her ear. "You can't say these things to me. I'll be sporting a hard-on for the rest of the night if you do." I nip at her neck and she releases a soft moan.

"Nolan," Harris call my name drawing my attention. "Switch and Wrath just left the warehouse. It's go time."

My mind immediately snaps out of the lust craving and into attack mode. I release Ashley and finish strapping my weapons to my body. King and Mia watch our every move.

"Please bring her back safe," Mia pleads. "I'll be here waiting once we get doc from the airport." I offer her a nod and move quickly as we file out the door and into the elevator. Adrenaline fills the small space as we reach the lobby and walk through. Heads turn in our direction and people move out of our way quickly. I'm in the lead with Ashley and Ace on each side. Ashton, Christian, Xavier, and Rush are behind us followed by Harris, Marks, and Ramirez. We walk out into the night air and a shiver passes over my body creating goosebumps on my exposed skin.

The three cars we borrowed from Ace earlier are idling at the curb. Ashley climbs into the driver's side of the

Shelby GT 500. Harris, Xavier and I follow. Ashton, Rush, Christian, and Marks get into the Dodge Viper and Ace and Ramirez climb into the Dodge Charger Hellcat. Ashley peels out onto the street and the other two cars follow, hot on her tail. She's dodging and weaving like a woman on a mission.

Ashton's voice comes into my head through my earpiece. We each have one for communication. "Let's go over the plan one more time."

"We're going to park down the street on the east side of the building. Ace's men will be watching the south, north and west side exits. Ace and Rush will have the three exits covered on the east side with the cars. The rest of us will use the fire escape on the south side of the building and enter from the roof. Stay away from the skylights. Once we're inside, we'll do a sweep of the office spaces on the catwalk, sticking to the shadows. When those are clear, Marks, Ramirez, and Harris will set up on the catwalk and watch for hostiles. Ashton, Ashley, Xavier, and I will go down to the ground level, extract Izzy and Redline and meet you all at the cars."

"What if Austin is there?" Ashley asks.

Dread fills my mind thinking about what could happen. He's been protecting Izzy, but will he come with us? "If he wants to come with us, he can. But I can't guarantee he will. We'll deal with that when the time comes. For now, let's focus on getting Izzy out."

Ashley's grip tightens on the steering wheel and her jaw is set. "Fine." She barks out through clenched teeth. "He's still my brother, Nolan. If any one of you hurt him, you'll answer to me," she growls.

"You all hear that? Do not do anything to Austin. He's been protecting Izzy by his own choice."

Copy that fills my head and I look over at Ashley. She's pissed. I rest my hand on her knee and she shifts slightly. It's a subtle move and I understand it. She doesn't bat my hand away as I gently grip her knee, but I can see the conflict passing on her face. "Ashley, I get it, he's your brother. You've got to focus on the job at hand and not what he's doing."

Her eyes cut to mine as she speeds up and passes cars in her way. The glare from the oncoming cars light up her face. "You don't get it, Nolan. He's here for a reason and it's not just to protect Izzy. They have something on him. I can feel it."

"Or, he has something on them. He did say that there's something bigger than what we know when you were in that hunting cabin. Maybe this is what he meant and he's trying to keep you out of danger." Her body relaxes, and she releases a small sigh.

"Maybe he knows how to take these fuckers down. We need a line of communication with him if he doesn't want to come with us."

"Good idea. Marks get a burner phone and give it to Ashley when we reach our destination."

"Copy that," Marks replies.

"My guys are following now," Ace says into the earpiece.

"Roger that. ETA five minutes out. Lock and load boys. Focus on the target. Quick and easy."

Ashley slows down, parks next to the curb and quickly shuts the car off. We wait for the others to follow and silence fills the air. Once everyone is present, we watch the abandoned building for any signs of movement for several minutes.

"My men are posted in their spots. Everything is clear on their end," Ace relays into our earpieces.

"Roger that, let's move," I respond.

Quickly and quietly, we all climb out of our cars. Rush and Ace pass us and disappear into the shadows. I grab the fire escape ladder and pull myself up onto the rungs. Hanging onto the ladder, I reach back down to help Ashley. She isn't tall enough to get it on her own. I lift her with one arm and Harris stays below, helping. She grabs the rungs and climbs up the ladder and we all quickly follow.

Once she reaches the top and disappears over the ledge, my heart pounds in my chest and my hands become sweaty. Fuck, what if someone guarded the roof and they just took her? I climb quicker, with desperation, when she pops her head back into my sight and gives me a nod. The moonlight casting a soft glow around her face and my breathing evens out. She's going to give me a heart attack one day.

I reach the top and lift myself over the ledge, landing quietly on my feet. I brush my hand across Ashley's shoulders and she stares into my eyes. No words are necessary, she knows she worried me. With a slight nod, she brings my attention to the corner of the building where a dark figure is slumped in the corner. Ashley holds in a giggle, proud of herself for disarming and taking down a big guy. I've got to stop doubting her, she's very efficient.

I quietly walk over to the corner with Ashley on my heels as we wait for everyone else to make the climb. The man is wearing all black like we are, and he's unconscious, bound and gagged. He's twice her size and has a good six inches on her. Shocked, I try to speak, but no words will form. Ashley closes my mouth, gives me a wink and walks back to the guys now on the roof.

I pass them and quietly make my way to the maintenance entrance. I try the handle, but it's locked. I snap my fingers and Ramirez appears. He picks the lock and backs away. Drawing my gun, everyone else does the same as I count down.

"On the count of three," I whisper into the mic. Ashton sets up on the one side of the door and puts his hand on the latch.

"One," everyone breaks off onto either side of the door.

"Two," I whisper again. We all get on the balls of our feet, ready to bounce.

"Three," Ashton pulls the door open and I enter first. Sweeping the room, I wait with my gun drawn, at the next door leading onto the catwalk for everyone else to get here.

"Again," I whisper.

Everyone sets up like last time in the small space and I countdown.

"One," guns are drawn, fingers on the trigger.

"Two," I brace myself, ready for anything.

"Three," Ashton opens the door and I walk out onto the catwalk and turn right, keeping my back flush against the wall. Ashley, Ashton. and Xavier follow me. Harris, Marks, Christian, and Ramirez turn the opposite direction. Signaling with my hands, I direct the four to take that side and clear the rooms. I set up next to the first door with Xavier next to me, Ashley passes me and sets up at the next door, Ashton goes to the door after hers. I try the knob and it's unlocked. Sweeping the room quickly, not making a sound, Xavier follows me in. There's nothing in here but dust, dirt, and a metal desk.

"Clear room one," I whisper into my mic. Turning toward Xavier I turn off my mic and whisper, "Look I know you're itching to go, but you need to stay with me. Don't leave my sight."

"I'm in way over my head like last time," Xavier confesses. "You won't get any arguments from me. If push comes to shove, I want you to trust me, please."

"Deal. We need to finish sweeping these rooms. Come on, let's go." I turn my mic back on.

"Clear room two," Ashley whispers in my ear.

"Clear room three," Ashton says next.

After we sweep and clear each room, we meet in the middle of the catwalk and regroup. I point to Marks to set up at the south end of the catwalk. He disappears into the shadows. Then I point to Ramirez to set up on the east side and he too disappears. Pointing to Harris, he also hides into the shadows to set up on the west side. That leaves, Ashton, Ashley, Christian, Xavier, and I at the top of the metal stairs. I point two fingers to my eyes and back at each. They all nod and we descend the stairs quietly.

This part has me on edge as we reach the bottom. We're wide open and anyone watching can pick us off one by one. We split apart at the bottom of the stairs. Xavier and Ashley follow me and Ashton and Christian go in the opposite direction. We hide in the shadows and quickly make our way across the warehouse. I spot Izzy curled up in the corner.

"Target located south end corner. Appears to be alone." I relay to my team.

We quietly make our approach toward Izzy. Xavier tries to pass me and get to her, but Ashley stops him. She shakes her head and he glares at her, not understanding why we're waiting. A shadow moves behind Xavier and Ashley pushes him against the wall, watching to see where the figure goes. It's heading our way, right down the middle of the warehouse.

"Hostile at your six. He's locked and loaded," Harris chirps in my ear. I push my body against the wall and wait for them to pass. Ashley has a palm on Xavier's chest and they're both against the wall, out of whoever's coming down sight. He passes us and walks toward Ashton and Christian. I can't see them, but I know they're there. Once his back is toward me, I sneak up behind him, channeling my rage and hate, letting the demon come out to play. I grab the guy's neck and squeeze hard, dropping him to the ground and dragging him back to the shadows. I could have killed him instantly, but instead, I knocked his ass out cold and have him disarmed, hogtied and gagged behind a crate.

"Hostile clear," I say into the mic, steadying my breathing and racing heart. Now's not the time to lose my head.

"Two more heading your way," Marks whispers.

I blend back into the shadows and watch as two more men strapped with AK 47's come into view. They split off in opposite directions. One turns toward Christian and Ashton and the other heads right for Izzy in my direction. I wait until he's right next to me and grab his neck. I squeeze with everything I have and he goes down silently. I drag him behind another crate, disarm, hogtie and gag him.

"Hostile two clear," Ashton says into the mic.

"Hostile three down," I return.

"All clear on our end," Ramirez responds.

"Let's get our package," I whisper.

I nod to Xavier and he quickly reaches Izzy. He gently shakes her and her eyes flutter open. Surprise is etched on her face when she sees him and tears form in her eyes. He lifts her off the floor and cradles her into his chest. Her hands and feet are secured with a thick rope. Izzy sniffles and her eyes collide with mine. She cries harder and breaks eye contact with me, burying her face into Xavier's chest. Ashton and Christian reach us and work on untying the ropes. Ashley is soothing Izzy hair and telling her everything will be all right.

"Wait," Izzy's voice croaks. "Redline is here too, but they separated us. I think he's in one of the rooms down here."

"On it," Ashton says.

"I'll go with you," Ashley offers.

Before I can stop her, the three disappear into the darkness. "Let's get you out of here," I tell Izzy. She nods her head but won't make eye contact with me, hiding her face in Xavier's chest.

"Nolan, we have him." Ashley's voice fills my ears.

"Good, let's move," I respond. I take the lead and find the exit on the east side. "Rush, Ace, we're coming out."

"Clear out here," Rush responds.

I open the door to Ace and Rush watching and waiting on opposite sides.

"Where's Ashley?" Rush asks, concerned.

"They're coming any second behind me," I answer.

"Coming out," Ashton grunts into the mic.

"Clear out here," I respond. The door swings open and Christian walks out first. Ashley and Ashton have

Redline propped between them. His head is down, and his feet are dragging behind him.

"He's had the shit beat out of him," Ashley growls. "He's unconscious." I quickly try to take Redline's weight off Ashley, but she pushes me away. "I got it," she snaps.

She's pissed. I can feel her eyes burn into mine and vengeance thrumming through her body. She's ready to fuck someone up. We all meet at the cars and together Ashton and her gently lay Redline down in the back seat of Ashton's car and she climbs in.

"What are you doing?" I ask, catching her arm.

She glares at me like I've lost my damn mind and I know I have. "I'm not leaving him, not now." She snarls and sits in the back seat. She has Redline's head in her lap and is staring straight ahead, avoiding eye contact with anyone. "We need to move now. Both Izzy and Redline need a fucking doctor. So, whatever your issue is, get over it and let's go." She tosses me the keys and sits back.

"Fine," I bark out and walk toward the car she was driving. Christian follows me. Xavier and Izzy are already at the car and I unlock the doors. We get in and I squeal the tires, peeling out of the parking spot. My grip on the wheel is so tight, I'm surprised it doesn't bend under my hands. Jealousy floods my body and sets my skin on fire.

"Relax man," Christian says.

"Relax? How in the fuck can I relax?" I shout. "This is such bullshit." I slam my hand onto the steering wheel hard.

"Bro," Xavier speaks up from the backseat. "Someone in her family is hurt really bad. How'd you expect her to act?"

"Fuck!" I hit the steering wheel again, ashamed of my actions. Taking a deep breath, I will myself to calm my racing heart down and get control. "You're right and I acted like a complete asshole. Fuck."

"She knows you're a jackass at heart man and she knows you love her. That's why this is hard on both of you." Xavier soothes from the backseat.

I peer into the rearview mirror and Ashton is right on my ass. I can feel his glare burning into me. Yeah, I fucked up going all caveman on Ashley. I don't know where my head was back there. I can barely make out her silhouette in the darkness. I catch Xavier's blue eyes in the mirror. He smirks before dropping his gaze and focusing back on Izzy. She's been quiet the whole ride and I'm concerned for her state of mind.

Now that we have her and Redline back, I need to figure out a way to get them up to the hotel room without suspicion. I swallow hard when a thought crosses my mind. "Fuck, the whole damn team knows what an asshole I am."

"We already know boss," Marks chirps in my ear, laughing. Fucker. I can hear the others laughing too.

"Fuck off, Marks," I reply. "Listen we need to get these two up to the room without raising suspicion. Anyone want to chime in without the comments on me being an asshole?"

"There's a service elevator that housekeeping uses to stay out of the site of hotel guests. We can use that," Ace responds quickly.

"That'll work. Do you have someone working there?" I ask.

"Asshole, I have someone everywhere," Ace snickers.

Of course, he has to throw the asshole part in. "Thanks, fucker."

"It's better than being a dick," Ramirez comments with a laugh.

"Seriously, guys and Ashley if you're listening, excellent work in there tonight. I mean that. If you all didn't do your part that could have been a lot worse. I want to thank each of you for stepping up and helping me get Izzy and Redline back. Ace, can you relay my thanks to your guys?"

"Already done," Ace answers. I can tell he wants to call me an asshole again by the teasing in his voice.

"That's what we're here for boss," Ramirez quips. Everyone but Ashley and Ashton respond, and my stomach drops into the seat at the thought. They must be pissed at me.

"I'll take the lead and get us to the service entrance of the hotel," Ace comes back on the line. I slow my speed down and Ace passes us quickly. Rush gives me the one finger salute with a smirk as they drive by. At least he isn't pissed at me. Ace turns on his right blinker and turns down an alley at the back of the hotel. His brake lights brighten up when he rolls to a stop. The door to the hotel flies open quickly and I'm out of the car fast, gun drawn. I can sense the others right behind me.

"Hey, calm down. Lower your fucking weapons asshole," Ace demands as he stands at the driver side door.

I glare at Ace and he stares right back, quirking an eyebrow. I turn my attention to the wide-open door and see a tiny woman quivering with fear, holding it open. Her brown eyes are wide with fright when she takes in the site of my massive frame crowding the space and my team surrounding her. Relaxing my stance and holstering my weapon I offer her a smile, but it feels more like a grimace. Man am I fucking up big time tonight.

"It's OK, Sarah," Ace soothes the woman. She relaxes when she hears Ace's voice behind me and I step back. Her eyes connect with his and something passes between their shared looks. I've seen that before. I don't want or need to interfere with that mess.

"Can someone help us," Ashley yells from behind me. I turn and walk quickly to the car she's in and lean in the back seat. Her jaw is set tight and she still won't look at me.

"Ash," I wipe a tear trailing down her cheek. "I'm..."

"Don't," she interrupts me, still staring straight ahead. "Not now Nolan. I don't need your apologies. I need to get Redline inside to see the doc. That's my main focus, not whatever's rolling through your head. We'll deal with this later." Her bottom lip quivers slightly.

"I get it and I acted like an ass. Don't shut me out, please," I beg.

She finally looks at me and the tears filling her eyes breaks my heart. "I'm not," she wipes away her tears and looks down at Redline's unconscious form. "He's really bad and I'm scared and extremely pissed."

"OK, let's bring him out and get him up to the hotel room. Ashton, Marks, and Harris get your asses over here and help. We need to lift him carefully so if there's any internal damage, we don't create any more harm." Ashton is at the driver side back door, lifting Redline's legs. I step inside the door and lift his shoulders. His head rolls to the side from the movement. "Someone steady his head." I bark out. Another set of hands reach beside me and hold his head still.

"On the count of three, Ashton you and Ashley push him my way. The rest of us, be ready to support his body and keep his head still. One, two, three." We all grunt at Redline's dead weight and get him out of the car. He's a lot heavier than he looks. Once we have him out of the car, we quickly walk into the service door and down a long corridor where Ace, Sarah, Xavier, and Izzy are waiting for us, holding open the stainless-steel elevator doors. We all pile inside trying to keep Redline's body steady. Izzy is tucked into Xavier's side and her face is buried in his chest. She's not talking or looking at anyone and I hope she isn't traumatized.

The elevator dings and the doors quietly whoosh open. Sarah steps out first with Ace right behind her. His massive body is protecting her without touching her as she turns and holds the doors open for us. He's watching her watch us, and I can see the pain in his eyes from having her so close, but not being able to do anything about it.

We carry Redline inside the suite and carefully lay him down onto the plush couch. I look at him for the first time since Ashley found him. His face is swelling and bruised badly, it's almost unrecognizable. Dried blood covers his hand and arms.

"Move please," I hear a soft female voice behind me. Spinning around, I come face to face with the doctor that patched Rush up after their kidnapping. Her long brown hair is up in a tight bun and she has a black doctor's bag in her hand and a no-bullshit attitude on her face. I step to the side so she can evaluate Redline. Her slender fingers open her bag and she pulls out her stethoscope and a blood pressure cuff. Ashley stays next to her, holding Redline's hand.

I let her do her thing and find Xavier and Izzy huddled in the corner with Mia and Christian. She's sobbing against Mia as Mia clings to her. Xavier has a look of rage that passes through his eyes when they connect with mine. I nod my head in agreement and approach Izzy.

"Izzy," I say softly. She picks her head up and cries harder. I pull her into my arms and run my hand through her dirty hair. "It's going to be OK. I promise." Her tiny body shakes under my grip and I do everything I can to hold my own tears back. My best friends and the only people who've treated me like family are hurt because of me. Revenge will be the only option for those who did this to us. Standing here holding onto the one woman who helped rebuild my broken soul I vow justice will be served to them all. Switch and Wrath are up for trial and I'm their executioner.

Chapter 29

Ashley

My eyes are ping-ponging between all the activity happening around me. Xavier, Mia, Nolan, and my best friend Izzy are huddling in the corner. Nolan's team is whispering to each other near the windows, Ace, King and the woman they call Sarah are in a different room. I didn't see where they went to. Rush is next to me watching Doc Amber take care of Redline out cold. I follow Nolan with my eyes and watch as he wraps Izzy in a comforting hug and her body shakes even harder.

"He'll be out for a while. I need to stitch up the cuts on his chest and arms and I gave him a shot for the pain. His nose is broken and his jaw is dislocated. I will have to reset them both, but I'd rather do it where he'll be staying for a few days instead of doing it now and then moving him and causing more pain. I'll let him rest for now. Was there someone else I had to look at?" Amber says.

"Yes, Izzy. Let me get her for you," I reply. Standing up from the floor, I walk over to Izzy. My feet are dragging with every step and it's taking everything I have not to break down and cry. My family's hurt and who knows what else.

"Izzy," I whisper, swallowing past the lump in my throat. She pulls her head from Nolan's chest and her green eyes are bloodshot from crying. More tears threaten to escape when she sees me. "Doc...," I clear my throat and try again, "The doc wants to look you over." I offer her a small smile and she nods her head.

"Do you want me to come with you?" Xavier asks. His voice is full of pain and anguish and his blue eyes are reflecting what he's feeling. Izzy shakes her head no and Xavier's face falls into a frown. Between Mia and I, we help Izzy up the stairs with the Doc in tow. I sneak a peek at the guys when we reach the top of the stairs. Xavier's fists are balled up and he punches the wall before collapsing against it. Nolan and Christian are surrounding him, stopping him from inflicting any more pain to himself. There's so much pain, heartbreak and anguish surrounding us all, I know we won't be the same after this. Izzy carefully sits on the bed and Amber evaluates her. Mia is next to her with her arm around her shoulders. I stay next to the door, protecting her from anyone coming into the room.,

"Where are you hurt?" Doc asks gently. Izzy points to her head, wrists, and stomach, still not saying a word. "Ok, lay back and I'll look you over."

Izzy does what she asks, kicking her dirty shoes off and laying on the bed. Tears are in her eyes when she closes them. Amber checks her heartbeat and lungs. Then moves to her wrists, which are raw from the ropes tied around them. She puts ointment on them and wraps them up with a white bandage. Then she shines a light in Izzy's eyes.

"No sign of a concussion and your lungs are clear. You're undernourished and I'm going to start an IV to rehydrate your body. Do you want a shower before I put your IV in?" Izzy nods her head and a smile graces her lips as she holds her belly protectively. "Ok, hun. Let's get you showered and cleaned up. I'm going to go and check on Redline and be back in a few minutes. Deal?"

Izzy nods her head and sits up. A squeak passes her lips, and she cradles her stomach, bending over. I run over to her and drop on my knees onto the carpet in front of her. "Izzy, what is it? What's wrong?" I run my hands over her back in a soothing motion.

"Cramping," she whispers. That's the first words she's spoken since we found her.

"Cramping? Like period cramps?"

"No," she answers quietly while holding onto her stomach tight. My eyes grow wide with realization.

"You're pregnant," I state. She nods her head and tears fall onto her jeans. I'm trying to hold back my own tears.

Amber is next to me quickly. "How far along are you?"

"Three months," she sobs.

"Any bleeding?"

"No. I just started cramping the night they took me from the apartment and threw me into the warehouse."

"Does Xavier know?" I ask. Izzy nods her head.

"I'll go and get X," Mia says through a lump in her throat.

"No, not yet," Izzy whispers. "He doesn't know I've been having cramps and I don't want him to know yet."

"It could be from lack of food and dehydration." Amber states. "Mia, can you run her a warm bath? That'll be easier than trying to stand."

"Yes," Mia replies and walks quickly into the bathroom. I hear the water turn on and there's a knock on the door. Izzy's eyes widen in fright and I move quickly to the door. Cracking it open, I'm face to face with Xavier and Nolan.

"How is she?" Xavier asks.

"She's OK. We're going to give her a bath and Doc is going to start an IV to rehydrate her."

"Can I see her?"

"Not yet. Let us get her cleaned up and settled in, then you can come in." Xavier swallows hard and drops his head in shame. "Hey, this isn't your fault. I know what you're thinking. So, stop it. There are no signs of a concussion or any other injuries. She needs to rest. We'll get her cleaned up and settled in."

"I should be in there taking care of her." The anguish in his voice breaks my heart.

"X trust us, please. She's going to be fine but wants us to help her. It's a woman and best friend thing. I promise as soon as Doc is done, you can be with her for as long as she needs you. Right now, she needs us."

"All right, but if something changes, you get me right away. I mean that Ashley. I'll be out here in the hallway waiting."

"Deal. Xavier, she'll be ok I promise."

"How are you holding up?" Nolan asks.

I peek back at Izzy and she nods her head. I step out of the room and shut the door behind me. I look up and see his whiskey eyes boring into me, pleading to talk to him.

"I'll be fine. Just worried about my family." I answer.

"Ash, I want to say I'm sorry for being an asshole." His big arms wrap around me and he pulls me against his chest. I try to fight against it but relax into his hold.

"I know. I heard it all on the ride over. Yes, you were an asshole, but I was also a bitch. So, basically, we're even." I answer. Nolan's arms tighten around me and I squeeze his waist. "What's the next step?"

"We're waiting to hear from Ace's guys about the drop. If they succeed in stopping it, we're going after Switch and Wrath. Then I'm going to find my kid and take him home." My body tenses.

I'm afraid to ask but I must know the answer, "Home where?" I look up into his eyes and press my fingers against his stubble covered cheek. My heart is beating hard against my chest afraid I will lose the one man that's ever captured my heart and broke through my walls.

"With you, Ashley. Wherever you are, I'll be there. If you want to go back to L.A. right away, so do I. If you want to go to Michigan with Xavier and Izzy for a while, I'll be there. I'm not leaving your side."

Releasing a breath I didn't realize I was holding, a sob escapes my lips and my body trembles in Nolan's arms. "Are you sure?" I ask through the lump in my throat.

"Absolutely. That is if you still want me now that I have a kid."

I raise an eyebrow at him, "Did you hit your head when we went into that warehouse?"

"No, but I need to know if you accept me and my baggage," Nolan laughs.

"You're a fucking idiot. You know that? I think one of those guys knocked you around a few times." I say with a grin, patting his cheek. "Of course, I still want you around. Just because you might have a kid, doesn't mean I don't want to be with you, you big oaf."

Relief fills Nolan's eyes and my heart soars with the smoldering look he's giving me. I want nothing more than the two of us alone, naked and sweating up the sheets, or couch or wherever we can find, but there are other pressing matters I must attend to and she's waiting for me inside that bedroom.

"I have to get back in there. Keep me updated on how it's going." I turn to Xavier, "I'll get you as soon as Izzy's done."

"Thank you, Ashley. Will you tell her something for me?"

"Of course."

"Tell her," his voice cracks and he pauses. "Tell her I love her no matter what and I'm right here waiting. I'll wait forever if she needs me too." Tears spill down Xavier's cheeks and he leans against the wall.

"I will," I promise. "I'll see you in a little while," I say to Nolan. His lips descend upon mine and gives me a soft kiss, making me wish for more. I pull away from his embrace and enter the bedroom without looking back. Mia and Izzy are in the bathroom and Amber is in the bedroom, setting things up for Izzy.

"Do you need any help?" I ask.

"No, I'm almost done. They should be coming out soon though."

"Ok, I'll go and see if they need my help." I want to ask her about Rush but decide against it and walk to the bathroom door and knock softly.

"Come in," Mia says.

I open the door slightly and walk inside. Izzy is still in the tub with bubbles surrounding her. She looks frail and weak sitting in there. "Do you need my help?"

"Sure, grab a towel. Izzy is done and I need help getting her out."

I grab a huge fluffy white towel off the shelf and hold it open. Izzy stands up and I try to hold in a gasp. Her bones are poking through her pale skin from lack of food, but her belly has a slight bump. A smile graces my lips when I realize what this means.

"What?" Izzy asks softly.

I wrap the towel around her and help dry her off. "You're going to be a mom," I exclaim. "A wonderful mom at that. I'm so happy for you Izzy."

Her eyes light up with excitement. "I've been afraid to think about it. I didn't want to get attached and have them take it away from me." I hear the slight tremble in her voice.

"You're safe now, Izzy. So, let's get you healthy and no one will ever harm you again. Does your dad know?"

She shakes her head as Mia is trying to dry it off. Her long blonde locks are shining and with the dirt and grime off her, I can see the deep purple bruising on her legs and arms. Anger thrums through my body thinking about someone hurting this sweet innocent woman.

We help Izzy in bed and once she's settled and doc puts her IV in, I get Xavier. He comes barging into the room, at her side in an instant and I leave them alone. Finding Nolan downstairs, I try to keep my temper in check, but the fury running through my veins is hard to control. My hands are trembling with rage.

I want to kill these fuckers for putting my family through all this bullshit.

"What's the word?" I ask approaching Nolan, Rush, King, and Ace.

"Nothing yet," Ace responds.

"Something's wrong. That meet was hours ago." Dread fills my stomach and I pace the room. "You should have heard something by now."

"I know, but I can't get ahold of anyone." Ace growls, dialing another number on his cell.

My eyes shoot to Nolan. "We've got to go there. Something isn't right."

"Marks, can you pull up footage of The Graveyard?" Nolan shouts.

Marks hurries to the laptop and after a few clicks, he searches the cameras. "Got it."

We crowd around him and watch. Ace's men move into position, hiding in the shadows. Marks fast forwards and nothing happens. No Switch, Wrath or the boat moving in for the shipment. Suddenly the screen fills with red and blue lights.

"Stop," I shout. Marks stops fast forwarding when we see the cops rush onto the pier where Ace's men are and handcuff them.

"Motherfucker!" Ace screams. "It was a fucking set up and now they have my men. That's why I couldn't get ahold of them. Fuck. This isn't good."

Suddenly Nolan's cell phone rings and he digs it out of his pocket. The caller ID says unavailable, but it's a New York area code.

"Yeah," Nolan barks into the phone. His fingers tighten on it so hard his knuckles turn white. "Listen to me, motherfucker. I'm done playing your games. I'm coming for you and you won't know when." He stops talking for a beat. "Oh, I'll be there, and you bet your ass you won't be walking away." His voice is low and deadly, and a smirk graces his lips. I've seen that smirk before. He's channeling his hate and rage and letting the demons he fights with daily take over. There's something different about him this time though. He's in control of the evil and God have pity on any soul who gets in Nolan's way because he will show no mercy.

Chapter 30

Nolan

White hot fury floods my veins when I hear Switch on the other end of the call. He's ranting about having the upper hand. Surprise motherfucker, I've got you right where I want you.

"You listen to me and listen good. I'm coming for you. There's nothing that will stop me now," I growl into the phone. Done listening to Switch, I hang up and squeeze my hands into fists. I need to feel pain, I need to dish out punishment for everything these assholes have done to my family.

"What are we doing?" Ashley asks as she gently puts her hand on my arm. I smirk and raise my eyebrows. She doesn't back down though. She keeps pushing me and shows no fear. She knows I won't hurt her and can be just as savage as I can.

I look around the hotel room. Eight sets of eyes are upon me waiting for direction. Each one with their own specific skills, but this time I can't use them all. There's only two I can use. The rest can go with us, but they can't interfere, they must stay in the shadows.

"Here's what we're going to do. Ashley and Ashton, you're with me. The rest of you need to hang back in the shadows. They're only expecting me, but I need to even up the playing field." I turn toward Ace, "You and King go back and see if you can get your guys out of jail. Take care of your men. I don't want you involved anymore. I've already caused enough damage to The Black Hearts."

"Are you sure?" Ace asks.

"Positive. Go and take care of them. We've got this, it's what I do." Man, it feels refreshing saying that. Ace and King leave without another word, leaving me with six. "Christian, I need you to stay here with Redline, Xavier, Izzy, Mia, and Doc. Your involvement stops here. We're about to get our hands really bloody and I don't want that to jeopardize your career."

"What? No, I'm coming with you, fuck that career." Christian growls.

"No, you're not. Your job is to protect and service, not judge and jury. Stay here and protect them." I walk over to Christian and rest my hand on his shoulder. "I need you here to protect my family while I stop any more harm coming at them. It's really important to me you do this, please."

"Fine," he snaps crossing his arms. "If anything happens to you or anyone else, I'll be there in a heartbeat." He isn't happy, but he must deal with it.

"Marks, Ramirez, and Harris," I turn toward them. "You three will be in the shadows. Observe but don't interfere. We'll communicate through our earpieces. I need you to stay out of sight, out of mind."

"I don't like this boss," Marks replies. "But you got it."

"Be ready for anything. If we need help, I'll bring you in, but I have a feeling Switch's head is getting too big and he feels no one can stop him. He's about to meet his maker." I smirk, cracking my knuckles.

"What about Ashley and me?" Ashton asks.

"You two will be with me. Don't let them get the drop. Wrath likes to be sneaky and will go for Ashley first, but you can handle her." I answer turning my attention to Ashley. Her honey eyes are narrow and she's ready for a fight. "One thing, Wrath will try to play off your emotions. Keep them in check and don't let her get the upper hand. That's how she beats her opponents in The Circle. She gets in their heads and tortures them with the things she'll do with their loved ones. Don't listen to anything she says."

"Got it," Ashley replies. "Nolan?"

"Yeah?"

"Let's make these fuckers pay for hurting our family."

I nod my head and pull her against me. I need to feel her body in my hands one last time. I lean down and kiss her softly, "They will pay for every time they did something to any of us. That's one promise I am making and keeping." I answer, resting my forehead against hers.

She wraps her arms around my neck, her body is flush against mine. "Don't make promises, deliver with actions. I'll keep Wrath off your back. She'll wish she never met me." Ashley offers me a devious smirk that pulls me closer to her. We're one of a kind and I'm one lucky son of a bitch for finding her.

"Ashton, you'll be watching my six," I tell him without taking my eyes off Ashley. She has a pull on me, I can't let go. "Watch for anyone trying to interfere and if they do, take them out. I don't mean unconscious either."

"You got it, boss. All right, let's lock and load." Ashton replies.

There's a flurry of activity around us, but my focus is on Ashley, ignoring the rest. Her arms are still around my neck and she hasn't broken eye contact. My eyes follow her tongue as she licks her lips, making the plump pink shine. Stifling a groan, I pull her tighter against me, so she can feel how she affects me. Her eyes shine with lust, but we don't have time. Fucking Switch. Another thing to file away and make him pay for.

"We should inform Izzy and X what we're doing," Ashley whispers, her fingers are gently ticking the back of my neck sending shivers down my spine.

"Yes, we should in just a moment. I want to savor this," I reply as my lips crash down onto hers. She moans and her lips part for my probing tongue. Digging my fingers into her hips, I yank her closer and explore every inch of her hot, wet mouth with my tongue, her taste on my lips. I break the kiss, panting heavily, my heart beating hard against my chest and all the blood flow has been redirected behind my jeans. "I needed that. Let's go talk to X and Izzy." I let go of Ashley's hips and take her hand.

Once at the top of the stairs, I knock softly on the door and peek my head inside. Izzy is sleeping with her back toward Xavier and he's laying down next to her, holding onto her waist. Doc has an IV set up next to the bed and a tube running down into Izzy's arm. It's just the two of them in here and Xavier shifts when he hears me. His eyes are red and swollen, and he holds a finger up to his lips. He gently kisses Izzy on the head and quietly climbs out of the bed. She doesn't move a muscle and her breathing is deep and even. Rubbing the sleep from his bloodshot eyes, Xavier stumbles toward the door and meets us out in the hallway.

"How's she doing?" Ashley asks. Her head is resting on my chest and I have my arms around her, holding onto her.

"She's doing OK. She keeps waking up every time she has a nightmare. I feel so helpless not being able to do anything about them. I can't chase them away anymore." His fingers flex into fists at his sides and swallows hard.

"You'll figure it out. Just keep doing what you're doing and comfort her. She's been through so much and all she needs right now is knowing you're safe."

"Thanks, Ash. I could help ease the nightmares after Marie, but this time it feels like I can't touch them."

"How's the cramping?" Ashley asks.

"Much better. She hasn't said anything since Amber put the IV in, but she's going to bring in an ultrasound machine to make sure everything is fine."

"What?" I ask. "Why would you need an ultrasound machine?" I furrow my eyebrows.

"You didn't tell him?" Ashley scolds Xavier.

"No," he shakes his head. "I didn't tell anyone yet, in case something happened."

"Tell me what?"

"Izzy's pregnant," Xavier blurts out. My heart drops to my toes and my stomach is churning.

"How far along?" I ask.

"Three months."

Ashley rests her hand on my beating heart, "Nolan, she's going to be fine. I only found out because she was cramping when I was in there with her or she wouldn't have said a word."

"But nothing since?" I ask afraid to know the answer.

"Not that she's said," Xavier answers shaking his head.

"One more thing for these fuckers to pay for," I crack my neck from side to side. "We're heading out to end this. If anything, and I mean anything changes with Izzy, you let me know immediately."

"I will. I know I said I want revenge and make these fuckers pay for what they've done, but I can't leave her." Xavier sighs.

"Hey, I'm going to see her for a moment while you two talk," Ashley says interrupting us and quietly opens the door, disappearing from my sight. My arms feel empty without her in them. I flex my hands and rest them against the wall I'm leaning against.

"I don't want you to leave Izzy either. She needs you more than we do. I will make sure they pay for what they did to both of you." A smile graces my lips. "You're going to be a dad. I'm happy for you." I really mean it. He's will make a great father. He's had a perfect role model.

"Thanks, I'm really nervous though and we still have six months to go." His eyes light up with happiness. "I just hope…" Xavier blows out a deep breath. "I hope we can get past this and raise our baby right."

"You will, together. Not only that, you'll have Ashley and me with the both of you and a huge family supporting you. He or she will have an Aunt and Uncle who will protect them."

"Can you imagine if it's a girl? Oh my God, she won't be able to date until she's thirty," Xavier says with a laugh.

"If it's a boy, we'll show him all the tricks," I grin.

"Definitely, he'll be a player like his Uncle." Xavier laughs.

"Can I see her before we go?"

"Yeah, come on." Xavier opens the door and we quietly walk inside. Ashley is sitting on the side of the bed, holding Izzy's hand. Izzy is sitting up and they're both smiling when we come in. A shadow passes across Izzy's eyes when she sees me, the smile falls from her face and she drops her head. I cross the room quickly and sit next to her, being careful of the tube for her IV. I pull Izzy into my arms and wrap her in a hug. Her tiny body shudders under me.

"I'm so sorry Nolan. Can you ever forgive me?" She sobs against my chest.

"Hun, you were forgiven the moment it happened," I soothe. "I never blamed or been mad at you. I know it wasn't your fault."

"I could have stopped them from making me do it, but I had to think about my baby and Xavier."

"Shh. You don't need to say anymore," I comfort her.

"Yes, I do. You don't understand. They showed me pictures." Her emerald bloodshot eyes look up into mine. "Did they really do those horrible things to you?"

I swallow hard and nod my head. "Yeah, they did when I was a teenager. But don't worry about that. They can't hurt me anymore and I won't let them hurt you."

"They told me if I didn't do what they said, they would do that to Xavier." Tears pour from her eyes, soaking my shirt, and her body shakes with silent sobs. "I didn't want to, Nolan. You must believe me."

"Yes, Izzy, I believe you. It's all right, calm down. No one will hurt either of you again. That's a promise I will make and keep. Ashley and I are going to end this for the last time."

"How? They have such a big reach," she sniffles. "I overheard that bitch talking to the asshole, and they said something about having a pull in California. She also said she had something on you that will make you come back to her."

"She has my kid I didn't know about until a few days ago. That won't make me go back to her. I'm going to get rid of them and get my boy back. Did they say anything about why they wanted Redline?"

Izzy shakes her head, "No. It doesn't make sense, they used him as a piñata. Each of their new recruits had to beat him until he blacked out. It was awful hearing the punches and kicks over and over and I couldn't do a damn thing about it." She wipes the tears from her eyes, "How is he doing, anyway?"

Ashley squeezes Izzy's hand, "he's still unconscious, but nothing major damaged or broken."

"That's because Austin saved him from them going to crazy. He saved me so many times too. I owe him my and my baby's life. When Wrath would come at me, Austin would step in and stop her. He has something on them and they're afraid of him."

"That's good to hear," Ashley whispers. Conflicting emotions pass across her face and she quickly schools her features and offers Izzy a smile. "We're going to get out of here and let you rest. We'll be back in a little while."

"Take care and watch your backs. I had a guardian angel looking out for me and he's watching out for the both of you too."

I give Izzy a soft kiss on the forehead and climb off the bed. Ashley gives her a hug and a kiss on the head. We walk out of the room and down the stairs. It's time to pay these two a visit. They're going to be dancing with the devil and the devil is me.

Chapter 31

Nolan

The moon is high in the sky, glowing brightly onto us as I drive the sleek grey Shelby GT 500 Ace left for us. Ashton, Ashley and I make our way down the dark street on the outskirts of The City with the rest of my team in the black SUV behind us.

"Boss, we have company," Marks chirps in my ear. "Three cars coming and picking up speed fast."

"Copy that. Hang tight boys, it's going to get dicey," I reply and punch the gas, shifting smoothly. We pull away from the cars following us and fly up Interstate moving at top speed.

"Fuck, Nolan. Watch out!" Ashley screams and braces herself against the seat, hanging onto the 'oh shit' bar when a car appears onto the highway and tries to sideswipe us. I jerk the wheel hard to the left and hit the median. Grass and dirt kick up behind me making the car fishtail. I tear back onto the highway and steady the car and my beating heart.

"You good boss?" Ramirez asks.

"Yup, I'm good," I reply, releasing a breath. "That was close."

"It's not over yet," Ashton says from the backseat.

I glance into my rearview mirror and see three cars surrounding the SUV, slowing it down. Every time my team speeds up, a car cuts them off making them slow down.

"Boss, I can't get past them. Get out of here and take care of business," Harris shouts into the comm pieces.

"I'm not leaving you behind," I shout back, zigzagging up the highway, passing cars left and right.

"Boss get the fuck out of here. There's more coming up behind us. We will take care of them and catch up." Harris orders.

"Nolan, we have to go, they're trying to stop us from reaching our destination. If they do, we're as good as dead." As soon as Ashton says the words, gunshots ring out. I glance in the rearview mirror; the black SUV and the other cars are nowhere in sight. "Keep going. Trust your team to do the right thing." Ashton reassures me.

Punching the gas, I shift again and race past the other cars on the highway. Looking in my mirror, bright headlights are right on my ass, not giving me any room. I speed up and they keep the same pace, inching closer and closer.

"Brace yourselves," I hold on to the steering wheel with a tight grip, turning my knuckles white. Ashley throws her seatbelt on and braces herself against the dash. Ashton tightens his hold on the seats. The car behind me nudges my back bumper, and the wheel shakes under my grip. The asshole behind me backs off, gains speed and hits me again, slamming into the rear end hard. I keep the car on the road, just barely. My heart is beating hard in my chest and my hands are sweating. Adrenaline is pumping through my veins and my fight or flight instincts are kicking in.

"Get us out of here," Ashley pleads from the passenger seat. I look from side to side trying to find an escape route. There's a break in the cars and a left turn exit approaches fast. I yank the wheel hard to the left and cut across several lanes and shoot off the exit, leaving blaring horns and bright lights behind me. I don't let up until I'm right on the hairpin turn, then I let up on the gas, grab the e-brake and turn hard to the right. We barely make the turn when I'm forced to repeat the process to the left.

"Who in the fuck made the roads?" Ashton grumbles from the back seat.

"I don't know but we're almost out and in the clear." I grit through my teeth. Another curve to the right descends upon us and I repeat the process. Relaxing my grip on the wheel, I check my rearview mirror at the same time Ashton turns around. I breathe a sigh of relief and calm my racing heart when I see no headlights in sight. "Pull up the GPS and see where we are."

Ashley fumbles for her phone and clicks on the app with shaking fingers as she steadies her own breathing. Her face is pale, illuminated by the glow on her phone. "We've gone too far. We're two exits away from the one we wanted."

"Is there a way back that isn't on the highway?" I ask.

"Yeah, but we have to go through some Podunk towns to get there and some windy mountainsides. I think it'll be best if we get back on the highway and head south. It's the quickest."

"All right keep your eyes open for any more trouble," I answer and whip a quick U-turn in the middle of the road. I drive back toward the highway, watching and waiting. Taking the turns to get back on the highway, no other cars are in sight. We ride in silence, the moon high in the sky creating an eerie glow of the treetops. Once I reach the exit, I check my rearview mirrors. There are cars coming up behind us, but they're too far back to cause me concern.

"Harris, Marks, Ramirez, are you back online yet?" Silence greets me on the other end. I try again. "Harris, can you hear me?" No response. "Marks, you there?" Silence. "Ramirez?" Nothing. "Where the fuck are they?"

"I don't know, but their phones are off too," Ashton answers from the back seat.

Turning left, a dreadful feeling sets in the pit of my stomach as I drive into the night. I turn down a dirt road and pull off to the side.

"Here's the plan. Since Harris, Marks, and Ramirez are missing, we need to do this with just the three of us. We won't have eyes on our six so it's up to us to watch each other's backs. The house I know Switch is in is at the end of this road. I'm going to hide the car here and we're walking to it through the woods. Remember to stay quiet and do not hesitate to take any of them out." I pull back onto the road and find a spot to hide the car. We quietly get out and make our way into the forest.

"Why is it when things are getting dicey we end up traipsing through the woods?" Ashley whispers.

"I was wondering the same thing," I respond and we both chuckle. "We're getting close, silence for here on out. We go in fast and hard. Don't ask questions. Switch will not hesitate to kill you, and neither will Wrath. We take them out along with Marcus, and we slice the head off the whole operation. Everyone ready?" We stop walking and check our weapons.

"Ready," Ashley whispers.

"Ready," Ashton responds.

"Let's do this." We come to the edge of the clearing and a huge old farmhouse lights up the night sky. Every light is on the first and second floor. Cars are parked haphazardly in the driveway and front lawn. The bass of the music is pouring out the open windows and creating a cover for us. Sneaking around the back of the old house, it's dark and deserted back here. I check the area for anyone patrolling the grounds and there's no one around. These guys are too comfortable and I'm about to change all that. Channeling my inner strength, we climb the back porch and I place one hand on the doorknob. I hold up three fingers signaling to go on my count. Lowering one finger, Ashton moves to the left of the door and Ashley moves behind me on the right. My second finger lowers and we aim our weapons at the door. My third finger drops, and I turn the knob cracking the door open. We all file into the back mudroom, staying low and silent. The music is vibrating the old wooden floorboards and we quietly creep into the kitchen doorway. The bright lights from the room cause me to pause before entering.

"We need to find the fuse box and kill the lights," I whisper in my earpiece. This is why I need my team. Fucking assholes for splitting us apart.

"I'm on it boss," Harris's voice comes across my earpiece.

"Thank fuck. What took you so long?" I tease him.

"Marks had to make a pit stop," Harris jokes.

"Fuck off," Marks responds.

"We're in the back mudroom, right next to the kitchen. You all locked and loaded?"

"You know it," Ramirez replies. "Let's put the women and kids to bed and play with the big boys."

The house plunges into darkness and chaos ensues. People are shouting and running around, trying to figure out what happened.

"Get Switch and Wrath out of here," I hear someone yell.

"What about the kid?" Another one asks.

"Fuck that kid, leave him." The same person barks out. I spot them moving into the kitchen and heading right for us by the flashlights on their phones. "Wrath doesn't even want the little asshole."

I hold up three fingers, signaling to Ashton and Ashley. They both give me a quick nod and prepare to take them out. The three men turn around and have their backs to us when they hear a noise from the living room. We each sneak up behind them and I don't see what the other two are doing. I know what I must do. Channeling my inner self, I grab the man from behind and without thinking twist his neck until he drops to the floor, not moving. I'll deal with the outcome later.

Moving quickly into the next room, I find two more men, strapped with AK 47's. They're looking all around and are scared shitless. I keep to the shadows, waiting and listening.

"What if it's that guy Switch warned us about is here?" One whispers.

"Kill him. Those were our orders. Kill him and anyone with him." The second guy answers.

"I've never killed anyone before. I don't know if I can do it." The first one responds.

"If you have a chance to kill him and don't, Switch will kill you. Which would you rather have?"

"I...," the first guy stutters.

"Listen, the first kill is always hard, but after that it gets easy and you don't even think about it anymore. Just do the fucking job or I'll take you out myself."

The flashlight shines in the first guy's face. He swallows hard and his face is pale. He's shaking and backing away from the second guy. "I can't do it, man. I didn't sign on for this."

The second guy brings up his rifle and points it at the first guy, "Then say goodbye you little fuckhead. Wrath and Switch don't want someone in their gang that won't kill for them." Not even hesitating, I sneak up behind the second guy and snap his neck before he even realizes what's going on. He collapses to the ground with a thud. I leer at the first guy who holds his hands up in the air, shaking so hard, his teeth are chattering.

"Don't…," he stutters. "Please don't hurt me. I never wanted to be here, but they made me," he pleads.

I approach him silently and watch his eyes widen with fear. He's just a kid, can't be any older than sixteen. Tilting my head to the side, I assess his stance. He's shaking, scared out of his mind. In that split second, I let him go.

"Stay still and don't move," my voice is low and deadly as I remove his AK 47 and pat him down, finding no other weapons. "Marks, one friendly coming out. He's wearing a green hoodie and blue jeans. No weapons on him."

"Copy that. Send him out the back. Ramirez is waiting," Marks responds. I grab the kid by the hoodie and make him walk in front of me toward the kitchen. Ashton steps out of the shadows, making the kid jump and shake even more.

"I got him," Ashton says and moves the kid through the kitchen and out of sight.

Ashley moves next to me and gives my arm a squeeze before we go into the next room. There's a set of stairs to the left and the dining room directly in front of us. We do a quick sweep of the dining room and come up empty-handed. Quietly making our way up the stairs, I'm in the lead and Ashley is right behind me, hanging onto my belt with one hand and her nine mil in the other. We keep our backs against the wall until we round the corner at the top of the stairs. Three closed doors line the left side of the hallway and I open the first door. The room is empty except for a twin-size bed and a dresser. We move onto the next two rooms and find the same thing, empty.

"Where the fuck are they?" I question, pacing the hallway. "Marks, Harris, Ramirez, did they sneak past us and get away?"

"Negative boss. No one's come out," Harris responds.

Replaying the layout of the house in my head, I flash through the images. There's two stories, lights on in every room except the basement and the attic. There is no door to the attic here. Shining my light above my head I see a pull cord by the stairs. They wouldn't be stupid enough to go up there, would they? A thump above my head has me moving fast toward the pull cord. I yank it down and a ladder falls with it.

Climbing up quickly, I keep my head low and aim my gun and the beam of my flashlight into the small space. Hearing a whimper from the corner of the attic, I climb up the rest of the way and shine the beam around, landing on a little boy huddled in the corner. He's shaking, scared out of his mind. Ashley walks past me quickly and reaches the little boy first while I'm paralyzed to my spot on the floor. I can't make one foot move in front of the other. She's whispering to the little boy and soothing him. I didn't believe it until now. I thought it was a ploy from Wrath until he peers up at me with matching brown eyes and shaggy brown hair. His clothes and face are filthy, and he's frightened.

"I got him," Ashton says from behind me. He picks the little boy up and takes him quickly down the stairs. Still glued to my spot, Ashley approaches me.

"He looks just like you," she confirms. "He told me they had him up here for a few days and he think they might be in the basement. He said they sometimes take him down there when they want to teach him a lesson in being a good boy." There's a hitch in her voice. I finally drag my eyes from the corner he was huddled in, to Ashley. She's furious with a glint in her eyes. "Let's finish this."

We quickly make our way down the stairs and into the living room. Neither of us saying a word when we cross the kitchen toward the basement door. It's heavy with several locks unlocked. I open the door and it creaks on the hinges. Shining my flashlight down the wooden stairs, we make our way down together. Memories flash through my mind when we reach the bottom. The pain and torture they inflicted upon me a few days ago in this very spot. This is where they took me and tried to beat me into submission. I can sense the evil lurking under my skin, ready to take over and turn savage. Metal beams and chains shine on my flashlight.

"Well, well, well. You finally decided to join us," Wrath sneers from the shadows in the dark corner. I shine my flashlight on her face. The face of a woman I thought I once loved stares back at me with big hazel eyes and her blonde hair is up in a ponytail. "Where's the little bitch?"

"Right here," Ashley says and steps out behind me. "This is going to be fun taking you down." She cracks her neck on her shoulders, stepping closer to Wrath.

"Not as much fun as what I'm going to have with you, once I kill him," Switch responds from another corner. He steps out of the shadows and has a gun pointed right at my chest. Fury pumps through my veins and the treacherous side I've kept restrained is thrashing against my chest trying to take over. An evil sneer crosses my lips.

"What's the matter Switch? Can't take me on one on one? Are you that much of a pussy?" I provoke.

His eyes narrow and he sets his gun down next to Wrath. "Oh, let's do this fucker. I've wanted you dead for a long time." He removes his shirt and his dark skin shines in my flashlight. He has his hands taped and his eyes appraise Ashley. That makes my blood boil. That's my woman he's looking at. "She looks even hotter in person,

I'll find out if she's just as hot with me pounding between her legs, making her scream my name."

"You will never touch me," Ashley counters next to me. There's no sign of fear in her voice or on her face. She's channeling her own fury and neither of these two knows who they're up against. She shifts her attention from Switch to Wrath, who's grinding her teeth and has fire in her eyes. "What's the matter, Wrath? Are you pissed he wants me and not you anymore?" Ashley taunts her.

"Slut!" Wrath screams and charges full speed. Ashley sidesteps her advance and swings her fist to the back of Wrath's head, sending her into the corner of the basement.

I turn my attention back to Switch who's inching toward his gun. "Bad idea," I growl and charge him. He spins at the last second and elbows me between the shoulder blades. That pisses me off and the devil shatters free from the chains I have him bound in.

With a sneer on my lips and fire racing through my veins, I attack again. I swing my fist and connect with the side of his face. Bones crunch under my knuckles and the sound is like music to my ears. Switch's eyes widen in surprise when he gains his bearing and looks at my expression. My muscles are bulging when I swing again, this time connecting with his nose. Blood flies everywhere and I keep attacking. Punch after punch, kick after kick, I continue to strike Switch, until he's a bloody heap on the floor, not moving. Straddling his limp body, I lean down so we're face to face, my breathing erratic, sweat dripping down my face and my adrenaline surging forth pushing me further.

"This is for everything you've ever put me through," I sneer and grab Switches head with my hands. He locks eyes with me and all the fight has left them. "This is for Izzy and Xavier," I twist his head in my hands and hear a crack. He turns limp under me and I stand up from his lifeless body. Remorse fills me, but I push it away. I'll deal with it later.

I hear a grunt from the corner of the basement and I turn to see Ashley has Wrath in a scissor hold, squeezing Wrath's neck with her thighs. She's slapping and clawing at Ashley's legs, but Ashley isn't letting go. Wrath's face is turning blue and her hazel eyes plead for me to help. Years ago, I would have helped her, but after what she did and the scars she created, I nod to Ashley and she drains the life from Wrath's body. Breathing hard, Ashley shoves Wrath's body off her and stands up on shaky legs.

"Are you ok?" Ashley asks with a tremble in her voice.

"Yes, we need to find Marcus," I respond, I know I need to go to her, but I can't right now. I'm not in control and I'm afraid if I do, I'll hurt her. I look around the basement, the chains clink together above my head and I remember everything they did. Soft hands are upon my back, soothing me. I turn around and Ashley's honey eyes are locked onto me, watching and waiting. Taking a deep breath, I pull her into my arms and my lips descend upon hers, taking everything she's offering. She opens her lips, welcoming my probing tongue.

"Boss, you down here?" Footsteps pound down the wooden stairs, but I keep my lips locked onto Ashley, shutting out all sound. It's just the two of us and she's grounding me to this world, not letting me fall. I pull away from our kiss and bury my nose in her hair, breathing hard and hold her.

"Thank you," I whisper in her hair. Her fingernails brush my neck and send a shiver down my spine.

"Anytime," she whispers back.

"Boss, we have an issue," Harris says from the bottom of the stairs.

"What is it?"

"Marcus and Shaun aren't here. We've searched this whole house, and they are nowhere to be found."

"Call Ace to see if he knows where they are. Maybe he found them already."

Ashley runs her fingers down my face, wiping away some of the blood from Switch. "How are you holding up?"

Looking around the basement, I can finally take it all in without revenge and pain. "It's going to take a while to reach the right mindset and put the past in the past, but as long as you're with me, I will be all right."

"Always, Nolan. I will always be wherever you are." A smile graces her lips. Even while taking lives tonight, she's smiling at me, lighting up my entire world. I hold her soft body against mine and everything clicks into place. All the pain and torture I endured in my life, my mother leaving me to these animals, my father's hard fists, Switch's mental pain, Wrath's ability to twist my mind, it all disappears, and a weight has been lifted off my shoulders. They can't hurt me anymore.

"Let's go home," Ashley states.

"That's the best plan I've heard. Harris, can you guys clean up down here?"

"You got it, Boss."

Ashley walks up the wooden stairs first and I follow behind, not letting go of her hand. At the top of the stairs, I turn around, looking into the dank basement. I push every painful memory away. Every scream, every taunt, every slash, and blood spilled stays down in that basement and will never affect my state of mind again.

When one door closes, another one opens and when we go outside into the sun kissing the horizon, I see the other door opening. He's laying his head against

Ashton's chest, sleeping. As I stare into his peaceful chubby face, and all my sins wash away bringing on a new chapter in our lives.

Epilogue

Nolan 6 month later

"Hurry! It's time to go," Ashley shouts from the bottom of the stairs.

I throw on a pair of jeans and a clean T-shirt. I grab my wallet off the dresser and shove it into my back pocket.

"Nolan! Come on, we're going to miss it," Ashley shouts again. I open the bedroom door and run down the stairs. I almost stumble into Ashley, but right myself at the last second. "Ready?" She asks. There's excitement in her eyes. I pause for a second and watch her. She turns away from me and bends down so she's eye level with our little boy. "Ok, Sherwood, where we are going is a special place to see some important people. Are you ready to be on your best behavior?"

Our little boy nods his head in excitement and she hugs him tight. It was quite a trial and error getting used to him being here with me, with us, but we managed. I thought Ashley wouldn't be able to do this, but she's stuck by both of us and she loves that little boy like he's her own. I couldn't have asked for a better outcome.

After we left New York City, Ashley and I took Sherwood back to Michigan. We promised Izzy and Xavier we'd stay and help them until after she had the baby, then we'd leave for Los Angeles. Sherwood suffered from nightmares the first two weeks here, but Ashley was there to soothe him and help him get past all the pain and torture he endured by giving him love, something he never had before.

I've been trying to convince Xavier and Izzy to come with us to L.A., but they don't want to leave their families right now and I don't blame them. They need love and stability to get through the mess Switch and Wrath created. With no sign of Marcus, we all breathed a little easier these last six month. Izzy and Xavier are doing great and so is Sherwood. Things have settled down and we're normal for once.

Ashley tried dirt track racing a few months ago, and she did great, but it's different from street racing. All summer long I raced, and she watched and afterword, I just thanked God for soundproof rooms because the noises she made set my skin on fire. I adjust myself thinking about all the different ways I make her body come to life.

"Nolan, are you ready yet?" Ashley asks with a smirk on her lips. She knows what I've been thinking about. "We have to go or we will be late."

"Yup, I'm ready. And, if I remember correctly, it's your fault we're late." I wiggle my eyebrows at Ashley and her face turns red. She couldn't keep her hands off me this morning or several times last night after my race. Ashley leans against me, her soft curves pressed against my hard ones, her lips inches from mine. She has a glint in her eyes and I have the urge to say fuck this and take her upstairs, again.

"Well, if you didn't look so good in that car, I wouldn't be tempted to wrap my lips," she nips the bottom of my ear with her teeth. "And body around yours." She soothes the nip with her tongue and my body lights with fire. Ashley turns away and I adjust myself in my jeans that just became too tight. Just words from this woman drive me crazy with lust.

Shaking my head, I hold out my hand and Sherwood's tiny grip clutch onto my big one. My heart melts from the sight of his familiar brown eyes gazing up at me like I hang the world. "Come on little guy, let's go meet the new member of our family."

We make it to the hospital in record time with Ashley driving. We hurry into the elevator and I let Sherwood push the button for the third floor. He's a smart little guy and is adjusting to his new life really well. The doors whoosh open and I look down at him. He's holding onto my hand and his gaze lands on mine. I watch him swallow hard and walk out of the elevator with his head held high and shoulders pushed back. I stop before we open the doors and bend down, so we're eye level.

"I know this is new and scary for you but remember Ashley and I are right here with you. We're not going anywhere and after we'll go get ice cream. How does that sound?"

His eyes widen and he nods his head so hard, his teeth rattle. Ice cream does it every time. I laugh, and he returns it. Before I stand up to walk into the maternity ward, Sherwood wraps his little arms around my neck and give me a big hug.

"Thank you, dad," his small voice echoing in my ears. Tears form in my eyes, it's the first time he's called me dad and my heart soars hearing it.

"You're welcome, son." Emotions clog my throat and I blink back tears. Ashley lays her hand on my shoulder, rubbing it soothingly. I peek up at her from the little arms wrapped around me and she wipes a tear trailing down her cheek and a huge smile on her face. "Come on, let's meet your new cousin."

Sherwood releases my neck and I stand up. He grabs my hand again and I take Ashley's other hand. Together the three of us walk into the Maternity Ward as a family. No matter where life takes us, what dangers are lurking in the shadows, we have each other. We have a tight bond no one will ever break. That's what family does. Through the thick and thin, we are in this together and will come out on the other side better and stronger than ever.

Thank you from the author.

There's so many people I want to thank for taking the time and investing yourself into my world. I hope you enjoyed Nolan's story and please, if you can, leave a review. This book had me in for a ride. There was so much emotion and heartbreak, love and hate, some days I didn't know which side of Nolan was going to appear.

I'm sad to see it end but look forward to the next series coming out. We will get into more depth of Rush, Redline, Noah, Quickshift and Hotflash as they battle their own issues and try to remember what family really means. And before you ask, Nolan and Ashley aren't done, yet. But they're done for now.

First off, thank you to all the wonderful readers who took a chance on me in book one, Racing Dirty. That was my debut novel and I had so much fun introducing you to a new world. One with heartbreak, tragedy and adrenaline filled action.

Thank you to my husband, Rex and children who understand when I get the itch to write, I can't get rid of it until I put the words out.

Sarah D, my Alpha, my sidekick. Thank you for keeping my head clear when I start to doubt myself. Nolan's book was by far the hardest to write and he put me through the ringer a few times. So, thank you for steering me when I strayed from the story and go all wonky (that's a word right?)

Michelle. There's so many roles you do. My PA, SIL, and without you, I'd be going crazy trying to keep up with everything. There's so much you do for me and I'd be lost without you. So, thank you for dealing with me #hotgilf.

Joy, Stormy, Katie, Holly, Krista and Courtnay – This is for you. Thank you for helping me in shaping this story and being there when I need to vent. I know I can be a pain in the ass, but you still love me.

Thank you to Callie at Literary Designs for creating my beautiful covers and all my teasers.

If you want to reach out and just chat my links are below:

J. Lynn's Badass Bitches – http://bit.ly/2m0i0w0

Like on Facebook – http://bit.ly/2qtxkpw

Follow on Amazon – http://amzn.to/2COi78o

Goodreads – http://bit.ly/2CHP2fCH

Bookbub – http://bit.ly/2HkczDZ

Books written by J. Lynn Lombard

Royal Bastards MC

Blayze's Inferno

Amazon: https://amzn.to/2DSLZ1x

Capone's Chaos

Amazon: https://amzn.to/34QUrNS

Capone's Christmas

Amazon: https://amzn.to/34QUrNs

Torch's Torment

Amazon: https://amzn.to/2Vh2Qax

Global Outlaw Syndicate

Deadly Rose:

Amazon: https://amzn.to/3lvyFCt

Savage Saints MC

Kayne's Fury:

Get it here: Amazon: https://amzn.to/2DbXmAl

Blayde's Betrayal

Get it here: Amazon https://amzn.to/2Z0yGoc

Stryker's Salvation

Get it here: Amazon https://amzn.to/2InXZKV

Rooster Redemption and Aces Ascension are coming soon. All are #FreeonKU

Find the stories that started all of this in the completed

Racing Dirty Series

Thrust Amazon: https://amzn.to/2AwrgJ7

Torque (book 2) Amazon: https://amzn.to/2H0JugS

Turbulence (book 3) Amazon: https://amzn.to/2KNuTaj

Printed in Great Britain
by Amazon